LEARNING TO TRUST AGAIN

SUGAR SPRINGS
BOOK 2

ALEXA ASTON

OLIVER-HEBER BOOKS

PUBLISHER'S NOTE: This is a work of fiction. Names, characters, places, and incidents either are the product of the author's imagination or are used fictitiously. Any resemblance to actual persons, living or dead, business establishments, events, or locales is entirely coincidental.

COPYRIGHT © Alexa Aston

Published by Oliver-Heber Books

0 9 8 7 6 5 4 3 2 1

 Created with Vellum

PROLOGUE

LOS ANGELES—SEVEN YEARS AGO …

Rory Addison opened her eyes, knowing her phone alarm would be going off any moment now. She always awoke out of habit before the alarm sounded but set it, just the same, whether it was for morning practice or a nap, which she had just finished to help her be fresher for tonight's competition. Once, Anya Moranova had handled all those small details for her. Her longtime skating coach had told Rory when to get up and when to go to bed. When to eat and when to train. She would have told her pupil what to think, but there had been no other time to think of anything but skating. Except for the books Rory sneaked into bed and read with a flashlight, she concentrated on skating during her waking hours.

Ice skating had been her life from a young age. She had shown promise early on and left her small Texas town, situated twenty miles east of Tyler, going with her mother to live at a training facility in Colorado. She didn't remember much about her life before she began training as an athlete, only that her father had chosen not to come with them. She still awoke sometimes, that final argument between her parents ringing in her head, her dad accusing her mom of choosing a stupid child over their marriage.

He had been right. Mom had always put her daughter first, at the expense of her marriage and career.

She sat up as the alarm on her phone went off, silencing it. It was the day of Worlds—the World Figure Skating Championship, the annual competition sanctioned and hosted by the International Skating Union—and the most prestigious, competitive event in the figure skating world. Only the Olympics garnered more attention than Worlds did. For the first time in more than two decades, the event was being held in the United States.

She left the bedroom and went to the living room of the hotel's suite, opening the curtains. Sunlight flooded the room. Calling for room service, Rory checked on her order, what she thought of as her game-day meal, although it was not a game she would play but a program she would skate. The outcome of tonight's free skate would decide if she would repeat as the Women's Singles Champion.

The hotel employee she spoke with already had received her order the night before and merely confirmed the time it was to be delivered to her suite. She thanked the woman and hung up.

She spent the next hour going through a mixture of Pilates moves and yoga poses. She never walked on the day of a competition, wanting to save her legs, but she did enjoy physical exercise, stretching her body and letting her mind float away as she ran through her familiar routine.

Once she finished, Rory hit the shower, letting the hot water sluice over her body and its aching muscles, which she had pushed to its limits leading up to this all-important competition. She wrapped herself in the luxurious bathrobe provided by the hotel and returned to the suite's living room. Five minutes later, her meal was delivered. Along with it came journalist Monica Wethersby, who must have been patiently waiting in the corridor for their scheduled appointment.

Rory ushered in both the server and reporter and then seated herself in front of the table, removing the lids from the plates. Monica, who had been following Rory for the past few competitions in order to write an in-depth profile on her, set her phone to record and placed it on the table between them. Still, the journalist took out a pad and pen as a backup, not wanting to miss anything from this rare interview opportunity. Rory hadn't given an interview in over two years, and she could almost see Monica salivating, ready to ask her questions.

The journalist's eyes skimmed the table. "Is this a typical pre-competition meal for you, Rory?" she asked.

"Pretty much," she said. "Although when I'm training, I space parts of this out in the morning. The yogurt and fresh blueberries are what I eat every morning before I go to the rink to practice. I take a break about two hours into rink time and eat the avocado toast I've brought with me."

She indicated the poached eggs. "These are the only addition on the day of competition. I like the extra burst of protein they provide."

"And this is all you'll eat before you go to the arena?"

"I had a protein shake this morning. I'll drink another one if I feel I need to do so. That would be right before I leave the hotel. I let my body tell me what fuel it needs. I've learned to listen to it over the years."

Monica made a note of that on her pad.

"Tell me your frame of mind today, Rory. What is it like, wanting to repeat as a world champion?"

She kept from rolling her eyes like a middle schooler

at the question. "As you know, Monica, I claimed the ladies figure skating world title six years in a row, starting when I was seventeen, until I turned twenty-two. So I do know a little bit about repeating."

"Yes, of course," the reporter said hastily. "I just wondered, though, what it's been like to come back from your injury."

She shrugged. "Injuries are a part of the sports world. Especially in figure skating. I've suffered from stress fractures in both feet, which is really common. They occur from the repetitive moves and motions from my jumps and landings in practice and competitions." She chuckled. "You would think I was a bone surgeon because of the way I can discuss metatarsals, sesamoids, and navicular bones."

Rory paused. "It was a hard landing a couple of years ago in warmups which caused me to roll my ankle and have to withdraw minutes before the final round. I knew when I came down, even though I'd warmed up and stretched properly, that I'd overstretched ligaments and would have to bow out from the competition in Madrid that night."

That had been a tough night for her. She had gone out in the warmups, conscious as always of how far she could push her body. She had given up her daily run when the stress fractures began occurring in her feet and now wore extremely expensive shoes, which cushioned her feet as she walked each morning. Walking helped her maintain her sanity. It was something to do away from the rink and allowed her to be introspective.

Putting on a bright smile, she knew the reporter would be dazzled by it. Rory was a beautiful woman and knew it, but she tried never to trade upon her looks, wanting her talent and intellect to speak for her instead.

"After I withdrew from the competition two years ago, I made changes in my routine."

"That's when you started spending less time in the rink, isn't it?" the journalist inquired.

She nodded. "I had enough experience on the ice. It's been home to me for over two decades. I wanted to keep up my strength and endurance and trained accordingly. I gave up running for walking. I started practicing yoga and Pilates. I also do strength training twice a week in the gym. I spend an equal amount of time on physical conditioning outside the rink, as I do inside on my routines."

"You famously choreograph all your own routines," Monica noted. "Why don't you leave that in someone else's hands, as other skaters at your level do?"

"Who knows me and my capabilities better than I do?" Rory asked. "I tailor my short program and free skate to fit my style and what I want to show the judges. I see the routines in my head before I ever commit them to paper and skate them in the rink."

"You're known for your unusual choices in music, veering away from the classics. You've even helped the careers of some lesser-known pop artists by selecting their songs for international competitions."

She shrugged. "I bore easily and want to choose songs that keep me energized. I select music which reflects my skills as an artist and athlete. Songs which play to my strengths. You have to realize that we skaters skate the same programs for months, if not a year or more, as we perfect it. I have to choose music which I can live with for that long."

"If you repeat tonight after last year's victory in the finals, that will give you eight world championship titles to go along with your two Olympic gold medals."

"Yes, I've been blessed to win gold at eighteen in my

first Olympic appearance and repeat as champion when I was twenty-two."

"You're twenty-five now, Rory, and will be twenty-six when the Olympics are in session. That's almost grand-motherly in the women's skating world these days. Will you skate for Team USA next year? And if you do, how many more Olympics do you have in you after that?"

She hesitated a moment, not certain if she wanted to answer the question, and she said so aloud.

"Monica, I take one competition at a time. The Olympics will happen next year, meaning there will be both them and Worlds back-to-back. I know my body has been under a great deal of wear and tear over the years. That's why I believe in only thinking about the current competition and not stargazing ahead."

"You have mentioned how you don't spend as much time in the rink as you used to in practice sessions, un-like other skaters. Besides training, what do you do away from skating?" Monica chuckled. "Most skaters I inter-view tell me they have no life off the ice."

Rory took a bite of her avocado toast and then said, "Two years ago when I had to withdraw, due to my ankle injury, I had to take a few months off from skating. It was at that time that I realized I had no work/life balance. No hobbies. At first, I binged a couple of old TV series which others have talked about. I'd never had time to watch them. Or any TV, really. *Game of Thrones* and *Breaking Bad*. I was obsessed—just as I was with skating —and would binge twelve to fourteen hours a day. I fi-nally figured out that was unhealthy. So, I started doing other things, cutting TV time to an hour or so a day. I picked up books from the bestseller list and started reading for pure pleasure. I've never cooked—never known how—and started watching Carter Clark's vlog."

"Oh, the sexy fireman turned vlogger turned Food

Network star," Monica said, making a notation on her pad.

"Yes. I decided if Carter Clark could teach me how to cook, he can do anything in my eyes." Rory laughed. "So, I read. I cooked. I binged TV in moderation. I started rehab. I've continued those hobbies ever since. I like myself better because I have hobbies and interests off the ice."

"You don't mention friends or family, Rory. What is your private life like? Are you seeing anyone on the skating tour?"

That was a question she wasn't willing to answer. It was an open secret on the competition tour just how many skaters hooked up with one another behind the scenes for short, intense, and very brief love affairs. Rory was no exception. She had been involved with everyone from an Olympic gold medalist and four-time world champion to an Olympic hopeful who turned out to be a dismal failure. He flamed out, leaving the tour to become a sports promoter. She was friendly to the other women on the circuit but not close to any of them. She'd been trained by her coach to be a competitor first and foremost—and competitors didn't get close to someone they would skate against, much less become friends with them.

Smiling brightly at the journalist, Rory said, "I would prefer to keep my private life private. I'm sure you understand that, Monica."

"Are you willing to say anything on the record about Anya Moranova?"

She stiffened. The reporter had just named her longtime coach. The woman who had discovered Rory while she was still living in Texas. The one who had convinced her mom to move them to the training facility in Colorado.

And the woman who had let Rory go on one night to compete while her mom wasn't in the crowd. Instead, she had been dying on an operating table.

Rory had always looked for her mom and the sweet, encouraging smile she gave her daughter during the brief warmup session that occurred before a round of competition began. Rory had gone out that night, the night of her second Olympics finals, and had not seen her mother sitting in her usual spot in the rink. Concerned, she had left the ice and found Anya, asking if the coach knew where her mom was.

"Ah, Aurora, your mother is here. I saw her earlier. Perhaps she merely has gone to use the facilities in order to be back in time to see you skate."

Rory had had no reason not to believe Moranova. Anya controlled every facet of Rory's life, and since her coach didn't seem worried, Rory was satisfied. She went out as the final skater of the evening, far enough ahead in the standings that if she skated a clean program and took no chances, she would easily take the gold medal for the US. She didn't look for her mom as she went out onto the ice. She never did at that point, always assuming her mom was present and watching, wanting to concentrate on the next few minutes of her performance.

That night, Rory's confidence soared and though she didn't need to, she took a couple of risks in her jumps, pushing herself physically and artistically. It paid off— and she won the gold by a mile to raucous cheers.

But it was only after the scores had gone up and Rory went out on the ice to skate a victory lap and sweep up flowers tossed to her that she once again saw the empty spot where her mom should be. She came to a halt on the ice and looked back to where Anya watched, a triumphant smile on her face. Though it wasn't her mom's habit to go to the kiss and cry area, Rory thought maybe Mom had done so. But only her coach stood there.

That's when Rory's gut told her something awful had happened.

She gripped the flowers she had already retrieved and skated off the ice, not speaking to Anya until they were behind the scenes. She had smiled and done a quick interview with ABC Sports, who broadcast those Winter Olympics, and then turned down the opportunity to go to the pressroom and speak to the cadre of international reporters present about her outstanding performance.

Instead, she had grabbed Anya by the elbow and led her to a janitor's broom closet, pushing the older woman inside and closing the door behind them. She demanded to know where her mom was.

It was then that Anya told Rory that her mother had been in an accident on her way to the skating arena. That she had been crossing the street in front of the facility when a car struck her. Her mother had been rushed to the nearest hospital in Paris and died halfway through the operation.

A fury unlike anything Rory had ever known filled her, but she had harnessed it, coldly informing Anya Moranova that her services would no longer be required. Ever.

She had left that broom closet and never spoken to or about her coach.

And never would.

"As you know, Monica, we parted ways several years ago. We had been together many years, and Anya taught me much about skating. However, I had ideas I wanted to try and decided to strike out on my own."

"But it's unheard of, Rory, for a skater on your level

not to have a coach. Or a nutritionist. Even an entire entourage. You have ... no one."

"I do have an assistant who handles things for me, such as flight and hotel reservations. She also books my rink time. Helps me gain the rights to music I wish to use in my routines. Other than that? I am pretty self-sufficient. I like being in charge of my destiny, from designing my own skating costumes to creating my choreography."

Rory stood. "I need to get ready now, Monica. Do my hair and makeup. Some stretching. Get to the arena. I need time alone to mentally prepare. Skate through my routine in my head. That kind of thing. I'm sure you understand. If you have any follow-up questions, you can text me."

She gave the journalist her cell number, cautioning her not to give it out and to use it wisely.

"I will, Rory, and thank you for spending this time with me. I know you're not one to do interviews, but I promise that you'll enjoy this in-depth piece I write. I'll email it to you even before I send it to my editor to see if there are any corrections you'd like me to make."

That generosity surprised her. "I appreciate that, Monica."

"And I appreciate your time, Rory. Oh, my reporter's nose is telling me you're holding back, but I respect that you wish to maintain some privacy. If you ever do want to fully tell your story, though, I would be honored to have that opportunity to work with you. Maybe once you end your ice skating career, we could work on your autobiography together."

Smiling, Rory thought that was the last thing she would waste her time with.

She saw the reporter out the door and then readied herself to go to the rink. Fortunately, no transportation needed to be arranged because the venue sat catty-corner from the hotel.

She pressed her costume, one she had designed herself. The deep blue reflected the color of her eyes and made her auburn hair stand out. Maybe once she stepped away from competing, she might see if she could have a career in designing competition costumes and practice wear for skaters. Being a skater herself, she knew what a perfect costume needed to consist of and thought her flair for design might be profitable.

Placing her costume in a garment bag, Rory gathered her athletic bag, slipping its strap over her shoulder, and then left her hotel suite. She knew enough to take the service elevator down and avoid the lobby, which would be packed with fans. She was in full competition mode now and needed to remain focused. Taking selfies and giving out autographs would rip her from her zone.

Coming out of the service entrance, she stepped into the hotel's parking garage. Security guards milled about, waiting to escort the bigger name skaters across the street to the arena. The same two men who had gone with her to practices and the short program competition moved toward her. Rory was comfortable with the pair and glad of their presence since she'd had a few disturbing emails recently.

"Can I take your bag, Miss Addison?" asked the taller one.

"No, I'm good. Just get us to the arena if you would."

They flanked her, walking from the dark garage toward the exit. A few fans waited there, calling her name. Most were teenaged girls accompanied by a parent. She smiled and waved, moving quickly as the hotel security people hustled her along.

But she did catch sight of a man in his late thirties. Her gut told her she'd seen him before entering a previous event. He looked at her intently. They locked eyes for a moment, and he called, "I love you, Rory," creeping her out.

She glanced away, wondering if he might be the author of the inappropriate, graphic emails.

Less than three minutes later, she was inside the bowels of the arena and waltzed through the security checkpoint.

"Thanks for the escort," she told the two guards.

"Give 'em hell, Rory," one said, grinning at her. "Bring home the title."

She smiled at him, determination filling her. "I plan to," she assured him.

The pair waved goodbye, and she turned, going to a large room designated for competitors to wait in until their time to skate. It had several large TV screens live streaming the competition, as well as food and drink available.

She nodded at a few of her fellow skaters. Other than that, she didn't interact with anyone. Some skaters were quiet. Others were engaged in serious conversations with their coaches. She liked that this facility only allowed the competitor and coach into this room. All entourage members had to stay outside.

Rory did some stretches and then changed into her costume. She checked her hair and makeup, seeing it was fine.

Then it was time for the final group to go out for their warmup session. Being in first place, she would be the last woman to skate this evening.

Rory did her time on the ice and then retreated to behind the scenes. She kept separate from the others, not bothering to watch her fellow competitors skate. She didn't care what they did. It was how she performed that mattered.

Closing her eyes, she ran through her entire routine from start to finish. Saw herself making the jumps successfully. So much of skating was mental, like a field goal kicker or a batter swinging his bat. It was a mind game you had to convince yourself to play —and win.

She rose from her chair, brimming with confidence, secure in her free skate of four minutes. She had integrated the required elements, building the spins and footwork seamlessly around her multiple jump combinations. Her combinations were more difficult than most competitors. Rory was known for her endurance, especially in this free skate portion. The weightlifting and strength training she had added to her workouts had paid off. She was going into tonight's skate at the top of her game.

Receiving the signal from an official, Rory moved to the entrance, adrenaline pumping through her. Her name was announced, and she skated to the center of the ice, cheers erupting to the rafters. Worlds hadn't been held in the US in many years, and the fans were hungry to see their country claim the title.

She waved to the crowd, her signature smile wide, knowing there was nothing like home field advantage.

Then Rory lowered her arms, readying herself, going completely still, her head bowed, waiting for the music to begin. When it did, she sprang into action, flying across the ice with grace and an innate poise which couldn't be taught.

Getting a few of the required elements out of the way, she moved into her first combination jump. She pushed off, floating in the air like a butterfly, then nailing her landing, knowing she'd gotten the height and spin needed for maximum points. She moved across the ice, knowing her routine was spot on, popular with the audience, and appreciated by the judges and skating aficionados.

She worked up speed and took off again, landing her quad/triple combo to thunderous applause. Everything was now a blur, time moving quickly and yet almost standing still as she worked her way through her free skate.

The last minute of the free skate approached, where her most difficult combination lay, followed by a beautiful end spin where she became a blur. Once more, she flew across the ice, gathering speed to launch herself into the air. She pushed off, stretching to the sky, rotating, her arms held tight against her body, the thrill of knowing she would win another championship filling her as she descended, a deep satisfaction for these hardwon, back-to-back world titles coming at her so-called advanced age.

As she swept her arms outward to balance for her landing, she heard a loud crack. Felt intense pain in her shoulder. Her arms fought the air, waving wildly as panic and hurt rippled through her body. Rory hit the ice wrong. Hard. Completely off-balance. She heard as well as felt her right ankle snap. Incredible pain shot through her, blinding, dizzying, unlike anything she'd ever known.

She lay on the ice a moment, seeing the red blood against the white, frozen surface. The silence which had filled the arena suddenly shifted to screams. People scrambled from their seats. She saw a group race across the ice toward her.

Someone asked her a question. She tried to answer, but no words came out. Her shoulder continued to throb, but it was her ankle screaming at her. Rory knew it was not a simple break. The fracture would be career-ending.

She was taken off the ice. Loaded into an ambulance. An EMT began talking to her, but Rory couldn't comprehend his words. She finally picked up on one.

Shock.

She must be in shock. That's why she now felt as if she were moving underwater, drifting, fighting. She felt him elevating her legs. Covering her with a blanket. Her teeth began to chatter. Her breathing was rapid and shallow. She heard something about an IV and felt the needle pierce her skin. The EMT was pressing on her shoulder. Confusion filled her.

After a moment, he said, "Good. Your BP is way better. We're almost at ER. They'll do a full workup and then get you some pain meds." He smoothed her hair. "You'll need surgery on that ankle. Maybe your shoulder."

Surgery. That meant pain. And rehab. It would be a long road to recovery. Rory knew that much.

More than that, she knew no more World or Olympic titles were in her future.

The Rory Addison she had been ceased to exist at that moment—and would never be seen again.

1

JULY—DALLAS

Walker Cox turned off his four-thirty alarm and rose, alert as usual upon awakening. He went into the bathroom and stared at his image in the mirror a moment.

"So, this is what thirty-six looks like."

He quickly got ready for his weekly 5AM racquetball session with Gideon Ross, his best friend since pre-school. The two men had grown up in a small town in East Texas and remained lifelong friends, even attending college together. While Walker had continued his education at SMU Law School, Gideon had joined the Dallas Police Department and was currently a detective. Both were divorced—and better off for it.

Walker left his high-rise condo on Turtle Creek, pulling his Beamer from the garage and heading for his exclusive athletic club a few blocks away. He'd been a member ever since he joined the prestigious firm of Sapphire & Sammons straight out of law school. The law office only had twenty-two attorneys and was one of the most exclusive firms which represented Dallas' rich and famous. And a few infamous, as well.

As he pulled into the parking lot, he only saw a handful of cars, one of them being Gideon's ancient truck. He'd offered to buy his friend a new one, but Gid was too proud and refused the generous offer.

He didn't have anything else to do with his money. When he first left law school, Walker worked one hundred hour weeks. Having made partner four years ago, he still worked ninety-hour weeks. The only difference was that he got paid a helluva lot more as a partner. Because he spent almost every waking hour working, he had amassed a serious bank account and investment portfolio. While he did drive the latest BMW convertible and wore custom-tailored suits, he didn't have the time to spend any more of his money. He would love to take a trip anywhere, especially to various Civil War or Revolutionary battlefields, being a history buff. But there was always another case to manage. Another client to try and satisfy. He might be sixty before he was able to cut back on his caseload and spend his hard-earned money.

Pulling in next to Gideon, Walker exited his vehicle and locked it, slinging his athletic bag over his shoulder. He greeted his best friend.

"You look hungover, Gid."

"I wish I had time for a drink. I've been putting in long hours on this serial killer case."

"Are you close to catching who's behind the murders?" Walker asked, already knowing the answer from his friend's dejected posture.

"Nope. And it's just getting uglier. This creep keeps sending snail mail letters to the newspapers and TV stations—and they keep giving him all the press and airtime he craves." Gideon raked a hand through his hair. "I don't think we're any closer today than we were four months ago when the murder spree began. The only thing we know for certain is that he kills redheads."

"Come on, let's go inside. Take your mind off the case for a while."

They entered the club and went to the desk. The place was old-fashioned, still run as if it were the 1960s. Walker signed in, noting Gid as his guest. He'd offered to pay for a membership for his friend. As usual, Gideon turned him down. Thank goodness Gid wasn't proud enough to keep them from playing their weekly game.

They headed straight to their usual court, passing other empty ones not in use yet. They played so early in order for Gideon to make it to work on time. Walker no longer had set hours at his firm and could show up whenever he wished. Usually, he was at his desk by seven or so, as early as any of their new hires, because his workload demanded it.

After playing three games, Walker had lost two of them and called it quits. They went to the dressing room, where they both showered and dressed for their workday. Both would save time and run an electric razor over their faces on their way to work.

"You have time to grab breakfast?" Walker asked.

Gideon nodded. "I don't even know the last meal I ate," he admitted. "Food sounds good."

They agreed on a local greasy spoon they frequented and were there in less than ten minutes. Janie came over and set down coffees for both of them.

"The usual?" she asked.

They both nodded, and the server left them.

"I should've said this before, but happy birthday, Walker. Are you celebrating with anyone tonight?"

He shook his head. "You know I don't have time to date. Hell, neither of us has time *or* inclination to do so."

"You're not kidding," his friend said. "I put in five years with Melinda. I can't tell you how many times she griped about having married a cop."

Gideon's wife had been one of the famous SMU campus beauties, and they had married immediately after graduation. Melinda came from a well-to-do Fort Worth family and had been thrilled when she landed SMU's star wide receiver, thinking he would go on to the pros and make a name for himself. Unfortunately, Gideon had torn up his knee three games into the season and sat out the rest of his senior year, missing the conference championship game and a bowl game. He'd worked hard to rehab the knee, though, and was disappointed when he went undrafted. Gideon tried to make it in the NFL as an unsigned agent but was cut from the final fifty-three man roster. He came back to Texas, and his servant's heart told him he could make a difference as a cop. Walker was surprised Melinda stayed around as long as she did. A Junior Leaguer living on a patrolman's salary was a long way to tumble in her family's eyes. The couple had divorced a few days before their fifth anniversary, and Gideon had only had a handful of dates ever since.

Walker's marriage history was no better. At twenty-nine, he'd married a fellow attorney, a Yale Law grad who worked for a competing law firm in his same building. Christine was ambitious and avaricious. She didn't think Walker was moving up the ladder as quickly as he should, especially since they were the same age and she'd just made partner at her firm. She divorced him six months after their spontaneous elopement, the ink barely dry on their marriage license. Christine had gone on to become one of the top attorneys in Dallas, and Walker had heard rumors that she was thinking of running for District Attorney in next year's election.

Janie placed their plates before them and then freshened their coffees, leaving them in peace once more.

"I thought thirty-six would be different," Walker admitted. "I knew I would make partner by then, but I also believed I would have a life. A wife. A couple of kids.

Definitely, a dog. I knew I would have to work long hours, but I thought I would have time to spend some of the money I made. I pictured living in a nice house. Taking a vacation each year, one with the family and a separate one with the wife."

He blew out a long breath. "I'll admit it, Gid. I'm lonely. Burned out."

And then Walker said something aloud that surprised even himself. "I think I'm done with Dallas—and this life."

Gideon's eyes widened. "You're going to quit Sapphire & Sammons?"

He nodded, liking the idea more and more, picking up a piece of bacon and inhaling it.

"What good is it to make a ton of money if you don't have someone to share it with?" he complained. "I can't help it. You know my parents. Campbell and Betty Cox are one of the great love stories of Sugar Springs. They are more in love today than they were forty years ago when they got married."

"What would you do?" asked his friend. "I assume you still want to practice law." He grinned. "Wouldn't want to waste all that education you got."

"Don't shit bricks, Gid, but I'm thinking about packing up and heading home to Sugar Springs."

Gideon let out a low whistle. "If you would've told me when I got up this morning that I would hear you say those words, I would have said that would be the last thing coming out of your mouth. Have you talked to your dad about this? Would you go to work with him?"

"No, but I'm going to call him. Mom actually spilled some beans last week. She told me that Dad is finally ready to retire. They want to travel the world. You know how much he loves to sail. They want to see the sights."

"And you think he'll ask you to take over his law practice, don't you?"

Walker nodded slowly. "That's what Mom told me. And she added to act surprised when Dad brought it up." He hesitated. "I'm seriously considering it, Gid."

"You should do it," his friend encouraged. "You don't have anything left to prove in Dallas, Walker. You've earned accolades. You've tried—and won—some of the most challenging cases to hit the headlines." Gideon's tone softened. "I understand that pull toward home. That feeling of belonging in a community. I also think you wouldn't have to work nearly as hard at being a lawyer in Sugar Springs as you do here in Dallas. You probably would put in half the hours you do now. Of course, it would mean less money, but you're already set as it is. I say go for it, buddy. Find a house. Find a girl. Get that dog. Have a life."

He heard the wistfulness in his friend's voice and said, "You could come home, too. You know that. Chief Hamilton would hire you in a second. Hell, he'd probably fire someone to make room for you on the Sugar Springs force."

Gideon laughed. "I don't know about that. Why don't you test the waters for me?" he suggested. "If you find happiness in Sugar Springs, then maybe I'll think about coming home one day, too."

They finished eating in silence, each lost in his thoughts, and then Walker said, "Let me get this. My treat."

He removed some cash from his wallet and handed it to Janie as they went out the door, making sure she had a generous tip.

They got to their cars, and Gideon threw his arms around Walker, hugging him tightly.

"If you go through with this, I won't think of it as

losing my best friend. I'll do whatever it takes to make time to see you," Gideon promised. "Just let me know when you've made up your mind."

"I will," Walker promised. "It'll be soon. I know that."

He slipped behind the wheel of his convertible and drove to his office in downtown Dallas, pulling into the parking garage and his reserved space, which carried his name, a privilege of being a partner. He was at his desk by seven-twenty and began going through his emails, his first housekeeping task each morning.

Half an hour later, an email notification flashed across his screen. It came from Elton Briggs, their managing partner, who was on a rare vacation to Belize. Walker wondered why Briggs was sending an email from there and decided to open it. He read the message with increasing shock.

To my colleagues at Sapphire & Sammons –

I regret to inform you that this will be the last communication we have. You see, I finally snapped. After three decades of grinding out hour after hour in devotion to this esteemed law firm, I've had enough. More than enough.

I quit—and I'm going out in glorious style.

Most of you know that I'm a wizard with numbers. I've also learned quite a bit about moving around offshore accounts from our esteemed client base. I'm sorry to announce this to you, but Sapphire & Sammons is bankrupt as of five minutes ago. I have moved out every single penny in the company's coffers. No account was left unmolested. I have taken retainers. Advances. Even funds from clients for current trial work. The planning that went into this was tremendous, but I have drained every dime from every account we possess.

Do yourselves a favor, gentlemen and our lone lady lawyer. Quit sweating blood and tears into this soulless law firm. Don't try to resurrect it from the dead, where I've buried it. I doubt you could because the scale of what I've done will be too great.

Find a life for yourselves, one which has meaning. That's what I'm going to try and do, something I should have done a long time ago. Don't try to find me. You and law enforcement won't be able to. I know how to bounce money all around the world ten times over, and I am not in Belize as I said I would be. I'm in a country which has a no extradition policy with the US. I'm fifty-five today. Maybe it's not too late for me to try and have a life. Go have one yourselves. Curse me now—but thank me later for what I have done—because I may have saved your souls with this clever—if highly illegal—move.

Whether you believe it or not, I wish all of you my very best.

Sincerely,
Elton Briggs

WALKER STARED AT HIS SCREEN, his jaw dropped in disbelief. He closed it, trying to wrap his head around what he had just read. He went through the email a second time to make certain he hadn't missed anything.

No, he hadn't. Elton Briggs had obviously siphoned off funds from every account the firm held. As the managing partner, Elton had access to all accounts at Sapphire & Sammons. Briggs would have been able to pull off what he said he'd done before anyone would have caught onto the scheme. Walker couldn't imagine the investigation which would follow. It would be a bloody mess. Even though no other partners or associates at

Sapphire & Sammons had broken the law, they all would be tainted by the brush used by Elton Briggs.

He supposed he should thank the managing partner, after all, because Walker knew what he now needed to do.

Writing a two-sentence resignation letter, he printed it out, signing and dating it. He glanced at his TAG Heuer watch and saw it was a few minutes until eight o'clock. Other than a few other attorneys, he was the only one in the office. The administrative assistants and paralegals didn't arrive until nine.

He scribbled a quick goodbye on a post-it to his admin and removed his checkbook from his briefcase, writing her a check for just under ten thousand dollars. She'd been with him three years and was a single mother. He wanted to make sure she had something to tide her over until she found a new position. After that, he typed a glowing letter of recommendation for her, printing out ten copies and signing each for her to use in her upcoming job search.

Opening the lap drawer to her desk, he left the letters, check, and goodbye post-it inside. Closing the drawer, her texted her a brief message to look in the drawer when she got to work.

Walker headed to the storeroom and collected two empty boxes. Quickly, he cleared his desk of the few personal items it held, seeing there was so little he needed to take that he would only need one box. Rising, box in hand, he placed his resignation letter on top as he headed to the door. He stopped at the receptionist's desk and tore off a piece of tape, placing it at the top of his letter.

Opening the office door, he taped the resignation to the front of the door and reclaimed his box of personal possessions, leaving his employee ID card on the receptionist's desk.

With a heart lighter than it had been since he left Sugar Springs for college half a lifetime ago, he returned to the parking garage and placed the box in his trunk. As he pulled out into heavy downtown traffic, he touched his mom's name. She answered, out of breath.

"Walker? What's up? I just got home from exercise class."

"It's time for Dad to make that call to me. The one where he offers me the chance to take over his firm." He paused. "I just resigned from Sapphire & Sammons, Mom.

"I'm ready to come home to Sugar Springs."

2

Rory finished dressing, nerves flitting through her. She had an interview with the principal of Sugar Springs High School this morning, and she wanted the job so badly she could taste it.

She had already run through her series of morning stretches, wanting to keep her ankle and the rest of her body strong. She had spent close to eight months rehabbing the fractured ankle she'd suffered the night of Worlds in Los Angeles seven years ago. The US Olympic Committee had been good to her in the aftermath, covering all her medical expenses. Not only from the ankle injury, but also the gunshot wound in her shoulder.

She would never understand why Ronald Smothers shot her. It wasn't as if she were some famous politician or movie star. Olympic skaters didn't have stalkers. The only bizarre incident she could recall that was a blot on the reputation of the ice skating world was when Nancy Kerrigan was attacked after practice and had to pull out of Nationals, which happened the following night. Eventually, police connected the ex-husband of Kerrigan's rival, Tonya Harding, to the attack. The scandal rocked the skating world. Beyond that, skating had returned to being quite tame, rarely suffering from scandalous headlines.

Until Ronald Smothers took aim at Rory.

The police had connected the frighteningly escalating emails she had received to Redman, who had a long history of mental health issues. It came out during their investigation that Rory favored the stalker's first and only girlfriend who had dumped him. A short time later, the former girlfriend had disappeared. No trace of her had ever been found. It was assumed that she was dead and Ronald Smothers had killed her, disposing of the body. He had evaded police and become a drifter.

It had been scandal enough that a gun had made its way into the event itself, and new security protocols had been put into place at athletic events around the world. That didn't concern Rory anymore.

She was no longer a part of that world.

Even before her long rehab began, her gut had told she wouldn't be able to come back from the ankle injury because of its severity. While the doctors assured her she'd be able to walk without a limp, she would experience twinges in her bones, both when the weather changed and if she were on her feet too long or pushed herself too much physically. She refused to go back and compete when she was aware she wouldn't be at the level she desired. It wouldn't be fair to her or her fans. Rory couldn't represent her country and let it down, so she had walked away from the sport which had been her entire life.

Thankfully, her previous stress fractures had taught her to have more of a balance in her life. She already enjoyed reading, cooking, and binge watching. She'd added crafting to that, as well, feeling a sense of accomplishment and pride in what she created with her Cricut device, making everything from Christmas ornaments to glass etchings.

What she wanted to do with the rest of her life had stood in front of her, and during those long months of rehab, Rory had decided she wanted to teach. Many in the skating world predicted she would go into coaching because of her success and experience. She wanted to stay away from figure skating, however. It really hadn't been the right kind of life for a child. Rory had been homeschooled from the time she was ten years old, thrust into hours of endless practice and training. Because of that, she had yearned to go to school and make friends. Anya had taught her to make no friends in skating. To look at anyone who put on a pair of skates and entered an ice rink as her competitor.

Going to college in the aftermath saved her sanity.

She had no reason to remain in Colorado, even though it had been home to her for fifteen years. Rory was a loner and had no friends there, only acquaintances. She had decided to return to Texas, a place she had left as a child, and thought of fondly. Though her mom was gone, her Granny Bea still lived in Tyler, and so Rory contacted her grandmother. They had always remained in touch throughout the years, and upon completing rehab, Rory moved in with Granny Bea. Her grandmother was what Texans would call a live wire, seventy years old and more active now than she had been when she was working. Granny Bea had owned a cleaners in Tyler and sold it for a decent profit. Her small house was paid off, and she offered Rory her guest room for as long as she wanted to stay.

Rory had applied for admission to the University of Texas at Tyler and started classes as a freshman in January, ten months after the incident at Worlds. She was able to finish her degree in three years, thanks to going to summer school, and did her student teaching the previous fall. In college, she hadn't made any friends. She was twenty-five to the eighteen-year-old freshmen, who thought her ancient. Though her name was recognized in countries throughout the world, those teenagers attending university classes in Tyler, Texas, had no idea who she was. She realized it was an American thing. Most Americans didn't keep up with figure skating, only becoming armchair experts once every four years when the Olympics were broadcast into their living rooms.

In a way, Rory reveled in the anonymity. She also soaked up her history classes. Her lifelong fascination with history led her to declaring history as her major. The practical side of her knew not much could be done with a Bachelor of Arts in history, though. That's why she had earned her teaching certificate and took a job in an elite Houston private academy upon graduation.

Bitterness filled her at the thought of how what had been the happiest three years of her life had become a nightmare, with Rory being asked to resign her position, her reputation damaged through no fault of her own. She had left her school a broken woman, heading back to Tyler and Granny Bea's welcoming arms.

Today's job interview was in Sugar Springs, a small East Texas town about twenty miles outside Tyler. Rory had already had three previous interviews in the past two weeks. None had panned out. Although her recommendations from her former principal and department chair were strong, she wondered if those who had interviewed her had connected her to Bradley Bolton and wanted to steer clear of her because of that. Today had to be different. It was mid-July. Time was running out. School would be starting in a month, and she was determined to win a permanent spot on a staff. She didn't care what she taught or where the school was located. She just needed to find a job.

She left her bedroom after a final glance in the mirror and found Granny Bea watching *Good Morning America*, her usual way to start a weekday.

Taking a seat on the sofa, she asked her grandmother, "What's on your agenda today? Book club? Gardening club?"

"A Red Hats Society luncheon," Granny Bea told her. "I have a new hat I'm wearing. I'll be the envy of all who attend."

Rory had never heard of the Red Hats Society before but had become familiar with it after moving to Tyler. It was a group of older women who wore purple outfits, topped by red hats. They held tea parties. Went to the movies. Even hit the bars, upon occasion. This year, Granny Bea served as the Queen of the Tyler Red Hatters, their leader for a year.

"I see you're dressed for another job interview," her grandmother noted.

"Yes, a position in Sugar Springs. For US and World History, according to the job board."

"I think you would be a perfect match for that, honey. I hope this will be the fit you've been looking for."

"I hope so, too, Granny Bea."

Rory had spent several hours crying on her grandmother's shoulder. For her former job. Her ex-fiancé. Her lost reputation. Granny Bea had let her granddaughter wallow—and then told her it was over. The past was the past. She had overcome hardships before and would do so again.

Granny Bea's grit and determination were something Rory wanted to emulate. She put everything about the past three years behind her and swore she'd never again speak the name Bradley Bolton aloud. She swore once she had been hired at a school, she wouldn't look at another man. She had no interest in dating anyone. Her heart had been bruised too badly. Rory doubted she would ever be able to trust any man ever again. She would grow new friendships and form a family with those friends. Their kids would be like her kids. But as far as dating and marriage went?

She planned to remain single. Forever. Through infinity and beyond.

She kissed Granny Bea goodbye and grabbed her keys, going to the used SUV she had purchased after arriving in Tyler. She had never owned a car—never even had a driver's license—until her retirement from skating. She enjoyed the freedom owning a car gave her.

Plugging in the directions to Sugar Springs High School on her cell's map app, Rory left town, heading west. She ran through a series of questions in her mind, ones she anticipated would be asked, and practiced her answers aloud.

When she arrived at the high school, she pulled into the front parking lot and saw a few scattered cars present. A large truck sat in a spot marked Principal Milton. She assumed he would be the one conducting today's interview. Walking the short distance to the building, almost melting in the heat, she was glad to step inside the building. Disappointment filled her when she found the hallway hot. She supposed the school district turned off its air conditioners in the summers to save money and hoped that the office would be cooled. She enjoyed the cold, having spent a majority of her life in it on the ice, and had had an adjustment to make living through the hot Texas summers again.

Signage pointed her to the school's main office, and she entered it. Sweet relief passed through her as the cool hit. No one was working in this area, and she figured the support staff wouldn't report back until new teacher orientation and staff development began next month. Rory made her way down a hallway, looking at the names on various doors. Two counselors. An assistant principal. At the end of the long hallway, a door stood open. Above it was a nameplate with Principal Milton's name on it.

Coming out the door was an attractive woman who looked to be close to sixty. The woman spied her and hurried down the hallway to meet her.

"Why, hello," the woman said, stepping to Rory and extending a hand. Rory shook it as the woman said, "I'm Betty Cox—and on my way out the door, literally and figuratively."

"Oh, I'm Rory Addison. Here for a job interview."

"You must be interviewing for Paige's spot. Paige Laramie. She taught history across the hall from me for eight or ten years. Well, as of five minutes ago, there's another position open in the Social Studies Department, Rory. I've taught several decades at Sugar Springs, finishing up with government and economics. If you're interested in either of those subjects, try to talk Joe Bob into letting you take my position instead of Paige's."

Rory knew exactly who Paige Laramie was. News had spread like wildfire through Tyler early in the summer when Tanner Haddock came to Sugar Springs to film a screenplay which Paige had written under the name Laramie Fisher. Tanner was one of the biggest stars in Hollywood and wanted to add directing to his résumé. Not only had he bought Paige's script to film, he had also had a whirlwind romance with the former teacher. Rory had hoped after her interview that if she drove around town, she might even get a glimpse at the filming going on.

"It's good to hear there are two positions open, Mrs.

Cox. I hope I can impress Mr. Milton enough so that I might be considered for one of them."

"It's Betty, dear, and if you get either slot, I'm sure Paige and I can sit down with you and walk you through things. I have amassed an incredible amount of material over my teaching career. I'm happy to pass along everything from lecture notes to handouts to tests in a variety of subjects. Paige would do the same."

"I've read why she's leaving teaching. Are you retiring, Betty?"

"I sure am, Rory. And happy to do so. Don't get me wrong. Teaching has been my life. I've spent every day of it here at Sugar Springs in the exact same room. My husband, Campbell, is an attorney here in town. He's finally ready to retire himself. We have our brand new passports, and we are going to see the world."

"That sounds so exciting. It'll be a new chapter in your life."

"We've led a quiet life all forty years of our marriage. We met here in Sugar Springs and began dating our senior year of high school. We went off to different colleges, Campbell to SMU and me to Baylor, but we always stayed in touch. We got married after graduating from college and then lived in Dallas for three years while he attended law school. I didn't teach then. I worked in various positions at SMU. In the library. As a research assistant. When Campbell graduated, though, we came back to Sugar Springs and I was hired to teach World Geography. Over the years, I've taught pretty much every course in our department, but I'm ready to see the world with my husband."

Betty paused. "I know you've seen a good deal of it, Rory. I recognize your name and face. I was sorry to hear about what happened to you. At least you got to travel and see so many wonderful places while you were competing. Maybe you can give me some tips on places to see as a tourist."

She laughed. "I'm afraid I would need to tag along with you on your world tour to see anything of note, Betty. I never really saw any of the cities I competed in. I liken it to someone on a concert tour who plays one night, hops on a bus, and sleeps the entire way to the next city, where they rehearse and perform again that night. Rinse and repeat.

"Figure skating was much the same. I would fly to the place where the competition was being held. Stay in a hotel close by. Put in practice time on the ice and then went through my short program and free skate on different days. Winners were declared and then it was either back to Colorado to practice or on to a new city and a different competition. Yes, I've been to Barcelona. Rome. Stockholm. Tokyo. Sydney. But I never really saw any of those cities. As a history major, I've worked my way through the history of the world."

She smiled. "Maybe one day I can see the famous places I've studied and taught about. I would say during my summers off from teaching—but you know how that goes."

Betty laughed. "The general public thinks that teachers have summers off, but that's far from being true. We have workshops to attend. Staff development hours to accumulate. Most teachers I know work on their lesson plans each summer and even revise tests so that they have time during the school year for the actual teaching and tutoring. Yes, Campbell and I would take a week or two in the summer to vacation, but we usually kept close to home. Hopefully, it may be different for you."

Rory held up both hands, her fingers crossed. "I just want to land this job."

"Joe Bob is all bark and very little bite," Betty revealed. "Whatever you do, don't back down with him. Stand your ground. He'll respect you for it."

Betty pulled out her cell from her purse. "I have a feeling you'll be hired today, especially with two positions open now. Why don't you come to dinner tonight with Campbell and me? I can fill you in on some of the ins and outs of the high school."

"And if I don't land the job?" she asked.

"Then still come to dinner. We can talk travel."

They exchanged phone numbers, and Betty wished her good luck before departing.

Rory continued down the hallway to the open door and knocked on the frame. A large man in his early fifties, balding, glanced up.

"I'm Rory Addison," she said, introducing herself. "I have an interview scheduled this morning for a position in the Social Studies Department."

He stood and came out from behind his desk, shaking her hand. "I'm Joe Bob Milton, Rory."

He indicated for her to have a seat in one of the chairs in front of the desk. She did so and liked that he sat in the one beside her instead of returning behind the desk.

"Let me tell you a little bit about us, and then I want to hear all about you," the administrator said.

The principal went on to give her various statistics about Sugar Springs High School. The size of the student body and number of faculty members. The recognition the school had received. The latest state test scores.

"Now, tell me about you, Rory, and why you think you might be a good fit for Sugar Springs High School."

"I'd be happy to, Mr. Milton."

His cell buzzed on his desk, and he reached over and

glanced at it before setting it face down. "Go on," he encouraged.

"I don't come from a traditional educational background," she began. "I was homeschooled from the age of ten, and I'll admit a pretty shoddy job was done regarding my education. I was always thirsty for knowledge, though. I read on my own, usually things related to history because I was drawn to it."

"Like what?" he prodded.

"*Night. Band of Brothers. The Red Badge of Courage. Johnny Tremain. The Grapes of Wrath. Roots. My Antonia.*" Rory paused. "Shall I go on?"

"No. I get the idea. What else? A homeschooler wanting to be a public school teacher strikes me as odd."

"You haven't read my résumé, have you?" she boldly asked.

He flushed. "No, I haven't. Been working on the master schedule and next year's budget to present to the school board. I just went online and saw a group of names. Yours was in the first batch of five."

"So, you're interviewing five of us?"

"Three. Two already found jobs by the time I contacted them." He paused. "The other two are coming in this afternoon. Frankly, they'll most likely be better candidates than you, Rory. Give me a minute if you would."

The principal reached for what she assumed was her résumé and skimmed through it. Then his gaze met hers.

"You only have three years' experience in the classroom, not counting your student teaching. One of the other applicants has taught a dozen years. The other almost twenty. Both in the public school system, whereas you've only taught in a private school. Offhand, I'd say they're better candidates because of that." He shrugged. "That's just the way it is."

She decided to take the bull by the horns, per Betty's advice.

"I'm better than both of them," she declared. "I think being homeschooled and then earning my GED opened my eyes. I went to college later than most, starting when I was twenty-six. I truly loved my last school, and I am up for a new challenge. I'm hungry, Mr. Milton. I'm smart. Enthusiastic. Loyal to a fault. Since I am a newbie to public schools, you can take me and mold me however you see fit. I can be a reflection of you and your philosophy regarding education. You're the strongest cheerleader for Sugar Springs High School. I want to be captain of your pep squad and support you however I can. I can sponsor any club you want. Teach as many preps as you can throw at me. Spend as many hours at school as necessary and beyond. I've been around the world, to over twenty countries. I know how to connect with teenagers. For goodness' sakes—I actually *like* them —even the unlikeable ones.

"I want this job, Mr. Milton," she said earnestly. "I need this job. And you need what I bring to the table."

He looked startled by her words, and then a slow smile crossed his face. "Did you happen to meet Betty Cox as she was leaving?"

"Yes, I did. We introduced ourselves. She told me she'd recently resigned, and I told her I was here for an interview."

"Well, you made a good impression on her, Rory. The text I received a few minutes ago was from Betty."

The principal reached for his phone and turned it around so it faced her, and she could read the message on the screen.

Hire her, you old fart. It'll be the best
decision you make this summer.

GRINNING, Rory's gaze met his. "Do you allow all your teachers to speak to you that way, Mr. Milton?"

"Betty's a former teacher now. And older than me. She's the one who broke me in when I was a first-year teacher many moons ago." He smiled. "She also helped me adjust to my role when I became principal here. If you won Betty over in just a few minutes—and she's a hard nut to crack—then you have something special."

"I know her spot and Paige Laramie's are open."

He chuckled. "Do you have a preference? The master schedule's already set. I can't go mixing things up now. It's either the US and World History classes Paige taught or Betty's gov and econ sections."

Rory considered it a moment. "My love of history wins out, Mr. Milton. If you are offering me the job, then I would prefer Paige's sections."

Milton let out a long breath. "Fine by me. You can keep Paige's room. She still hasn't come to clean out her things. Promised me she'd do it this week."

The principal reached for his phone and typed a quick message. Looking up, he said, "That was to Betty, letting her know I'd taken her advice." He glanced at his watch. "Let me call Paige now. She should be at her lunch break. They're filming in our gym today."

He tapped his screen and held the phone to his ear. "I've just hired your replacement, Paige. Do you have time to come up and meet with her? Name's Rory Addison. Okay, good."

Milton hung up. "She said for me to bring you down

to the gym. She's eating and will finish up by the time we get there."

Rory rose and offered her hand. "Thank you, Mr. Milton. I promise that I won't let you down."

As he walked her from the office, he said, "You'll make some mistakes, but I think Betty is right. You'll do just fine at Sugar Springs High School."

He stopped in an office and removed keys from where they hung on a board. "Your room key. Cabinet and desk keys. The marked one lets you in the front door in case you want to come up and work on a weekend."

They made their way to the gym, Milton pointing out the cafeteria, which was full of people.

"The craft services set up there to feed the cast and crew while they're filming here at school for a few days. We have a lot of students from our drama department volunteering on this production. And our very own Sarah Meinholdt, the speech and drama teacher, has the lead role in the movie."

Rory had read about that online, how Chloe Turner had left the production after a week due to creative differences between her and director Tanner Haddock. She couldn't help but wonder if the teacher turned film actress would also leave her teaching position if the movie proved to be successful.

Milton showed her the auditorium and indicated the Social Studies wing as they moved through the building. He told her she would need to sign her contract and asked her to return at nine-thirty tomorrow morning, promising he'd take her to the administration building and introduce her to the superintendent and Director of Human Resources.

When they reached the gym, the hallway had a few people milling about.

"Paige?" the principal asked.

"Inside," someone said.

They entered the gym. Thankfully, the air conditioning was on in this part of the building. Then her heart began beating in double-time as they approached who had to be Paige Laramie, deep in conversation with the incredibly handsome Tanner Haddock.

Paige turned as they arrived. "Thanks for bringing Rory down, Joe Bob. Go back and finish up that budget," she teased.

"I'd ask to trade with you, but I know that would be a lost cause," the principal said and left.

"Hi, Rory. I'm Paige," the screenwriter said, offering her hand. "This is my husband, Tanner."

"Husband?" she squeaked.

He laughed and also offered his hand. Rory couldn't help but be starstruck by the actor's charisma and good looks. "Yes, we got married on the Fourth of July. We'll wait and take our honeymoon once we wrap this film."

Tanner leaned over and kissed his new wife. "I'm going to grab something to eat while they work on the lighting." He turned back to her. "Nice to meet you, Rory."

"Same," she managed to get out.

After the actor left, Paige said, "I know it's a little overwhelming meeting him, but Tanner is from a small town. Way smaller than Sugar Springs. And you're a star in your own right. I've watched you skate on TV during the Olympics."

"That was pretty long ago."

"You brought home the gold twice. Made Americans proud." A shadow crossed Paige's face. "I'm sorry about what happened to you. I guess your injury prevented you from further competition."

"It did. That's when I went to college and earned my

teaching degree. I'll be taking over your sections this coming year."

"I'm happy to leave everything. My gift to you. Use what you can and junk the rest." Paige laughed. "Now Joe Bob can get off my back about cleaning out my room. Let me show you to your new home away from home."

The screenwriter took Rory back the way she and Milton had come, pointing out more than the principal had. When they reached a room at the end of a wing, Rory took the keys Milton had given her and opened the door.

"Betty Cox is across the hall from me. Maybe. Maybe not. I've heard rumors she may be retiring. We're friends, but I've been so busy with this shoot all summer that I haven't had time to visit with her."

"Betty turned in her resignation this morning," Rory informed her. "I met her as she was leaving Mr. Milton's office."

"Call him Joe Bob. He'll get a big head if you keep up the mister stuff."

Quickly, Paige showed Rory everything in the room and pulled four notebooks from a shelf.

"These contain my lesson plans for each semester for both courses, along with lecture notes and various keys for assignments. As I said, use anything that looks good but make it your own. This room. The kids. It's yours now, Rory."

"Are you sad to walk away from this?" she asked, seeing Paige's eyes had misted over.

"Yes and no. I love the kids. I love teaching. But writing is in my blood. I've sold three scripts now as Laramie Fisher. Stepping away from teaching and focusing on writing full-time is what I want to do. I've had some good times in this place, though. You will, too."

"Thanks for everything, Paige."

"Let me give you my number. Just in case you have a question about something."

"I promise not to overuse it. Or sell it to the press," Rory teased.

They traded cell numbers, and as they walked back to the gym, Paige asked, "Where are you living now?"

"With my grandmother in Tyler. I left a teaching job in Houston and moved in with her while I've been looking for a new position. I lived with Granny Bea when I went to college in Tyler."

Paige's brow furrowed and then she said, "It would be a lot more convenient for you if you lived in Sugar Springs."

"Oh, I definitely want to move here. I don't want a twenty-mile commute each way."

"Why don't you move into my house? It's only a few blocks off the square. I was going to see about renting it out but since you're taking my classroom, it would be nice if you also stayed in my house. I'm not sure what I want to do with it in the long run, so I can't make any promises. I do know we'll be going to Greece and then back to California for Tanner to edit his film, so we won't be in Sugar Springs for a good while. You're welcome to live in it for the entire school year."

She was flabbergasted. "I ... that is ... I would like that. Very much."

"Great. We should be through shooting about two weeks or so from now. Definitely by the end of the first week in August. That would give you time to move in and get settled for a few days before school began. I don't want to push you into this, but it would be nice to know my house was being taken care of by someone I trust." Paige laughed. "And I know we don't know each other, but you're a fellow teacher. It's an instant bond."

"I'm happy to stay in it for the upcoming school year.

Let me know the rent. I can write you a check for the first month."

Paige shook her head. "No, I don't need rent. If you'll simply cover the utilities—electricity, water—and take care of the place, that'll be enough."

When Rory protested, the former teacher waved her hands. "Honey, I know what the pay is. You won't be making much. I already have a new place to live with Tanner. I just need someone to look after my house here. I don't really need the rent money now that I'm selling screenplays. Just keep the grass cut and the utilities paid, and we'll both come out fine."

"If you're sure."

"I'm positive." Paige glanced at her watch. "I need to get back on set. Can you meet me here tomorrow at eleven-thirty? I can use the lunch break to take you to the house and make sure it's okay with you."

"That's perfect. I'll be here."

"Come to the gym early. Say eleven. You can watch a little of the filming before we head out." She grinned. "I think you might appreciate seeing Tanner work his magic."

She felt the blush heat her cheeks. "I'd like that opportunity. For now, I think I'll stay in your room—my room—and get familiar with things."

Paige smiled, looking around the classroom. "I remember how proud I was to call this my room." She hugged Rory. "I hope you enjoy it here in Sugar Springs."

After Paige left, Rory strolled around the room, thinking how she would arrange the furniture, which now stood in the hallway. She knew custodial crews shampooed carpets, painted, and cleaned windows each summer and wondered when she would be able to get in to put her touch on the place she would spend the better part of each day for the coming school year.

Her cell rang, and she saw Betty Cox's name on the screen. Answering it, she said, "Hi, Betty. Mr. Milton showed me what you texted him."

"Well, I wanted him to know my opinion of you as I walked out that door, Rory. I think you'll be a fine asset to Sugar Springs High School and the Social Studies Department."

"I'm in my room now. He took me down to meet Paige Laramie, and she brought me upstairs. Gave me everything in the room. I have so much to look over and explore."

"Paige and I always kept the most important things in notebooks. I called them our bibles."

"She gave me a fall and spring one for each history course. I noticed they're in school colors, red and blue."

"Those notebooks will be your lifeline. Skim through both so you have an idea of the big picture, and then concentrate on the fall curriculum. That would be my advice."

"I'm happy to take everything Paige handed down to me. I'm only selfishly sorry that I won't have you across the hall from me, Betty. I think we would have had a lot of fun together."

The older woman laughed. "Joe Bob is probably happy I won't be there to cause him trouble. I do hope you're still planning to come to dinner tonight."

"I wouldn't miss it."

"I just found out we'll be four this evening. My son is coming to eat, as well. I haven't seen him since Christmas."

"Oh, then I should come another time," she protested.

"No, I insist you come tonight. I'd like you to meet

him and my husband. I'm just calling to confirm the time with you. Five-thirty okay? We tend to eat early."

Betty said she would text the address to Rory, and they hung up. She called Granny Bea and got her voice-mail and left a message that she wouldn't be home for dinner but would be back later this evening.

Then Rory did a quick spin in place, squealing for joy.

She had a job. A place to live.

And a fresh start in life. Far away from that bastard Bradley Bolton.

3

W alker got out of his car and entered the diner. Janie met him, handing over a cup of coffee to him.

"Your other half is in your usual booth," she told him. "He's already ordered for you both."

He went to the back of the diner and slid into the booth. Gideon nodded a greeting.

"You set to go?" his friend asked.

"Yes. I rented a small U-Haul. It's got all my clothes and cartons of law books. A couple of paintings I'm partial to. It's sad to boil down a life of thirty-six years to just a few boxes."

"You're leaving all your furniture behind? You paid a fortune for it, Walker."

He nodded. "Renata said the place will show really well with the furniture still there, as if it were staged. You know I have zero taste. That's why I hired an interior decorator to come in and furnish the place from top to bottom when I moved in. Besides, I don't have a place to live. All the furnishings were tailored to fit that space. No, Gid, I want a clean break from the past. New life, new start. Old furniture, nice as it is, stays behind."

Walker remembered the day he had moved into the

high-rise four years ago. He had made partner and had always loved the Turtle Creek area of Dallas. Pride had filled him when he signed the papers making the condo officially his. Unfortunately, he'd barely been home to enjoy it. His life had been consumed by work. One thing he did know which had to change was the amount of time he spent in his office. That was just one of the reasons he was returning home to Sugar Springs.

"How did your meeting with the detectives go yesterday?" Gideon asked.

"I told them everything I knew—which was next to nothing. I explained my relationship to Elton Briggs. How he'd been the consummate professional, and how Sapphire & Sammons and all the partners had trusted Briggs completely. He'd been employed there for decades. They didn't indicate they knew where he might be, just reaffirmed that the firm had been bled dry. Let's just say I won't be getting my last paycheck," he finished.

"What about your clients? I know you said you resigned, but did you talk to any of them?"

"No. Leaving the firm, I thought it would be unethical to contact them. From what I read in the newspapers, however, a majority of our clients immediately jumped ship and quickly found new representation. Actually, a lot of them went to Christine's firm, which doesn't surprise me."

"Do you think she'll run for District Attorney next year?"

Janie arrived, setting down their plates and pouring fresh coffee.

After the server left, Walker answered, "Probably, but I don't care. We aren't in touch. Haven't been since our divorce. Besides, Dallas is in my rearview mirror as far as I'm concerned. Except for you, Gid. I still wish you would take up my offer and move into the condo."

"No, there's no reason for me to do that when you can sell it and make a profit. Use that to buy something in Sugar Springs. I couldn't make your mortgage payment anyway on my salary."

"You wouldn't have to. I told you that you could live there as long as you wanted, rent-free."

Gideon's mouth set stubbornly. "And I told you I didn't need your charity. Besides, I'm barely home as it is. It doesn't matter where I live. I stumble in. Grab a few hours of sleep. Shower and change clothes. Then I'm out the door again."

"Has the task force come up with any solid leads?"

"Not one," his friend said flatly. "I don't know what it's going to take to catch this killer. Whoever he is, he's batshit crazy to do the things he's done to these women. No, that's not right. He *is* crazy—like a fox. If he's ever caught? I'm sure he'll have the slickest lawyers plead insanity for him. It would take someone totally off their rocker to commit these kinds of murders."

"I hope you can find him soon. For your peace of mind and that of the citizens of Dallas," Walker said. "I suppose I won't be having any visits from you until this case is solved."

"Nope. It's all hands on deck, twenty-four/seven. When I do come, where will you be?"

"I'll need to find somewhere to live. I don't want to be living with my parents in my mid-thirties. I will stay with them at least until the sale of the condo goes through. After that, I'll definitely need my space, whether I rent or buy something. I love my mom, but she will absolutely smother me with love and attention."

"I'm envious, Walker," Gideon said. "You're leaving behind one life and entering a new one. Well, not exactly new. We both know what life is like in Sugar Springs."

"It will be a slower paced life. I know that," he said. "And the law I practice will be dabbling in a little bit of everything. Yes, I may have to go to court occasionally, but it won't be the type of high-profile cases I usually argue. I'll be writing wills. Doing estate planning. A little criminal law. Personal injury and bankruptcies. A variety of things. It should keep things interesting."

"Remember, you can always come back to Dallas if you miss it," Gideon reminded him. "Try Sugar Springs and see if it's a fit for you. If it isn't, any law firm in Dallas would be happy to have you sign on as a partner."

"No," Walker said firmly, shutting down those thoughts. "I realize now I was flaming out. I want to keep practicing law, but I want the kind of life my dad has had. Doing something he loves. Staying busy—but not too busy. He managed to spend time with his family and serve his community."

"Are you thinking about a family? I know that was a sticking point with you and Christine. That she only mentioned not wanting kids after you got married."

"Definitely. We're thirty-six, Gid. I want to be married again. My little starter marriage of a few months gave me a taste of what marriage could be. Not that Christine was home enough, but when she was. I enjoyed those rare occasions when we cooked together. Snuggled on the couch and watched a movie. Made love without rushing out the door. I'm hoping to find the kind of life my parents have lived all these years. My gut tells me it's waiting for me in Sugar Springs."

They finished breakfast in companionable silence, and this time Gideon picked up the check. They went to their cars, and Gideon threw his arms around Walker, squeezing tightly.

"We always keep up by text. Even when we don't have time to see each other because of work. I expect you to keep that practice up," his friend said. "As soon as my case ends, I'm due for some vacation time. A bunch has stacked up. I'd love to spend it in Sugar Springs with you. Fishing. Drinking beer on the porch. Just chilling."

"Sounds good to me, buddy."

Walker drove to his high-rise for the final time, leaving his car and the attached trailer parked in front of the building. He went up to his condo, walking through each room slowly, his eyes sweeping over things to make certain nothing of importance had been left behind.

Going back downstairs, he told Jimmy at the concierge desk goodbye, slipping him and the doorman envelopes with a hefty amount of cash. Then he drove the short distance to Renata's real estate office in order to drop off his set of keys.

The realtor brightened as he stepped into her office and said, "We have a showing at nine this morning, Walker. A recent widow who has a sizeable house on White Rock Lake. She's looking to downsize—and has a good friend in your building she would love to be close to. The way she talked to me, I can almost guarantee you that she'll buy your condo."

"Just let me know, Renata. I can drive into Dallas for the day to sign any kind of papers."

"I think this might happen today, Walker. Why don't you delay leaving town for a couple of hours and let me show her the place? My gut tells me once she sees it, she'll make an offer. I'll be listing her house soon. She could move in right away to your place and give me time to get hers ready to put on the market."

It wasn't as if he had a set timetable. "Okay. I can do that."

"Why don't you be back here at the office by ten-thirty?"

"I guess I'll see you then."

He handed over his keys and went back to his car, wondering how he would kill the next couple of hours. He decided to leave his car with the trailer attached at Renata's office and used a ride share to go to NorthPark Center. The giant indoor mall was one of the first built in the nation and a place he'd enjoyed going to at Christmastime, seeing all the decorations and watching the man who played Santa Claus talk to large groups of children, telling them stories about the North Pole.

Though the stores were closed at this time of the morning, the mall was opened. He walked a few laps, killing time, seeing other walkers Most looked to be of retirement age, with a few sets of moms pushing strollers thrown in. He hoped Renata was right, and he could tie up the sale of his place today. If he did, he wouldn't have any reason to return to Dallas, unless it was to see Gid. Walker took another ride share back to the realtor's office, where the receptionist said Renata and Mrs. Finegold were in the conference room discussing the sale.

"I can have you wait in Renata's office if you'd like, Mr. Cox."

Before he could reply, Renata appeared. "Good. You're here. Come meet Mrs. Finegold, the new owner of your condo." She leaned close and whispered, "She went fifteen percent above asking price, thanks to the furnishings staying."

Walker did so and had an interesting conversation with the elderly woman while Renata drew up the closing papers. Mrs. Finegold had lived an unusual life, traveling around the world with her executive husband. They had finally settled in Dallas when their children were teenagers, and all three still lived in the area. The widow had lost her husband two months ago and told

Walker that their six thousand square foot home was just too much house for her with him gone.

"I have a dear friend who moved to your building when she lost her husband three years ago," Mrs. Finegold told him. "That's why I was familiar with it. Renata is friends with my daughter, and I called her up, asking if she wanted to not only sell my house but if a spot in your building might be open."

The widow's eyes twinkled. "When she told me she had a brand-new listing in it, I knew I wanted it before I even saw it. You are quite generous in leaving your furnishings behind, Mr. Cox. The décor goes perfectly with each room, much more than the furniture I could bring. This way, having a furnished place, I can have an estate sale after my children have chosen the items they wish to have. You have made this quite easy for me. Might I ask where you are moving?"

"Actually, I'm leaving Dallas," he revealed. "I'm from a small town in East Texas, just outside of Tyler. A place called Sugar Springs. My father is an attorney in town there, and I will be taking over his law practice now that he's retiring."

"My, that sounds wonderful, Mr. Cox. I wish you all the best in your new chapter in life."

"And I wish you the same, Mrs. Finegold. I'm glad my place is going to someone who will take care of it."

An hour later, Walker was finally on the road. He called his mom first to give her a heads up that he would be arriving today.

She answered on the second ring. "Hello, Walker, dear. Guess what I did today? I turned in my resignation to Joe Bob Milton."

"Oh, I guess that's why I felt the earth tremble earlier this morning," he teased. "So, it's official, Mom?"

"It is. As much as I've enjoyed what I've done all

these years with the kids, I'm ready to do for myself now. I can't thank you enough for agreeing to come home and take over your father's practice. If you hadn't agreed to do so, I'm not sure he would have been willing to step away now."

She told him she had his old room, which she had turned into a guest room, ready for him.

"How much are you bringing with you?"

He chuckled. "Not as much as you'd think. I have my clothes and law books. A couple of odds and ends that are in boxes."

"You can store those in the garage, dear. I'm so looking forward to seeing you."

"Would you make your chicken enchiladas for me tonight?" he asked. "It's been a long time since I had them."

"I'm one step ahead of you, honey. I was already making them for dinner tonight."

"You rarely make that recipe. Why out of the blue? To celebrate putting in your retirement papers?"

"That—and the fact I invited a new teacher from Sugar Springs to dinner this evening. She was going in to be interviewed by Joe Bob as I was heading out. We chatted for several minutes. She's a lovely girl, and I wanted to welcome her to town. I hope you don't mind that she'll be at dinner tonight."

"No, I don't mind. As long as you don't try to do a little matchmaking."

"Are you opposed to getting married again, Walker Cox?" Her tone was sharp, that teacher tone she used on him at times when she was displeased with something he'd done or said.

"That's not it, Mom. In fact, I *do* hope I'll find someone in Sugar Springs. I just don't need my mommy to find a wife for me. This big boy will do it himself in his own good time."

Betty Cox laughed heartily. "I'll see you when you get here. Oh, would you mind stopping by the bakery and getting something for dessert?"

"Bakery? No, ma'am. If I'm choosing, it'll be coconut pie from Ida Lou's. See you soon."

Walker called his dad's cell next.

"Hello, son," Campbell Cox said. "How is the news from Dallas?"

"I met with the police yesterday and need to make myself available if they have further questions. I doubt they will. They're getting the same song from everyone they're interviewing. No one knew what Elton Briggs was going to do. It wasn't as if he were siphoning off funds slowly. It was well planned and executed, done in one fell swoop. Clients have been abandoning the firm in droves. There really is no more Sapphire & Sammons, except in name only."

"I know how disappointed you are by this turn of events, Walker. Maybe it's for the best, though."

"I hadn't told you or Mom, but I had been thinking about resigning my partnership the very day this all broke. I had breakfast with Gid that morning and told him I was ready for a big change in my life. How I'd thought about returning to Sugar Springs. And that was before you hit me up with your retirement and asked me to step into your shoes."

"My handing the reins of the practice over to you is perfect timing then," Dad said, sounding pleased. "I'm just glad it's you, Walker. I've built something special here over the decades. This firm has a relationship with so many different people in the area. They'll like the continuity of you taking over for me. Family is important in this neck of the woods."

"I agree. I'm on my way out of Dallas now, Dad. I just sold my condo to a spry widow. She's bought it and all the furnishings, so it looks as if I'll be starting from scratch. See you for dinner tonight."

Walker concentrated on the road ahead. The one which would lead him to Sugar Springs—and a new kind of life.

4

Rory wished she could have stayed in her new classroom until it was time to head over to Betty Cox's for dinner. Unfortunately, two things prevented her from doing so.

One, her stomach rumbled, letting her know it was time to eat. Two, the lack of air conditioning was starting to get to her. There was no way she could remain in this stifling heat. She collected the precious notebooks, which she would comb through carefully before she started her orientation training and staff development sessions. Slinging her purse over her shoulder, she locked the classroom door and made her way downstairs. She returned to her car and placed the notebooks on the back seat and thought she might drive around and find somewhere nearby to grab a bite to eat, as well as see a bit of Sugar Springs.

Pulling from the front parking lot, Rory circled the school, seeing a second parking lot on the back side, which was full. It looked as if the gym was the closest entrance to the building. All these cars must be from the cast and crew who were filming scenes there.

She still couldn't believe her luck today. She'd been hired to teach two subjects she enjoyed although this would be her first crack at teaching World History. She had met Paige Laramie, who graciously gave Rory ownership of a treasure trove of teaching materials so that she wouldn't have to start from scratch in her preparations. Finally, Paige had provided Rory a place to live, and the cost would be substantially less than what she had paid in Houston.

Even if she had been splitting the bills with Bradley.

Rory decided to drive by the house now, just to see its location and what it looked like. Plugging the address into her map app, she reached it in just a few minutes. As she pulled up to the curb, she sat in the car, staring at the cute frame house.

A place to live. A new beginning. A chance to repair her damaged reputation. She couldn't ask for anything more.

She drove a few blocks farther, finding herself in the heart of Sugar Springs, a large town square with a beautiful gazebo in its center. She parked her car and turned slowly to see what stores were located here. She saw a pharmacy and hardware store. A bakery and insurance office. A law office, which she wondered if it might be where Betty Cox's husband was located.

Food-wise, she had her choice of eating at a pizza parlor, Romano's, but she didn't want that much to eat. That made her decision easy, and she decided on the diner. She grabbed the world history notebook which held the fall curriculum. She could skim over it while she ate a light lunch and then possibly go to the local library and find a quiet spot to spend the rest of the afternoon with the notebook. While she felt comfortable teaching U.S. history since she'd done so the past three years, she would need to familiarize herself more with what she was to teach in the other subject.

It was one-thirty when she entered the diner, and

only a handful of tables and booths had people still eating. A woman with abundant white hair and sparkling blue eyes met her.

"Table for one?" she asked.

"Yes. A booth if I could have it."

"You got it, honey."

The woman led Rory to a booth which looked out over the square and asked, "Is this okay?"

"Perfect." She slid into the booth and placed her notebook on the table.

The woman handed her a menu and smiled. "I'm Ida Lou. I own this place. Looking at that notebook, with Sugar Springs' mascot splashed on the front of it, I'm guessing you're a teacher."

She grinned. "That's a good guess. I was just hired this morning to teach history at the high school."

"I know you aren't the new head football coach, so you must be taking Paige Laramie's place in the Social Studies Department."

"You're very well informed, Ida Lou." She stuck out her hand. "I'm Rory. Rory Addison."

The two women shook hands, and Ida Lou said, "Well, it's nice to have you in town. I don't know where you're living now, but if you need a realtor, I can point you in the right direction."

Knowing how gossip spread through a small town, Rory wasn't ready to explain how Paige was allowing her to live rent-free in her house and so she said, "Thanks, but I've already arranged for a place to live."

Ida Lou handed her a menu. "Take your time, honey. Just wave when you're ready to order."

As she perused the menu, her stomach growled. She had a feeling Betty Cox would feed her pretty well tonight, and so she didn't want to fill up, especially since it was already so late.

Motioning for Ida Lou, she handed over her menu. "I'll do the Cobb salad and an iced tea, please."

"Sweet tea?"

"No sugar for me. Plain is fine." That was the former athlete in her talking.

"Coming right up, Rory."

As the older woman headed toward the kitchen to place the order, Rory opened her notebook. At the front was an outline of the materials to be studied during each grading period for the fall semester. She spent her time studying the outline, thinking of those places and eras. In world history, she would be teaching topics such as Ancient Greece and Rome, the Middle Ages, and the Renaissance and Reformation the first half of the year. She already knew in U.S. history that she would cover the nineteenth century after the Civil War and through the end of World War I in the twentieth century.

Ida Lou returned, bearing both salad and tea. Rory lost herself in the magic of Paige Laramie's notebook, filled with all kinds of goodies. As she read through everything, she made some notes of ideas she had herself and how she might implement them.

When she finished her salad, Ida Lou took it away and said, "Stay as long as you'd like, Rory. You can see the place is empty. You aren't in anyone's way. By the way, your lunch is on the house as a welcome to Sugar Springs."

She started to protest and thought better. Instead, she expressed her gratitude to the diner's owner.

Ida Lou chuckled. "I figure you'll spend some time here as it is over the next year. Glad to have you in Sugar Springs, honey."

Rory had thought after lunch she might go to the library, but she was comfortable in the booth and decided she would stay until it was time to go to dinner at Betty's house. She intended to leave a generous tip, however, for the time she would spend in the diner.

Though she was absorbed in the notebook's materials, she sensed when someone new entered the diner. Glancing up, she heard Ida Lou say, "Hello, stranger." She threw her arms about the man who had entered.

He was as hot as they came.

He was dressed casually in a T-shirt and cargo shorts, which showed off his muscular calves. He looked about six feet, with a lean, athletic frame. His hair was dark brown. She wished she could see what color his eyes were.

Immediately, she lowered her eyes and began reading again, feelings rushing through her that she wished to banish. She had been celibate as a nun when she'd left the skating world and earned her college degree and had only been involved with one man during her teaching years. A man Rory had thought she would marry.

A man who betrayed her on every level possible.

He was why she'd sworn off men. She couldn't trust them. Any of them. Not after what she'd gone through the past year.

She'd last had sex the week before Christmas, more than half a year ago. The day the news broke. She hadn't even thought about sex in all these months.

But right now her body was coming alive. Tingling because of the smokin' hot guy who'd just walked in. She would need to put those thoughts on hold. Being in a small town, gossip spread quicker than wildfire. As a teacher, she would be under extra scrutiny by the citizens of Sugar Springs, especially the parents of her students, and those students, as well. Rory would have to be discreet in her social life. As it was, she worried about a student or parent Googling her and linking her to the scandal with Bradley.

She told herself again she was done with men. They were a thing of the past. Instead, she would establish herself in town and make certain her reputation remained spotless.

Then she sensed the stranger coming her way. With the entire diner empty of customers, she wished he would sit at another table far from her.

Instead, he came right up to her and asked, "May I sit a few minutes with you?"

Rory looked up, struck anew by his good looks now that he was next to her. His eyes were brown like his hair, the color of melted dark chocolate. He had cheekbones that could cut glass and lips so sensual that she found herself holding her breath.

Still, she told herself she wasn't interested and gazed at him coolly.

"There are a ton of other places you can sit. Choose one of them."

She dropped her gaze back to the page, hoping her dismissal would make him leave.

He slid into the booth across from her anyway, smiling the most charming smile Rory had ever seen. It was a smile that made her glow from within, and she figured many women must have been dazzled by it. By him.

Putting on her best teacher frown of disapproval, she asked, "Why did you sit uninvited?"

"Because I'm new in town—and I want to get to know you," he declared boldly, causing a ripple of desire to run through her.

He continued, saying, "I grew up here, though. Ida Lou can vouch for me. I'm not some serial killer, so I hope you'll talk to me a few minutes."

"You must think my standards are pretty low if the only people I might rule out might be murderers," she retorted.

Ida Lou brought a to-go cup to the table and placed it in front of the man, whose name Rory still didn't know.

"Thanks, Ida Lou. And would you let this lady know I'm not a serial killer?"

The older woman's eyes widened in surprise, and then she burst out laughing. She swatted him on the shoulder. "You are such a tease, Walker. Behave yourself."

Ida Lou left them, and Rory studied him. "So, your name is Walker. And you used to live here. That means you've been somewhere else. Where?"

"I left for college half a lifetime ago and never came back," he said, taking a sip of his drink. "After graduation, I decided to stay in Dallas when a job opportunity came up. My best friend from Sugar Springs, Gideon Ross, also took a job in Dallas as a policeman. Two small-town boys in the big city, raising hell." He grinned. "And we're still best friends today. In fact, I had breakfast with Gid this morning before I left Dallas."

A longing filled her. She had no friends from her childhood years. No friends now at all. She'd made several during her three years of teaching in Houston, but everyone avoided her like the plague after the scandal hit. No one would eat lunch with her at school. Every time she entered the teachers' lounge, conversation died until she left the room. No one invited her to go anywhere for pizza or a drink or to see a movie. Everyone eyed Rory with suspicion. Those last months in Houston had been as isolating as her time in skating, with no one to lean on.

"What about you?" he asked. "What do you do in

Sugar Springs?" He glanced down at the open notebook on the table and back up at her. Smiling, he said, "You have to be a teacher."

"I am. I'll be teaching history at the high school this coming school year."

Surprisingly, a wistful look crossed Walker's face. "I love history. Always have. Majored in it and political science in college. I have always longed to travel and see the places I've read about, especially battlefields of the Revolutionary and Civil Wars. You'd think by my age I would've been a lot more places, but my job kept me tied up, working long hours."

"You never took any vacations?"

He shrugged. "Not really. I just didn't have the time. Work was too demanding." Determination filled his face. "That's going to change now. I'm going to start a new job. I'm actually going to buy into that work/life balance philosophy."

"I understand exactly what you mean," she said quietly. "Before teaching, my previous job had me working —or thinking about it—around the clock. I'm really looking forward to building a new life for myself here in Sugar Springs."

She offered her hand across the table. "I'm Rory, by the way."

He took it—and took her breath, as well. Just his touch caused her heart to speed up and her mouth to grow dry. He clasped her fingers and shook them before he released her hand.

She wanted to curse him. He looked so cool and collected, while a maelstrom brewed within her. Rory placed her hands in her lap, squeezing them together, trying to get control of herself.

Ida Lou appeared at their table, bearing a box in

hand. "Here you go, darlin', your favorite. Try to share it if you can, Walker."

He laughed heartily. "Maybe I should've asked for two pies."

"You could have, but I only had one coconut in the back. Play nice and share with your folks."

Walker passed a folded bill to the diner's owner, and she slipped it into her apron and walked away.

Sliding from the booth, he said, "Rory, it was very nice to meet you. I hope we'll see each other around town."

"Maybe," she said noncommittally, thinking it would be a very poor decision on her part to spend any time with a man who made her feel the way this one did. She wanted to get off on the right foot in Sugar Springs and earn the respect of her students and other adults. She was done with men.

Done. *D. O. N. E.* Done.

Walker picked up the box and gave her a wave and that beautiful smile again. Rory was thankful she was sitting because it would've been hard to remain standing with him showering such a sunny smile on her.

She refused to watch him leave the diner and lowered her gaze, trying to concentrate on the notebook in front of her. Her focus was shot, though. She cursed him inwardly. He had disrupted her concentration. She didn't think she would be able to get it back.

Rory collected her things and went to Ida Lou, pressing a twenty dollar bill upon her.

"Honey, I said it was the house."

"I know what you said, but I also know tips are the lifeblood of any place serving food. I'll be back, Ida Lou. Thank you for your generosity today."

Going to her vehicle, she placed her notebook on the back seat. Locking the SUV again, she walked the square, going into various stores and browsing, trying to keep her mind on anything except the brown-eyed flirt who'd left such a strong impression upon her.

She left and Googled where the Sugar Springs library was located, driving to and exploring it. She introduced herself to Ruth Hilton, the librarian, who was thrilled to meet her and told Rory she'd be happy to work closely with her on any projects she assigned to her students.

The women spent a happy hour together, perusing the social sciences section, which was much larger than Rory would have expected. Ruth told her some of the projects Paige had had her students work on throughout the year, and Rory told the librarian she would be in touch once she had familiarized herself more with the curriculum.

She went to the restroom in the library to freshen up a bit before heading back to her car and plugging in the directions to Betty Cox's house. Driving the short distance to it, she parked and went to the front door, bearing a candle she'd bought on the square as a hostess' gift.

Ringing the doorbell, she smiled brightly as the door opened. Her smile faded even as the one on Walker's face grew.

"Hi again, Rory. We never traded last names. I'm Walker Cox. Betty is my mom. Come on in."

5

――――――――

Walker saw the bright smile on Rory's face dissipate. Wariness filled her eyes as he stepped back and ushered her inside. In all fairness, he hadn't known who she was when he talked with her in the diner. Yes, his mom had told him she'd invited a new teacher to dinner this evening, but she'd never mentioned Rory by name.

On the other hand, he'd played it pretty close to the vest himself, not mentioning he was a lawyer. He'd talked in vague terms because it had become second nature to him. After his marriage to Christine imploded, Walker had developed trust issues where women were concerned. He rarely dated, in part because of his demanding work schedule, but mostly because he simply didn't trust women anymore. He knew it was unfair to lump all females into the same category as his witchy ex-wife, but it didn't stop him from being irrational and doing it anyway.

When he'd walked into Ida Lou's diner, though, he'd been struck by the woman he saw sitting in the booth. She was the only customer in the place, and Walker found himself drawn to her in some inexplicable way that couldn't be explained. Which was crazy because he was very good with words. He wrote clear, concise briefs. His arguments in court were known for their simple, persuasive language. Mr. Sapphire himself had sat in to hear the closing argument at one of Walker's trials and later told Walker that he'd never heard a closing so eloquent and yet straightforward. So, words weren't an issue. Usually.

But Rory Addison had almost had him tongue-tied. Still, he'd gone into attorney mode as he'd sauntered over to speak with her, displaying his usual, outward confidence. Something about her spoke to him, and he wanted to get to know her better. When he'd arrived home with tonight's dessert and placed it in the fridge, his mom had mentioned that she hoped Rory liked coconut.

That's when Walker put two and two together and realized the intriguing teacher whom he'd met in the diner was the new hire at Sugar Springs High School his mom had invited to dinner this evening.

Something told him fate was working on his behalf.

Something else also told him Rory Addison would not be easy to know. He had a sixth sense about people, reading them well after having spent so many hours choosing jury members. Rory was an example of the old adage, *still waters run deep.*

Walker had always been up to a challenge, no matter how large or small. He was ready to learn as much as he could about Rory tonight.

At least as much as she'd let him know.

Wanting to put her at ease, he closed the door and said, "Come on in. Mom and Dad are in the kitchen. It's this way."

He turned his back, hoping she'd follow him. She had to. She seemed to be a decent person and wouldn't make a scene. At least, that's what he was hoping. Suddenly, he worried about her feigning being ill and fleeing like a deer caught in a car's headlights.

He stopped halfway to the kitchen and turned. "I didn't know you'd been invited to dinner when we met. Well, I did—but Mom didn't tell me your name. Only that she'd invited a new teacher to dinner. I didn't realize it was you. I promise, I wasn't trying to pull a fast one on you."

"I understand," she said primly. "We didn't exchange last names. If we had, I would have asked if you were related to Betty."

"Would knowing I would be here tonight have kept you from coming to dinner?"

"Probably," she said honestly. "I don't have time for games, especially with someone like you."

"Games? What are you talking about? And just what kind of person do you think I am?" he asked, puffing up in anger, thinking it was totally out of character for him to lose his cool.

She eyed him knowingly. "You're very confident, Walker. Almost to the point of being cocky. You came onto me in the diner. Betty's son or not, I'm simply not interested."

"In me—or men in general?" He thought it a fair question.

She took a deep breath. "I'm coming off a broken engagement. I have no plans to take up with anyone anytime soon. I want to focus all my energy into my new job. Being in another relationship this soon is off the table as far as I'm concerned."

"I can understand that," he said quietly. "I was married once myself. Several years ago. It only lasted six months, and I still feel like a fool. I really haven't dated since then. Mostly because of that hectic job I told you about, but part of it was I don't think I have it in me to give my heart to someone again. My ex-wife was not the woman I thought she was."

Rory nodded in understanding. "I can relate to that. My ex-fiancé betrayed me in the worst way possible. I suppose I should be glad I dodged a bullet and didn't marry him, else he would have dragged me down with him even more than he's already done."

Before Walker could ask what she meant by that, his mom appeared and said, "Why, there you are, Rory. I see you've met my son."

"Yes, he told me he's moved back to Sugar Springs recently."

"As of today," Mom said, turning and beaming at him. "We're so glad he's back. Not just because Walker is mine and Campbell's pride and joy and only child, but he's agreed to take over his father's law practice."

"Ah," Rory said. "That makes sense. His presence will allow you to start your wonderful extended vacation."

"Did I hear vacation?" His dad walked out, extending his hand. "Hello, Rory. I'm Betty's other half. She tells me you're new to the faculty at Sugar Springs."

"Yes, I'll be teaching history come the fall semester."

"Rory is taking Paige's sections, honey. But everything's on the table. Let's move to the kitchen. We can talk more there."

Walker liked that even with a guest, his mom had them eating in the kitchen. He had spent so many meals at this table, sharing his life with his parents, asking their advice, listening to them also talk about their day. He blinked a few times, surprised he was misty-eyed by those memories.

"Pass me your plate, Rory, and I'll serve you some chicken enchiladas," Dad said. "Betty makes better ones than you'll find in any restaurant."

They passed around the salad, along with sides of rice and refried beans, and everyone dug into their food.

"This is amazing, Betty," Rory praised after a bite of the enchilada.

"Mom's known for her chicken enchiladas," Walker told her. "She only makes them on special occasions."

"Well, I suppose you coming back to Sugar Springs would be one," Rory said.

"No, Mom made these for you. She didn't know exactly what day I'd be arriving home. But today was a good day," he shared. "I sold my condo in Dallas to a very nice elderly lady with a friend in the building. Packed the few belongings I have and came back to where it all began, here in Sugar Springs."

As they ate, his mom said, "I know neither of my two will know who you are, Rory, but I have to brag on you." Mom looked at him. "Rory is a figure skater."

"*Was* a figure skater," Rory interjected. "I'm just a teacher now who enjoys doing a little Pilates and yoga to try and stay in shape."

"I played sports in high school," Walker said. "I was a better third baseman, but I also played defensive back for the Sugar Springs Knights. Gideon Ross, my best friend, was our star wide receiver and earned a scholarship to SMU. We went to school there together."

A wistful look crossed Rory's face. "I wish I could have had the typical college experience. I was an older student, though."

"But you had wonderful experiences which others only dream about, Rory," his mom insisted. She looked to him. "Rory was an Olympian. She won gold medals in two different Winter Olympics."

"What?" He looked at their dinner guest. "You skated in the Olympics? And won gold?"

Rory smiled bashfully. "Yes, I began skating at a

young age. We lived outside Tyler, and I took lessons there. A coach discovered me and thought I had great potential, so my mom and I moved to Colorado for me to train."

"If you won Olympic golds four years apart, you were competing at an elite level for many years," he said, in awe of her accomplishments. "I'm going to assume you also vied in competitions around the world for the US."

"I did. But that's all behind me now. I've been teaching for three years. First in a private school and now in Sugar Springs."

"Why don't you think about living here while Campbell and I are gone?" Mom offered out of the blue, knocking him for a loop.

"Hey, what about me?" Walker protested.

"This house is large enough," Mom insisted. "You'd both have plenty of space. And you've said you want to find a place of your own anyway, Walker. Rory could act as a caretaker for the place. Campbell and I wouldn't even charge you any rent if you promised to water my flowers and plants."

"Actually, I'm not only taking Paige's spot on the faculty, but she's allowing me to rent her house for the upcoming school year," Rory revealed.

"I thought you could stay here, Walker," Dad said. "While we're gone."

"How long are you going to be traveling?" he asked. "I know you mentioned doing a vacation, but I have no idea where you plan to visit."

"Well, I tried to talk your mom into sailing around the world in a sailboat. She said we might want to start on a bigger ship first, but she's still ready to see the world now."

"What your father is trying to say is that we're going on a cruise. Several cruise ships, to be exact. I've found one which leaves out of Galveston in mid-August. It goes to Central America, through the Panama Canal, and travels down the western side of South America and back up the eastern side. Then it goes throughout the Caribbean and docks in Florida. That's the first ship and leg of our journey."

"The second sails to the UK from Florida," his dad said. We'll stay on it for a while, see places in the UK and then go to the Mediterranean."

His parents took turns describing stops on the rest of their itinerary, both sounding so excited. He realized in that moment how much he loved them—and how much they loved each other, even after forty years of marriage.

"Eventually, we'll make our way back to the west coast," Mom finished. "We'll fly home from California after docking in mid-May. So, we'll be gone about nine months, almost an entire school year." She sighed. "No grading papers. No irate parents. And no faculty meetings! I think it will be heavenly. But I wonder what this next year will bring for the two of you?"

Walker hoped he would be settled into his law practice. That he would have found a home to purchase. He glanced toward Rory.

And maybe love?

He was certainly attracted to her. Moving back to Sugar Springs, he would need to get the lay of the land again. While his mom had kept him up on local gossip, he preferred seeing for himself what single women might be available. Rory had already told him she had an ex-fiancé and no interest in dating right now. He would need to look other places because even if he'd had a terrible experience at marriage and hadn't dated —much less trusted—women these past six years, he was interested in finding a partner and building a life together with her in Sugar Springs. If he could be half as happy as his parents, he believed his next marriage could be a success.

They had dessert, and Rory raved about the pie.

"Nothing like an Ida Lou pie," he told her. "Anytime I come back to visit Mom and Dad, I always make sure we have pie from the diner."

"Delicious as this meal has been, I need to get home to Tyler," Rory said, standing and picking up her plate. "Let me help clean up before I go."

"No, dear," Mom said. "You're a guest, and you need to get on the road. When do you sign your district contract?"

"Tomorrow morning. Joe Bob Milton said to report to him at nine-thirty, and he'll take me to the administration building to meet with the Director of HR."

They all rose, and his mom went and embraced Rory. "I hope to see you before we leave town."

"Thank you for a lovely dinner," she replied. "I appreciate the gesture and hope everyone at the high school will be as warm and friendly as you've been, Betty."

"I'll walk you to your car," Walker offered.

"No, that's all right," Rory said.

"I don't mind," he insisted, seeing she did mind. He figured she'd be too polite to say anything more in front of his parents.

They reached her car and he asked, "What do you have planned after signing your contract?"

"I'm supposed to meet Paige at the high school. They're shooting scenes there tomorrow. She said I could watch some of the filming, and then she'd take me to see her house during the lunch break."

"When can you move in?"

"Probably around the end of the first week in August. It will depend upon when they finish filming."

"After you see the house, you'll be hungry. How about meeting me at the diner? We could have lunch. And more pie," he added, trying to tempt her, not quite ready to give up on her just yet.

Rory frowned. "I made friends with your mom. Not you, Walker. Thanks—but no thanks—to lunch," she said brusquely. "You're acting as if we've been on a date when we simply shared a meal at the same table. I thought I made myself perfectly clear before. I am not interested in you and have no desire to see you socially. I am simply in Sugar Springs to teach. Period. I will be cordial if our paths cross, but I have zero interest in you."

She opened her car door and slid inside, quickly starting the vehicle and pulling out without so much as a wave goodbye.

As he watched her taillights fade, Walker knew there was more to her story. A stunningly beautiful woman—an Olympic champion, nonetheless—turns up in a small town in East Texas. She was more prickly than a pear when it came to men. Especially him, it seemed.

He liked puzzles and vowed to get to the bottom of this one.

6

Walker returned inside the house and heard noises coming from the kitchen. He went to see if his mom needed any help cleaning up.

"Where's Dad?" he asked, knowing how his father always helped in the kitchen after guests had left for the evening.

"He received a call and retreated to his study. Sounded like business to me."

"Then I guess it's you and me on dish duty," he said, picking up a dish towel.

Although his parents owned a dishwasher, it was rarely used in their household. Betty Cox had once shared with her son that some of the best conversations she'd ever had with her husband had occurred as they washed and dried the dishes together after dinner each night. He had always remembered that, and when he came home on infrequent visits, he tried to do the same so he had alone time with his mom.

She filled the sink with hot water and dishwashing soap and slipped on a pair of yellow rubber gloves, picking up the first plate and scrubbing it before passing it along to him to rinse and dry.

"What do you think of Rory Addison?" he asked, curious about Mom's take on the former Olympian turned teacher.

"I liked her from the moment we met. Of course, I almost felt as if I already knew her, after watching her on TV for so many years."

While Walker enjoyed watching the summer Olympics, especially the track and field events and swimming relays, he had never really gotten into the winter version of the games. Living in Texas, where it snowed once in a blue moon and only a dusting at that, he had never known much about winter sports such as the luge and slalom. His mom, however, had always been drawn to figure skating competitions.

"What was she like on the ice?" he asked.

Mom smiled. "Rory was a thing of grace and beauty. She was definitely an athlete, though. She could complete some of the most difficult jumps, far better than any of her competitors. But it was her artistry on the ice that drew me in. Rory was a beautiful young woman and had a way of interpreting the music unlike any other ice skater I've ever watched."

She paused. "Why do you ask?"

Walker decided not to hide his interest and said, "She intrigues me."

Mom gave him a sympathetic look. "I know you haven't really dated much since you and Christine ended things. Do you think you might be interested in Rory?"

He shrugged. "Maybe. Probably." He grinned. "Definitely."

Betty Cox laughed. "Rory is smart, Walker. I know she would certainly challenge you. I sense something in her, though. A sadness."

"She told me she had an ex-fiancé. It wasn't what she

said—but the way she said it. The breakup was fairly recent, and she's not ready to date yet."

"Hmm." His mom handed over the 9x13 glass dish the enchiladas had been baked in. Walker rinsed it, waiting for what she would say.

"You've never been one to back away from a challenge, honey. I think you would be good for Rory. And I think she would be good for you. Don't move too quickly, though. Try to be friends first and then see if you can build upon that friendship. Your father and I were friends from the beginning and have remained each other's best friends for all these years."

He finished drying the casserole dish and set it on the counter. "She didn't seem interested in me one whit," he admitted. "I think I've given her the impression that I'm some slick city lawyer who's a smooth talker. She pretty much told me she wouldn't be dating anyone anytime soon, me, in particular. She wants to devote her time to her new job."

Mom clicked her tongue. "Rory is new in town. She's going to need to make some friends. Keep trying, son. Something tells me that the two of you might be able to build something special together."

He switched topics, asking her more about the trip she had planned, and they finished the dishes as they spoke.

"I think I'll turn in," he said. "I'll see you in the morning."

"Are you going to go to the office with your father?"

"Probably. We'll figure it out." He bent and kissed her cheek. "Goodnight, Mom."

"It's so good to have you home in Sugar Springs, sweetie."

Walker returned to his boyhood bedroom, which looked nothing like it did during his years growing up.

His mom had kept some of his things for a while since he came home occasionally from Dallas on the weekends during college, but after he began law school, she turned his bedroom into a guest room. Gone were his rock band posters from the walls and the many trophies he'd accumulated over the years, both in sports and academics. He did like knowing he didn't have to rush to find somewhere to live on his own. Properties didn't open up in Sugar Springs very often. With his parents being gone for almost a year, it would be best for him to stay in the house and act as its caretaker. He would want to meet with Tamara Heath, however, and let the local realtor know he was in the market for a home. Not just anything, but a large, sprawling house for the family he wanted to have sooner rather than later.

He grabbed his tablet and slipped off his shoes, stretching out on the bed, pillows braced behind his back. He searched for Rory Addison online and decided he wanted to see her skate before reading anything, so he pulled up several videos of her at various competitions. Some were at various world championship competitions, while others were videos of her Olympic events. Walker was struck by the combination of pure athleticism and artistic grace in her performances.

Rory was mesmerizing on the ice.

He clicked on a fifth video, glancing at the title and seeing it was another world competition. He wondered how many she'd competed in and how many titles she'd brought home to the United States. Walker watched her skate, and it brought a lump to his throat. It was obvious she was a fierce competitor but had such unabashed joy as she skated.

This video was different from the others he'd watched, though. Her program was coming to an end, and Walker anticipated the last combination of jumps she would perform. From the commentators on each video, he'd learned that most of the skaters did their hardest jump combinations early in their programs, when their legs were fresher. Rory had a tendency to save the most difficult jumps for the very end, which spotlighted her physical endurance. He was amazed at the height she got, flying off the ice and spinning in the air. This time, though, something happened. Something awful.

Something unimaginable.

As Rory came out of her last rotation, he saw her body jerk in an odd way, mid-air. It threw her off-balance, and she hit the ice incredibly hard. Although he didn't hear the break, he could tell from her face that she had landed wrong and broken something.

Then horror filled him as he saw blood on the ice, her body still.

The video continued. People rushed out on the ice to her. It abruptly ended.

Why hadn't he heard about any of this? Then he shook his head as he saw the date. The incident had occurred seven years ago. Seven years ago, he had been putting in incredibly long hours while being a newlywed and trying to squeeze in sex whenever he could. He'd had no time for news, much less following a sport he had never watched before. Nuclear war might have happened, and Walker wouldn't have known, his head buried in case files or his cock inside his new wife.

Curious now, he went back and searched for articles about Rory. He decided to start at the beginning, reading a couple of online biographies. They noted that Rory came from a small town in East Texas and was plucked from obscurity to come and train in Colorado. He read about her storied career in awe. The string of world singles titles in a row. The two triumphant Olympic appearances, both ending in gold.

And then the shooting and career-ending injury.

Rory never spoke about the incident to anyone and never competed again, but her shooting had affected the skating world tremendously. Though some speculated she would go into coaching since she had parted ways with her own coach several years before the shooting, she left the figure skating world behind. The last thing in the official biographies said Rory was attending college, which he already knew because she held a teaching degree.

Walker decided to dig deeper now, fascinating by her story. Googling her name coupled with teacher, he found a few sites, one with her picture in a yearbook from a private school just outside of Houston. It was the typical teacher pose, one he'd seen over and over from his mom's lengthy career. He wondered why she had left this school, though. She seemed happy and smiling in the few pictures he found. He went a few pages deeper into his search—and that's when he found what he was looking for. She was mentioned, almost as an afterthought, in an article about Bradley Bolton. Rory was cited as Bolton's fiancée. Walker then dived into this man.

What he found turned his stomach.

Bradley Bolton was on the faculty with Rory and had been an English teacher and girls' wrestling coach. Apparently, he had been having an affair with Aimee Withers, one of his athletes who was eighteen years old. When news of that affair came out, a huge scandal ensued, and Bolton had voluntarily resigned from his teaching position last December. Since then, five other young women had come forward, all speaking of how the educator had groomed them, telling them how special they were and how much he loved them, but that nothing physical had happened until each girl turned eighteen. The affairs had been intense but brief, with the wrestlers then each moving on to college.

And Bolton targeting another young woman the next year.

Because every relationship had the appearance of consent, and the fact the girls were all of legal age when the relationships were consummated, no criminal charges could be filed against Bolton. Still, the community uproar was great enough to cause him to resign. Walker didn't bother to pursue where Bolton was now.

He closed his tablet and set it on the nightstand next to the bed, deeply disturbed by what he'd read. So, this was the man Rory Addison had been engaged to. He assumed they had been living together since they were engaged. He couldn't imagine how this betrayal would have hit Rory. No wonder she seemed so untrusting toward men.

Knowing something about the school business from his mom's many decades in it, Walker knew Rory would have been painted with that same brush of scandal. Though guiltless, she would have been lumped in with Bolton. Parents would have despised her. Students would have gossiped about her. Other teachers and administrators would have frozen her out. He figured she had finished out the school year, and her contract had not been renewed. Even if it had been by some wild chance, it would have been too uncomfortable for her to remain teaching in that school.

Now that he knew why she had come to Sugar Springs and had a handle on her background, Walker knew he would need to proceed with extreme caution. For a moment, he wondered if he should even try to do so. He would be the first to admit that he was damaged goods himself, untrusting of women after his experience with Christine.

Yet there was something about Rory that tugged at his heart. He wanted to protect her. Get to know her. See if anything might be possible between them. Perhaps his mom was right, and he shouldn't try to pursue a romance with her. Instead, he should aim for friendship to begin with. If they could become friends—if they enjoyed one another's company and got along—then just maybe they might have a chance to deepen the relationship and see where things went.

How Walker would do that, he had no idea. Although Sugar Springs was a small town, it did have about thirty thousand people in it. If he were a teacher at the high school, he would have a better chance of running into her and getting to know her. Being an attorney, however, their paths might not ever cross unless Rory needed legal advice. Something told Walker he would be the last attorney she might seek out in times of trouble.

If she wouldn't come to him, then he would need to come to her. He didn't want to appear as if he were stalking her, but he wanted to try to run into her if he could. She had said she would be signing her contract in the morning at the school's administration building and then going to meet Paige Laramie at the high school, where they would go to see Paige's house. Walker had met Paige twice and liked her quite a bit. He'd been surprised when his mom told him that Paige had been writing screenplays on the side under a pseudonym. He was even more shocked when Mom told him Paige was engaged to Tanner Haddock. Walker might not follow pop culture much, but even he knew who Tanner Haddock was.

Walker decided that he would need to see if Paige

Laramie might be willing to broker a meeting between Rory and him. Just a way that he might be able to run into Rory and spend some time with her.

He readied himself for bed and decided he would ask his mom and Paige for help tomorrow. As Scarlett O'Hara so famously said?

Tomorrow is another day.

And Walker planned to make the most of it.

7

R ory left the house for her usual morning walk. She had already spent twenty minutes doing a PiYo routine she enjoyed. Even though she was no longer a world-class athlete, she liked doing the stretches and clearing her mind, using the combination of Pilates and yoga.

What she really enjoyed most, however, were her long walks. She usually put in three to four miles each morning, and it was sometimes the best part of her day. She had done a lot of lesson planning in her head on those walks, as well as a lot of soul searching these past few months. Especially after Bradley's scandal hit the news and social media sites.

As she walked down the street, she still couldn't help but feel the taste of bitterness at what her ex-fiancé had put her through. He had been nice-looking, with all-American looks. She had never doubted him. Not once. Bradley had always been attentive to her. Yes, he was gone a lot, but that was the life of a coach, especially a wrestling coach whose competitions involved weekend tournaments. Rory gone to a few of them in the two years she had dated and been engaged to Bradley, but he had told her it wasn't necessary because he understood how boring it was to her. He encouraged her to stay home and get her papers graded so that when he did come home, they would be able to spend quality time together.

The sex had been good. Not outstanding. Her fiancé had little interest in foreplay, wanting to move to the main event every single time. Rory had felt so lucky to have landed a man such as Bradley—with looks, charm, and intelligence—that she had pushed aside the tiny doubts in her head when she wished he would think about meeting her needs every now and then and not make every sexual encounter about his pleasure.

When the news broke that Bradley had been sleeping with Aimee Withers—and the other young women who had then stepped forward—it had been a severe blow to Rory's confidence. She wondered what had been wrong with her. Why she hadn't been enough for Bradley.?

She had been the one to move out of the apartment they shared. The only saving grace had been that the news had come out just as their winter break began. She was able to clear out her things and find somewhere new to live in the two weeks they had off for the holidays. She broke off all contact with Bradley, from deleting him on her phone to blocking him from all her social media accounts. Unfortunately, she'd had to shutter all social media once people began posting horrible things about her, accusing her of knowing what Bradley had done. Saying she had encouraged him. Some of the vicious posts had even speculated that she, too, was sleeping with students on her own or that she'd participated in threesomes with Bradley and his various girls.

He had tried for a while to win her back, leaving notes on her car or flowers at her doorstep. She had no idea how he knew where she'd moved and wound up breaking her lease, moving again to try and put even more distance between them.

What hurt more than his betrayal was how she was treated at school. Every adult froze her out. It was as if she were the one who had been sleeping with students. Everywhere she went, Rory saw judgment in the eyes of others and how they believed she was the one lacking in morals, not Bradley Bolton. The friends she'd eaten lunch with told her she was no longer welcomed at their table. No other tables in the staff lounge invited her to join them, and she ate lunch—when she could keep it down—by herself in her room every day. Not a soul greeted her when she came in every morning and checked her mailbox. No teacher sat with her at faculty meetings. People stopped replying to her emails. It was as if she were totally alone in the world.

Her students had watched her warily. None of them outright confronted her and said aloud what they were thinking, but she saw the smirks and found graffiti scrawled on their desks, which she had to clean on a daily basis.

By spring break, Rory was lonely, isolated, and frustrated beyond belief. Although she had signed a contract which ran for another two years, she couldn't see how she could remain in such a hostile environment. Coming back from spring break with her resignation letter written, she was ready to offer it to her principal when he called her in that first day, telling her he thought it would be best if she didn't return to campus in the fall. Immediately, she handed over the resignation letter she'd brought with her and quickly left his office. It had been the only time any staff member had spoken to her, and it would be the last time any did so until the semester ended. Rory had run through her checklist that final day, turning in her keys and teaching materials, not bothering to ask for any references. All her evaluations had been excellent up until that point. The one time an assistant principal observed her class that spring, she had been given marks so low that she was ashamed. It wouldn't have done any good to challenge the evaluation, though, and she let it slide. She knew having no letters of recommendation had hurt her in her job search, but she was too proud to beg and doubted anyone would have given her a good recommendation.

She headed back toward Granny Bea's, grateful that Joe Bob Milton had taken a chance on her. Yes, Sugar Springs was a small town, and he was trying to fill two positions quickly at a late date. Rory vowed to be the best teacher on campus and let nothing distract her.

Especially Walker Cox.

The attorney was handsome as sin and just her type. Where Bradley had been blond and blue-eyed, Walker was his opposite, with dark brown hair and eyes the color of melted chocolate. She could feel the spark between them and was determined not to see that fire lit. She worried that her past association with Bradley Bolton would come out and the town of Sugar Springs would judge her accordingly. She needed to keep to herself and keep Walker Cox at bay, devoting all her time to her classroom and her students. If she could build a solid reputation as a hard worker this year, she might think about dating in the far-off future. For now, though, any kind of relationship was off the table. Especially with Walker, whose air of confidence told her that he knew just how handsome and charming he was. Well, she was one female who would be immune to falling at his feet.

Rory reached home and showered away the July sweat, carefully doing her makeup and dressing in a sleeveless, knit dress, which she belted to give it a little definition.

She went into the kitchen, where Granny Bea sat sipping her coffee, *Good Morning America* playing softly in the background.

"There you are, Rory," her grandmother said, smiling. "Can I get you something to eat?"

"I'll just grab a bowl of cereal and toss in some blueberries," she said, beginning to do so.

"How was Sugar Springs?" Granny Bea asked. "Did you get to see your new classroom?"

Rory had called to let her grandmother know she had landed the job and that she wouldn't be home until late. This was their first opportunity to talk, though, and so Rory told her everything. How she would be teaching US and World history, taking the place of Paige Laramie.

Granny Bea's eyes lit up. "I've been following everything happening in Sugar Springs with her. I can't believe she's now a screenwriter, and they're filming a movie she wrote in her hometown."

She grinned. "And she's also Mrs. Tanner Haddock now."

"What?"

She explained how Paige and the Hollywood superstar had recently wed and that they would be taking a delayed honeymoon after filming had been completed in Sugar Springs.

"I actually got to meet Tanner," Rory bragged, knowing her grandmother had a crush on the superstar. "He is extremely nice and probably the best-looking man on the planet."

Both women chuckled, and then she continued. "They will go to Greece for a honeymoon and then return to California, where Paige said Tanner would be working on editing the film he directed this summer. Because of that, Paige's house will be vacant, and she asked if I wanted to live in it for this upcoming school year."

Rory elaborated on the generous offer Paige had made, telling Granny Bea she would be moving to Sugar Springs in a couple of weeks once the house was unoccupied.

"I know you'll be glad not to have that commute each day." Her grandmother took Rory's hand and squeezed it. "I'll miss having you here, though, sweetie. It's been nice."

Tears misted in Rory's eyes. "I can't thank you enough for letting me live here, both during college and then this summer while I looked for a job. Without your support, I don't know what I would've done."

"You've gone through some rough times, my dear, but you've come out stronger for them. This job in Sugar Springs will be a new start for you. And hopefully, you will come to see me every now and then."

"Of course, I will."

Rory then told her grandmother about having met Betty Cox and how the woman had been close with Paige. She showed Granny Bea one of the notebooks Paige had gifted to her, explaining how much easier her transition would be from private to public school because of the wealth contained within these sets of notebooks.

"Unfortunately for me, but fortunately for Betty, she has just retired. She and Paige were very close, so I will have another new teacher across the hall from me this year."

"I hope you make good friends with her." Granny Bea's eyes twinkled. "Or him."

She frowned. "You know I'm not interested in seeing anyone. I need some time to heal."

Her grandmother clucked her tongue. "You've had

plenty of time to heal. It's been seven months since you cut that bastard loose. I say it's time to climb back into the saddle and take the ride of your life. On your terms."

Could Granny Bea be right?

"I did meet Betty's husband and son at dinner last night. Campbell Cox is an attorney in Sugar Springs, and he'll also be retiring soon. He and Betty are going to go on a cruise that will leave next month and circle the world. They'll be back sometime in the middle of May."

"I would love to do something like that," her grandmother declared. "Maybe I can get some of the Red Hats together, and we can do a trip like that." She paused. "What about the son? Is he also a teacher, or is he a lawyer like his daddy?"

Rory swallowed. "Actually, he is an attorney and just moved back to Sugar Springs yesterday. He had been practicing law in Dallas, and he plans to take over his dad's law practice."

Her grandmother's eyes sparkled with mischief. "So, what does he look like?"

"He looks like sin on a stick," Rory declared, using one of her grandmother's colorful sayings.

Granny Bea burst out laughing. "Well, somebody's got to take on that stick. Why not you?"

"I think he's a little too cocky for my taste." She glanced at the time on the microwave. "I need to get going. I have to be back in Sugar Springs to sign my contract, and then Paige invited me to watch a bit of the filming today. During lunch, she's going to take me to her house and let me see it."

"Then I won't keep you, honey. I need to go get ready myself. I've got book club this morning. We're going to be discussing another Jodi Picoult novel today."

Rory gathered her purse and went to her SUV, hoping she would be as active as her grandmother when she reached her seventies. Granny Bea wasn't only in a book club, but she also belonged to a cooking club, a gardening club, and did volunteer work at one of Tyler's library branches.

As she drove to Sugar Springs, she thought about what her grandmother had said. Maybe Granny Bea was right. Maybe she should climb back in the saddle and aim for a bit of a social life once she moved to Sugar Springs. Rory decided she would be open if anyone asked her to do anything, male or female. She had hungered for friendship for months and was ready to forge new ones in her future hometown.

The only person she was iffy about was Walker Cox. Her ex-fiancé had oozed confidence and charm. Walker Cox did the same. She declared she would be immune to the man's charms and would be open-minded enough to go out with anyone except the handsome lawyer.

Joe Bob Milton called when she was entering Sugar Springs, telling her he had a meeting which had come up unexpectedly.

"Sorry I can't accompany you to the administration building, but HR knows you're coming."

He provided the address, and Rory headed for it instead of the high school. She parked and went inside, introducing herself to the receptionist. The woman looked a bit puzzled, as if she had seen Rory before but couldn't remember where. Rory used to get that all the time but not so much these days.

She was escorted to the office of human resources, where its head walked her through the contract and had her sign it. She was given a welcome pack, which included the district's yearly calendar for the next two years and also a list of local businesses, many of which gave teachers a discount on goods and services. She noted that one of them was Ida Lou's diner and decided after she toured Paige's house, she would stop there for lunch.

The director gave her the schedule for new teacher orientation, as well as the agenda for the week before school when teacher staff development would occur.

"If you don't mind, I'll forward your cell number to Joe Grafton, the Social Studies Department Chair. I'm sure he'll be in touch with you soon. We'll have three new faculty members this year at the high school. You, Pam Holland, who's just been hired to take Betty Cox's place, and whoever the new head football coach will be. I've just been informed I need to hunt for one."

Rory thanked him and returned to her vehicle, driving to Sugar Springs High School, and parking in the rear lot next to the gymnasium, where filming was taking place this morning.

She gave her name at the door and was admitted by a student volunteer, who showed her where to go. Slipping into the gym, Rory sat in the front row of the bleachers, watching a scene being filmed. The actress in it was electrifying. Rory had read where Chloe Turner had left filming early in the production, and the local speech and drama teacher, Sarah Meinholdt, had taken over for her. Rory didn't think this teacher would be in the classroom much longer. Once this movie came out, directors would line up to work with her. Sarah's teaching days would be a thing of the past.

Another student approached her. "Are you Miss Addison?" he asked.

"Yes, I am," Rory confirmed.

The tall teenager smiled. "I'm Freddie Otts, and I'm serving as Mr. Haddock's assistant on this film." He pointed to the actress Rory had been watching. "That's Miss Meinholdt, our drama teacher. She got a bunch of us jobs on the crew as volunteers. Miss Laramie—

Mrs. Haddock, that is—told me to tell you they only have one more scene to film. Then she'll be right with you."

"Thank you, Freddie. Are you still a student here, or have you recently graduated?"

"I'll be a senior. I've already taken the classes you'll be teaching, but it's nice to have you at Sugar Springs High School, Miss Addison."

Freddie left and Rory watched one more quick scene being shot. After it was completed, Paige joined her, giving Rory a hug.

"Let's take my car," Paige said, and they went to the parking lot.

They chatted comfortably until they arrived at the house Rory had driven by yesterday.

Paige took her inside, saying, "It's small, but cozy, and there's plenty of space for one person. Here's the living room. TVs already hooked up to cable if you don't mind continuing to pay that bill."

They went to the kitchen, which had an eat-in area, and then to the two bedrooms.

"I use this one as my office and the other to sleep in."

Paige took her outside to the backyard, where a plethora of flowers bloomed.

"I'm not certain I have your green thumb," Rory confessed.

"Don't worry. Max McAllister is our biology teacher, and he always has plenty of advice where plants and landscaping are concerned. You can ask him anything. I just do what he tells me to do—and things grow. So, Rory, do you think my place will meet your needs?"

"I love the layout and its location," she declared. "It's the perfect size and really close to work."

Paige told her she would stay in touch in order to give Rory an idea when filming might be completed so she would have an idea about when she'd be able to move in.

"I'll take my clothes but leave everything else for you. Furnishings. Linens. Dishes, pots, and pans. Make this house your home, Rory."

She hugged Paige. "Thank you for your generosity. It's great to have landed a job and already know where I'll be living for the upcoming school year."

"I need to get back to set now, but would you mind if I made one quick stop on our way? I've got to sign some papers at Campbell Cox's office. Campbell has represented me as a screenwriter, but he let me know that he's retiring soon. With Tanner and I moving to California, I'm comfortable with switching over to his lawyer now that we're married. It's just makes sense."

"Sure," she said, hoping that Walker wouldn't be there.

A ding sounded. Paige read the text and typed something back. "Okay, we can go now."

They parked on the square and went inside the law office, where Paige greeted the receptionist.

"Hi, Margaret. Let me introduce you to Rory Addison. She's going to be taking my spot at the high school."

The receptionist, who looked to be in her mid-thirties, grinned broadly. "Oh, I know your name, Miss Addison. I took ice skating lessons as a kid and have always followed figure skating on TV ever since. You are the best skater I've ever seen. The US hasn't come close to winning gold in the Olympics since ..."

The woman's voice faded, and she looked embarrassed.

Trying to put her at ease, Rory said, "Thank you for the compliment, Margaret. It's nice to be remembered so fondly."

What she hated was that this woman's last memory

of Rory skating was seeing her shot on national TV. It seemed as if the incident would forever haunt her.

Paige said, "I'm here to sign—"

"I've got the papers right here," a familiar voice said.

She turned and saw Walker stepping from an office. Her heart sped up, and she cursed inwardly, angry that he was here.

And looked so hot that she felt herself growing warm.

"Dad had to be in court, and he left them with me. He said you'd already talked over everything with him and would merely need to autograph the document," Walker continued.

"Yes, this is just a separation agreement, which will allow me to have another attorney in California represent my interests in the film business," Paige said, accepting the sheaf of papers Walker handed over. She signed and handed them back. "There you go."

Paige's phone rang and she answered it. "Oh, no. All right. I can handle it now. Tell Tanner not to worry. I'm on it."

She hung up. "I need to go put out a fire pronto." She looked to Walker. "Sorry, I forgot to introduce you. This is Rory Addison."

"We've met," he said.

"I hate to ask, but would you mind dropping Rory off at school where her car is?" Paige asked. "I've got to drive to Tyler and pick up some prop that is desperately needed for a scene later today."

"Oh, I can walk," Rory said. "It's not far from here."

"No, I'm happy to drive you," Walker said. "Go take care of business, Paige. It was good seeing you before you head off to California."

"Good seeing you again, Walker. Thank so much." Paige hugged Rory. "I'll be in touch."

She hurried from the office and Walker said, "I was about to head to Ida Lou's for some lunch. Do you have time for a quick bite?"

Despite her better judgment, Rory heard herself saying, "Yes. I'd like that."

8

Walker couldn't believe how smoothly everything had gone.

He had gotten up this morning and gone for a run. When he returned, he told his mom he was interested in getting to know Rory better—and needed her help. He explained how he wanted to see Rory today, knowing she would be in town to sign her contract and see Paige's house. Quickly, they had put together a plan and Betty Cox had called Paige, bringing her into the loop. They had worked out a brief timetable, where Betty would call Paige soon after she had arrived at the law office. Paige would invent some reason she needed to leave immediately, leaving Walker to get Rory back to her car at the high school.

His mom loved being included in the scheme, giving him a knowing look, but never saying *I told you so*.

His dad had told Walker at breakfast not to come into the office since it was a Friday. Campbell Cox had to be in court in Tyler that morning for what he said would most likely be a one-day trial. Walker decided to go in anyway to begin familiarizing himself with files. Besides, he needed to be there when Paige arrived with Rory in order for all the chips to fall into place.

Margaret, his father's longtime receptionist and assistant, had greeted him with enthusiasm, and he let her know that he intended to keep her on in the same position if she were willing to remain and work for him. She assured Walker she would do so, and he knew having Margaret in the office would make the transition into working in Sugar Springs that much easier. She had been helpful in pulling several files for him, explaining the last open cases that his dad was working on closing before turning the office over to his son.

Walker had even met with a walk-in who had come in with no appointment, wanting to see about having a will drawn up for himself and his wife. The client was new to the area, and they had just had their first baby, a time when many couples began thinking about wills and estate planning for the first time. Walker took information from him and told his new client that he would have things prepared to sign by Monday. He'd wanted to set an appointment for the man and his wife to come in to sign the copies and then realized with the new baby, that would be a struggle. He offered to come to them, which the man had been thrilled about. Walker realized that *this* was small-town law at its best, working around his clients' needs and helping out when he could, even in out of the box ways.

That had kept him busy until shortly before Paige was to drop by with Rory. Paige actually had already made plans to stop by the office to sign documents which would end her business relationship as Laramie Fisher with Campbell Cox because she would be seeking representation in California, where she and Tanner Haddock would make their home.

Walker's heart beat faster when he heard the jingle from the bell on the door and heard Margaret greeting Paige and Rory. He had picked up the sheaf of documents from his dad's desk and walked out to meet the pair. Things had gone smoothly and Paige had left, leaving him here with Rory. It surprised him when she agreed to have lunch with him. He realized he hadn't made the most favorable impression upon her and hoped to rectify that now.

"Shall we?" he asked, ushering her out the door.

He had an idea and said, "I know I just suggested Ida Lou's, but I have a hankering for Romano's pizza. It's the best I've ever eaten, and I haven't had it in a while. Would you mind a change of plans?"

He saw the wariness in her eyes. It saddened him, knowing how hurt she must have been by her ex's actions.

"All right," she said cautiously.

"We can still walk there." He pointed at the pizzeria. "It's just across the square."

"I passed it the other day," she told him, falling into step with him. "I did a quick tour of the shops on the square after Joe Bob offered me the job."

"Paige is close with the Romano's daughter. Vivi. They were several years behind me in school, but everyone goes to Romano's. After football games. School dances. That kind of thing."

"So, I suppose you didn't know Paige in school since she was much younger."

"No, but I've gotten to know her a little since she and Mom have been good friends the last decade or so. Once Paige came to teach at the high school."

"I know I'll have big shoes to fill," Rory said. "I've gone through the notebooks Paige left me. She's really creative and has a ton of great lessons."

"You'll make your own mark," he assured her. "Just follow the curriculum—and your heart. The kids will take your lead. That's what Mom always says."

They arrived, and Walker opened the door for Rory, who stepped inside the pizza parlor. The lunch rush was over since it was just after one o'clock. Only a few tables were occupied, patrons finishing up their lunches.

"We can seat ourselves," he said, walking to a booth in the back corner.

Rory slid into one side of it, and he sat opposite her.

"Thanks for indulging me today. It's been a long time since I've had a Romano's pizza. You're in for a real treat. Mrs. Romano comes from Italy, and she and Mr. Romano know pizza."

Just then, Mrs. Romano came to their table, and he rose to greet her.

"Walker Cox!" she exclaimed. "It's good to see you. It's been a long time."

"Yes, ma'am, it has. I can tell you that no place in Dallas makes pizza as well as Mr. Romano does." He hugged her and seated himself, indicating Rory. "May I introduce to you Rory Addison? She will be taking Paige's slot at the high school this year."

Mrs. Romano smiled warmly at Rory, offering her hand. "It's so nice to meet you, Rory. Paige is like a daughter to us. My Vivi and Paige have been best friends since they were little girls."

Rory shook the owner's hand. "It's lovely to meet you, Mrs. Romano. Walker tells me that your pizza is the best he's ever eaten."

Mrs. Romano turned her gaze back to him. "A little birdy told me that you were coming home to roost, Walker."

"Yes, I am. I've resigned from my law firm in Dallas and will take over Dad's practice soon."

Briefly, he told the older woman about the trip his parents would take around the world.

"I have been pushing my husband to also retire. I'm

trying to convince Vivi to come back and take over the place for us."

Mrs. Romano turned to Rory. "My daughter works at a very exclusive Dallas restaurant. So does my son, Dante. He is blinded by the lights of the big city, but I think my Vivi might come home once I convince my husband that it's time to hang up his apron. I'm working on him now. I think I will wear him down sooner rather than later. I want to go back to Italy and see relatives. Stay a long while. Maybe for good." She shrugged. "We'll see. In the meantime, what can I get you? Whatever you want. It's on the house. To welcome Walker back and you to Sugar Springs, Rory."

He looked to his companion. "Is there any topping you don't like?"

"Not when it comes to pizza. Order for me," she told him. "But I would like a sparkling water if you have one, Mrs. Romano."

Walker told Mrs. Romano the toppings they would have on their pizza, and she left them.

"She's very friendly," Rory said. "Ida Lou was, too. Is everyone in Sugar Springs so nice?"

"Mrs. Romano will think of you as extended family because you're taking Paige's spot on the faculty. And once you have one of Mr. Romano's pizzas? You will probably stop in at least once a week."

"Do they do takeout? I don't often eat out. I'm guilty of being a workaholic and will pick something up and bring it home with me so I can keep working while I eat."

"They do." His gaze met hers, and he was drawn in by her deep, blue eyes. "Thank you for taking the time to have lunch with me. I know I'm not your favorite person, but I appreciate you giving me this second chance."

"I suppose I was too quick—and too harsh—in my

assessment of you," she said honestly. "Your parents are lovely people." She smiled. "I'll give you the benefit of the doubt simply because Betty and Campbell produced you. With those genes, you can't be all bad," she teased.

Mrs. Romano arrived with their drinks and salads, and they dug into them.

After a few bites, Rory said, "This salad is excellent. Ice-cold. The dressing is so flavorful. I could eat this salad every day for lunch and be happy."

"Can I get to know you a little better now?" he asked.

A guarded look crossed her face. "How?" she asked quietly.

"We could pretend this is a date. A speed dating one. Have you heard of that?"

"I have, but I don't know what it involves."

"Just answering a quick series of questions which are intended to help you get to know someone a little better."

"This *isn't* a date," she said stiffly. "I want to make that perfectly clear."

"I know that. I'm just hoping we can become friends. All my friends from my years growing up here have left Sugar Springs, so I'm starting from scratch. Since it's as if we're both new in town, I was hoping we could become friendly. If not outright friends."

"What do you want to know about me? And you have to answer the same questions I do," she insisted.

"All right. Favorite food?"

"Hummus and pita chips."

"That's your *fav*? Something . . . healthy?"

"It's my go-to snack food. Sometimes dinner. I've eaten it a lot."

"Favorite food indulgence then?" he pressed.

This time, a smile crossed her face. "Brownies. With a little bit of vanilla ice cream to accompany them. I don't eat sweets very often, though. I suppose that goes back to my figure skating training. My coach made me watch every bite that went in my mouth."

Something in her tone let Walker know she had no fond feelings for this coach. To smooth things over, he said, "I would go with a cheeseburger. There's nothing like a juicy burger off the grill, smothered in cheese. And grilled onions and mushrooms on top, of course. Favorite TV show?"

"Buffy the Vampire Slayer," she said automatically.

"Why?"

"I like that Buffy was smart. Capable. Fierce. She never backed down from a challenge, even when she felt vulnerable."

Walker thought her response telling and that it most likely described Rory herself.

"You?" she pressed.

He laughed. "I wish I had one. Honestly, I haven't watched TV since I was about ten. From that time on, my entire life was sports and school. And scouting. You are in the company of an Eagle Scout, you know."

She crinkled her nose. "What does that mean?"

Briefly, he explained the different ranks in scouting and how a scout could obtain the rank of Eagle Scout.

"My independent project was to build half a dozen little libraries scattered around Sugar Springs and fill them with donated books."

"That's a worthwhile project. What sports did you play? I think you mentioned baseball last night."

"I was a decent athlete. I played defense in football and third base on the baseball team. I was too busy in my teens to watch any TV. College was the same way. When I wasn't in class or studying, I was cutting loose and having a little fun. Then came law school, which was an intense three years. Summers, I clerked in various law offices in Dallas to gain experience and beef up my résumé. After that, I put in a good ninety to hundred hours at my firm every week. It left little time for something trivial like TV. My priority was to get in a workout before I went to the office each day, which meant usually getting up at four or four-thirty. I was lucky to be home by ten at night. Maybe you can give me an idea of some shows to binge on. I'm hoping now that I'm in Sugar Springs, my hours will be a lot fewer and that I'll have some free time on my hands."

To get to know you better.

"Favorite place you've ever been?" he asked.

Rory shrugged. "I have so many places I want to go. Actually, places I want to go back to. I traveled quite a bit to various competitions around the world, but I never got to see the cities I competed in. I would love to go back as a tourist to Paris, Rome, and London. They would definitely be on my travel wish list. What about you?'

"I'm interested in history, especially the Revolutionary and Civil Wars, so I'd most likely go to some of those battlefields. Gettysburg. Antietam. Bunker Hill and Yorktown."

"I'm surprised you haven't already been to those places since they're in the U.S."

"Mom and Dad were frugal. Our vacations pretty much consisted of a few days hitting the beach in Galveston or camping in Tyler State Park. As an adult, I made a fantastic salary, especially after I made partner at my firm, but there was never time to enjoy my earnings. My life was so hectic. One day, I looked up, and I didn't even recognize myself anymore. That's when I knew I needed a change and decided to come home to a quieter life in Sugar Springs."

He gazed at her intently. "You've seen my parents.

They're more in love now than when they wed forty years ago. I want what they've had, Rory. A job I love. One which doesn't consume me. A wife who's my best friend and lover. A family I can raise here in Sugar Springs. And a dog," he insisted. "Especially a dog."

A wistful look crossed her face. "I never had a pet. I was gone too much to have one, either long hours at practices or weeks on the road, competing around the world. It wouldn't have been right to leave a dog or cat alone so much. I moved in with Granny Bea during my college years and once again, I found myself too busy for a pet. Besides, I never would have imposed upon her and brought an animal into the house."

"What about when you were teaching?" he nudged, wondering if she'd say anything about the past few years.

"I thought about getting a dog, but Bradley—my ex —wasn't fond of animals. I should have known from that, that he couldn't be trusted. A dog would've sniffed out his true nature," she said, bitterness lacing her voice.

Wanting to lighten the mood, he said, "Then maybe we both should get a dog. Now that I'm back in Sugar Springs, I won't be working such long hours and will have time to train one and spend time with him or her. You could do the same. I've been to Paige's house. It's got a nice-sized backyard."

"That would be really nice," she said softly.

"Once you've moved in and gotten settled, maybe we can both go to Tyler to the animal shelter. Or even check here in Sugar Springs. Sometimes a local vet will house animals looking to be adopted. I'll look into that and get back to you." He hesitated, hoping his next words wouldn't push her too hard. "Would you mind if we ex-changed cell numbers?"

Her gaze burned into him. "All right," she agreed.

They traded phones and input their numbers, trading back. Walker felt this was a huge step for Rory.

Mrs. Romano arrived with their pizza and set it on the table. "Here you go, my lovelies. Enjoy!"

He served the first slice to Rory and then took one for himself. He felt he had made good progress already in getting her open up some. If they both adopted dogs, they could work together on training them. Maybe even attend a class in dog obedience together.

One thing Walker did know?

Rory Addison was definitely someone he wanted to get to know better. His gut—and heart—was telling him that she was The One.

9

Rory put the last of her clothes into her SUV. She did not have much to take with her to Sugar Springs. She had always traveled light, going to competitions around the US and world with little more than a single suitcase and backpack. Even in her apartment near the training facilities in Colorado, she hadn't possessed many personal items. She had donated all her skating trophies to the US Figure Skating Committee, and they were housed in Colorado.

The only items from her skating days she held onto were the two gold medals she had won, and even then, she had kept those in a drawer, too humble to display them. She didn't own physical books. Instead, she kept everything on her Kindle. She didn't have music or movies, choosing to stream those on her tablet. In a way, it was a little sad that she was thirty-two years old and had so little to show for her life. The only things besides clothes in the car were her school items. She had five large boxes filled with files from her three years of teaching. Lesson plans. Examples of student projects. Old lecture notes from college which she referred to from time to time.

She was fortunate that she could rent Paige's house

because it contained everything she would need. She might have to purchase an item or two, but the kitchen was fully stocked, as was the linen closet. Paige and Tanner had left Sugar Springs two days ago, filming on *Shadows of the Past* now completed. Rory had retrieved the keys from Paige and hugged her new friend goodbye, wishing her well as the Haddocks left to honeymoon in Greece. Paige assured her that the drawers and closets were now empty since she had shipped her clothes and personal items to Tanner's place in Malibu.

Entering Granny Bea's house, Rory said, "I think I have everything. If I've forgotten something, I can pick it up later this weekend. Are you ready to come and see Sugar Springs and my new place?"

"I most certainly am," Granny Bea declared. "Are you sure you don't want me to follow you over instead of riding with you, honey? That way, I would have my own car and be able to drive home."

"No, I'd like you with me. I want to drive you around town and show you all the places I've come to know in my new hometown."

The two women went to the SUV and chatted the entire twenty miles to their destination. Once there, Rory took Granny Bea on a tour of Sugar Springs, starting with the town square. She pointed out the diner and pizza parlor, both reminding her of Walker Cox. She had enjoyed their lunch together, probably a little too much. She hadn't seen Walker since that day two weeks ago, however. Rory had come to Sugar Springs several times since then, getting her classroom arranged the way she wanted and organizing her closets and file cabinets.

While at school, she had met Pam Holland, who would be across the hall from her and take on Betty Cox's gov and econ classes this upcoming school year. Pam was a couple of years older than Rory and had twins who were three years old. Her husband was a software engineer with a Dallas firm but had been given the opportunity to work from home. Since Pam had grown up in Sugar Springs and still had family nearby, she had convinced her husband to come here to raise their twins in a small town. Rory already liked her fellow teacher, who had been teaching in a Dallas suburb the last dozen years and hoped they would become fast friends.

She pointed out a few stores on the square and then Walker's office. They had texted back and forth several times over the last two weeks. Walker had settled in at the firm he'd now taken over, while Campbell Cox had exited gracefully and would be leaving with Betty in a week's time for their trip around the world.

Rory had grown eager to hear from Walker and wondered if she might explore a relationship with him. Fortunately, he hadn't pressed her to do so, keeping the tone of their texts light and friendly. She had let him know that she would be moving in today, and he said he would stop by and see if she needed any help.

She then drove Granny Bea to the high school and took her inside, giving her a tour of the school and showing where her new room was located and what she had done to it.

"You've created a nice home away from home, Rory," her grandmother praised. "Although I never saw your classroom down in Houston, I like how warm and inviting this one is. Especially the curtains."

Rory had made the curtains for the classroom, as well as working on some design ideas for skating costumes the past week. She felt she had a good handle on what she would be teaching this year, and she liked taking some downtime to fiddle with designs.

"I suppose I should take you to Paige's house now. No, my house," she corrected. "I doubt Paige and Tanner will ever live in Sugar Springs again. She told me they'll make Malibu their base but will travel to wherever Tanner films over the next few years. He grew up in a small town in Oklahoma and has a house and some land near his parents. That's where Paige said they'll eventually move in order to raise their family once they have kids in school."

Granny Bea laid a hand on Rory's arm. "I think you've found a home here, honey. I hope you, too, will be able to find a good man and have a family of your own."

Walker Cox's image came to mind, and Rory dismissed it. "We'll see, Granny Bea."

They left the high school and drove the short distance to the cottage she would live in during the next school year. Her heart sped up when she saw Walker leaning against a car in front of her house. The fact that he had been waiting for her brought a thrill that she wasn't ready to think about just now.

She pulled into the driveway and climbed from her SUV, waving at him.

He waved in return, coming to the driveway where she'd parked. "I'm a welcoming committee of one," he said, opening the passenger door and helping Granny Bea from the vehicle. "Hello. I'm Walker Cox," he said, introducing himself. "You must be Granny Bea. I've heard all about you."

"My, Rory didn't tell me a handsome young man would be here to greet us."

Walker grinned shamelessly. "You better watch it, Granny Bea. I'm single—and hear you are, too."

Her grandmother laughed in delight. "Are you one of Rory's new friends from the high school?"

She hadn't mentioned Walker to her grandmother, not wanting to reveal the fragile friendship she'd begun to forge with this man.

"I'm not a teacher. I'm a teacher's son," he said. "My mom taught at the high school for decades, across the hall from where Rory will be teaching this year."

"Oh, you're Betty Cox's son," Granny Bea said. "Rory has mentioned Betty to me and how kind she's been to my granddaughter. Do you live in Sugar Springs?"

Walker laughed. "I do now. As of two weeks ago, I moved home and have stepped into my dad's shoes. He's been an attorney in Sugar Springs for many years. He's now retired, along with Mom."

"Oh, they are the ones taking the cruise around the world. Rory told me about that. How do you find Sugar Springs now, Walker, having been gone so long?"

Walker answered, looking directly at Rory. "I find it's as accommodating as ever, Granny Bea. I am looking forward to making new friends—and especially spending time with your granddaughter."

Her grandmother looked to Rory and back to Walker. "I see," she said sagely. Then to Walker, she added, "My granddaughter is my best friend in the world, young man. I would do anything for her. Do you understand?"

A long moment passed before Walker nodded. "I most certainly do, Granny Bea. I'll tell you now, my intentions are honorable—and I plan to pursue Rory—because I find her interesting. Honest. She's someone I want in my life on a permanent basis."

Rory found her cheeks heating with his words, which took her completely by surprise. Calling him out, she said, "I thought we were going to be friends."

His eyes twinkled as he said, "Oh, we're definitely going to be friends, Rory. And I hope a whole lot more."

The air sizzled between them, and Granny Bea burst out laughing, saying, "You can start by bringing in the boxes from the car, Walker."

"Yes, ma'am," he said. "I know how to take direction from a strong, Southern woman, having been raised by one."

Rory took her grandmother's elbow and hurried them into the house, not bothering to gather anything from the car.

Once inside, she gave her grandmother the tour, and they found a large bouquet of flowers on the kitchen table. A note was attached to it, and she opened it.

I HOPE *you'll be as happy here as I have been. Love, Paige*

"MY, THAT WAS A THOUGHTFUL GESTURE," Granny Bea said. "So, when were you going to tell me about your young man?"

"He's not my young man," she insisted. "He's Betty's son. I agreed to try and be friends with him. No more."

Her grandmother took Rory's hands in hers. "I know you've been terribly hurt by men, Rory, starting with your own father years ago. I know you hoped to start a life with Bradley, and his betrayal almost did you in. That's behind you, though. Look to the future here in Sugar Springs. I think it will be bright for you."

Granny Bea paused. "And I want you to promise me that you will give Walker a chance."

Rory squeezed her grandmother's fingers. "I'm scared to death," she admitted. "I feel the attraction between us, and I just don't know if I can make it through being burned again."

"You're strong, Rory. You always have been. At your core is a steely determination unlike anything I've ever known. I have no doubt you can do whatever you wish to do. Don't close your heart to this man because of what you've experienced in the past. Take one day at a time, but take each day and cherish it. Get to know him. If it's meant to be, it will work out. If it doesn't, you lift your head high and march into the next day and the day after that. But don't let what has happened to you before color your future. Learn from yesterday. Live for today. Look forward to tomorrow."

Tears sprang to Rory's eyes, and she hugged Granny Bea fiercely. "When did you get to be so wise?"

"I have lived a hard life myself, and romance never worked out for me. I've learned to be happy with what I have and who I spend my time with. You must do the same." Her grandmother grinned mischievously. "And let me know how he kisses."

"Granny Bea!"

Rory left the kitchen and went to bring in a load of clothes. She passed Walker along the way. He carried clothes over each arm.

"I've been putting these on the bed. I know women. You'll want to hang them in some fashion that makes sense to you."

She followed him back into the house and bedroom, where she saw other clothes on the bed and the two suitcases she had packed with things such as shoes, socks, and underwear sitting in a corner.

"I put the boxes which I was betting contained school stuff in the study," he said. "One more trip to the car, and it should be emptied. And then I'm treating you and Granny Bea to lunch."

"No, I should be treating you after all the work you've done."

"You didn't have that much stuff, Rory. I was happy to bring it in. Didn't even break a sweat. I'll be back."

She returned to the kitchen, where her grandmother was opening cabinets. "It seems as if you have everything you'll need, dear. I was looking to see what I might give you as a housewarming gift."

Rory hugged her grandmother. "I don't need a thing from you." Releasing her, she continued, "Walker asked if he could take us out to lunch. Would you like that?"

"I most certainly would. I'd like to get to know your young man a little better."

She didn't bother correcting her grandmother, knowing it would fall on deaf ears. Walker returned with the last load of clothes. She followed him into the bedroom as he placed them on the bed.

He dusted his hands together and said, "You travel pretty light."

"Old habit," she said. "Besides, Paige left me with everything I might need. I don't think I'll need to buy a single item."

"Well, I've worked up an appetite. How about we head to Ida Lou's? If you don't mind, I'll have Mom and Dad meet us there."

"That would be really nice, Walker."

She gazed at him a moment—and then did something spontaneous. Something she had wanted to do since she met him.

Rory stepped to him and looped her arms about his neck, pressing her mouth softly to his. His arms slipped around her, and he stepped closer, their bodies flush against one another.

The kiss was lingering. Sweet with a bit of pressure. His lips felt right against hers, even though she knew they both held back. She felt the warmth of his body. Smelled the tang of his cologne. Yearned for more, but knew now wasn't the time.

Walker was the one who broke the kiss and stared down at her. "We'll definitely continue this later," he said huskily. "But we shouldn't keep Granny Bea waiting."

He cradled her cheek with his palm. "When I kiss you again, Rory, it's going to be for hours."

She shivered, thinking how she wanted the same. She longed to explore his mouth. His body. She had never had such an intense response, both physically and emotionally, to a single kiss.

Stepping away from him, Rory said, "Let me know when you're ready, Walker. Because I'm more than ready to see what happens between us."

10

Rory followed Walker back to the kitchen and told Granny Bea, "My car is now empty, and Walker wants to take us to Ida Lou's."

Her grandmother's brows arched slightly. "Oh, that's the diner you've mentioned, isn't it?"

"Yes, ma'am," Walker said. "It has some of the best food I've ever eaten. Pot roast. Chicken fried chicken. Stuffed peppers." Winking, he added, "Don't tell my mom I said that. If you don't mind, Granny Bea, I'd like to ask my parents to join us. They'll be leaving in less than a week, and I'm trying to spend as much time with them as possible."

"By all means," her grandmother said. "Rory has spoken so highly of your mother. I will be happy to meet her."

"Then let me give them a call. Excuse me a moment."

Walker turned away and made the call as Rory said, "How do you like the house overall?"

"I think you'll be quite happy here—and I like this man, Rory. Very much."

Her cheeks burned, remembering the kiss from only a few moments ago.

"I've told you. He's not my man," she said quietly.

Granny Bea's eyes twinkled with mirth. "But he wants to be. And I think you should give him a chance. Remember what I said, Rory."

"I'm going to give Walker a chance. I promise."

Her grandmother took one of Rory's hands in hers. "It's hard to learn to trust, much less to learn to trust again when you've been hurt. I hope this works out for you."

"So do I," she said fervently, acknowledging aloud something that she had been pretending didn't exist.

Walker turned back to them. "Mom said they'll meet us there. We can all go in my car if you'd like."

"You mean that fancy sports car sitting by the curb?" Granny Bea teased.

He laughed. "Yes. It's the one thing I indulged myself in during my Dallas days as a lawyer. I realize it's not very practical." He grinned. "But I sure look good in it."

They went to where the BMW convertible sat. Walker opened the passenger door and helped Granny Bea into the front seat, while Rory climbed into the back behind the driver's seat.

He got behind the wheel and drove them to the town square, which was crowded with it being a Saturday.

"It might be hard to get a table at Ida Lou's," Walker noted. "I hope you don't mind if we have to wait a bit."

He escorted both women to the diner, and they stepped inside. Rory saw Betty and Campbell standing by the door. She made the introductions, and her grandmother thanked Betty for taking Rory under her wing.

"I never had a daughter, but if I had," Betty said. "I hope she would have turned out as lovely as Rory. I recognized her from the moment we met because I'm a figure skating fan. In talking with Rory, though, we've bonded as teachers."

The door opened again. None other than Pam Holland entered, accompanied by her husband and twins.

"I'm so glad we ran into you, Rory," Pam said. "I've been singing your praises to Sam."

More introductions were made, and Rory bent to meet Griff and Callie, Pam's three-year-olds.

Walker knelt and asked the twins their names. Griff began telling them all about someone called Iron Man, and Walker encouraged the little boy. She saw the enthusiasm on Walker's face, and her gut told her this man would make for a wonderful father.

She asked Callie about what she wore, not the usual shorts and T-shirt of a hot August day, but something that resembled a Halloween costume.

"I'm Elsa," Callie declared. "I watch *Frozen*. I love Elsa and Anna."

Pam laughed. "We took the kids to Walt Disney World last month for the first time. Callie got her Elsa outfit there and wants to wear it every single day. I'm afraid she'll wear it out by the time Halloween comes around." She chuckled. "We should have bought two."

Ida Lou came to greet them. "Sorry. It's busy. Are you all together? It's going to be hard to seat you if you are, but we can pull some tables together."

Pam said, "No, that's all right. We can eat together another time. They were in front of us, Ida Lou. Please seat them first."

"Will do. Follow me," the owner said, and they were shown to a booth for four. Ida Lou stole an empty chair from a neighboring table. Betty and Campbell slid into one side of the booth, while Rory moved into the other. Walker saw that Granny Bea was seated at the head of the table before he took a place in the booth next to Rory. He slipped her hand into his beneath the table.

A warmth spread through her. She wasn't used to

such small, intimate gestures. Her brief affairs on the figure skating circuit had all taken place behind closed doors, with no signs of the relationship in public. As for Bradley Bolton, he was not a fan of public displays of affection, telling her he didn't think it was appropriate they show their feelings for one another in public because they were both teachers and should show some restraint in front of their students.

Rory had respected his feelings—even agreed with him to an extent—but couldn't ever recall Bradley taking her hand. Not even when they were alone. Cold as he'd been, his disinterest in foreplay should have been a red flag.

In that moment, Rory realized she had deserved better than Bradley.

She turned and smiled up at Walker, who returned her smile and squeezed her hand lightly. Somehow, this simple gesture of holding her hand meant more to Rory than all of the other times she had had sex with a man. Because it felt genuine. Whether things worked out between her and Walker remained to be seen, but for the first time in her life, she understood that she warranted more from a man than she had been given in the past.

Ida Lou brought them menus and chatted a few minutes, telling Granny Bea how happy she was that Rory had come to town to teach at the high school.

"I'm so glad that my granddaughter has found a good place to teach and call her home," Granny Bea said.

"Don't worry, we'll take care of Rory for you," Ida Lou assured the older woman. "Let me get you some drinks, and then I'll take your orders."

Ida Lou soon returned with the drinks they'd requested and reeled off the special of the day, which was chicken fried steak, mashed potatoes, and butter beans.

Everyone ordered, and Campbell asked if Rory had gotten moved in.

"Yes, thanks to Walker's help."

"She didn't have much. Unlike Mom," Walker teased. "She's probably going to take six suitcases with her on your cruise."

"No," Campbell said. "We each are taking two suitcases. That's it. Anything we buy, we'll ship home."

They talked some about the places the Coxes would see on their extended vacation, and their lunch arrived shortly after, delivered by a server Rory had not yet met.

The meal was a happy one, with many stories traded and the food tasty. Betty told Rory she would have her over for dinner one more time before they left late next week for Galveston, their departure point for the first leg of their journey.

When lunch ended, Walker drove them to her new house. Parking in front, he said, "Why don't you unpack and get settled, and I'll take Granny Bea back to Tyler?"

"Oh, I can't ask you to do that," Rory protested.

"I'd like to help out in any way I can," he said, adding, "Once I get back to Sugar Springs, I can swing by and see if you need any more help."

The look in his eyes let Rory know Walker wanted to do more than help her unpack.

"Sure," she said casually. "That will be fine."

She told Granny Bea goodbye and got out of the car, waving goodbye as Walker drove away. Going inside, it only took her a few minutes to hang her clothes in the closet the way she liked, by color and season. Opening the suitcases, she put away all of her intimate apparel and then went to the bathroom, finding a place for all her makeup and toiletries.

She then went to the kitchen and familiarized herself with where everything was located, changing a few items around to better suit her. She thought about going to her study and opening up her school files but wasn't in the mood to do so. A buzzing filled her. One of anticipation. Rory knew Walker would be back and when he came, things would change between them.

To distract herself, she retrieved one of her sketchpads and her colored pencils. Sketching soothed her, and she still thought she might be able to design figure skating costumes and exercise wear at some point. It had been a dream she'd put on hold once she'd become involved with Bradley. He had told her she had been gone from the figure skating world too long and no one would be interested in her designs. That she should concentrate on teaching and put her glory days behind her.

Rory had done so without question but now wished she had stood up for herself to him. Bradley had been a couple of years older than she was and had seemed so wise and mature. She knew now it had all been a front. She regretted that she had lost confidence in herself because he had used her, making her a woman he could refer to as his girlfriend and then fiancée so that he could hide behind her and their relationship, even as he pursued young women.

Rory cleared all thoughts of Bradley Bolton from her mind and took up one of her pencils, soon losing herself as she drew. She was startled when she heard a knock on the door and glanced at her watch, realizing it must be Walker, who'd had time to drive Granny Bea to Tyler and return to Sugar Springs.

She went to the door, her heart pounding violently, and opened it. Walker stood there, looking impossibly handsome. He smiled at her, a true smile that not only touched his sensual lips but reached his eyes. She realized now the smiles Bradley had given her had always been false ones. That her ex-fiancée had held back emotionally.

Rory decided from this moment forward, she would never think of Bradley again. For the first time in her life, she would put herself and her needs first.

Smiling, she asked, "Won't you come in?"

She stepped aside so Walker could enter and closed the door behind him. Turning, she found his arms going about her, drawing her to him. They stood close together, neither speaking, merely drinking in each other.

"This feels so right," he said, his voice a low rumble.

She looked up at him. "I don't want to move too fast —but I'm feeling things I've never felt before, Walker. It's a little bit frightening, to be honest."

"Thanks for admitting that," he said. "I'm pretty much scared shitless myself."

"Why?"

"Because I don't want to mess this up. Can we sit?"

Rory nodded, and he released her, his fingers threading through hers as he led her to the sofa. They sat on it, their fingers still linked.

"I want to be as transparent as possible with you, Rory. I want you to know the real Walker Cox."

"I want the same," she told him. "You can ask me anything. I need to get to know you." She swallowed. "To learn how to trust you. And I'll admit that's not going to be easy for me."

"Trust has also been a huge issue for me. I dated for fun in college. Not a lot during law school because I was too damn busy. Then I started at Sapphire & Sammons. Putting in a hundred hours a week, it barely left me time to brush my teeth, much less have a relationship with someone. I did meet another attorney at a competing firm at a bar association dinner, though."

Walker paused. Rory saw pain flash in his eyes briefly.

"Her name was Christine. We had a whirlwind romance. She was bright. Beautiful. Ambitious." His tone turned bitter. "More ambitious than I would have ever guessed. We only dated briefly before we got married at the courthouse. I knew within two weeks that we'd made a huge mistake. The marriage didn't last another six months, but it was over long before that. Ever since then, I've only had a handful of dates. I closed my heart because I'd been hurt so badly."

He squeezed her fingers. "I finally made the decision to come home to Sugar Springs. I'm thirty-six. I want more than just to be an attorney. I want to be a husband. A father. I need to be a better man than I was in Dallas and contribute to my community."

Walker shrugged. "That's my story in a nutshell. I wanted you to know all about my background going forward. I see potential with you, Rory. With us. I feel that physical spark between us, which frightens me in a way. I had that with Christine—and it blinded me to the truth about her. So I'm clear with you. I want to take things slowly."

Rory was moved by his openness and what he had revealed.

"You've shared a lot about yourself in just a few minutes. I owe you the same." She hesitated and then plunged in. "I told you that I had an ex-fiancé. He was a fellow teacher. We met at school. Began dating. Moved in together although we kept that quiet. We got engaged though he never gave me a ring. I was expecting it last Christmas."

She had been looking directly at Walker but now had to turn away.

"He wasn't the man he represented himself to be. I

think now that I was merely a cover for his activities and that I never would have received a ring from him, much less spoken our vows."

She swallowed, the ache in her heart causing her throat to grow thick with unshed tears.

Then Walker's hand cupped her cheek, turning her toward him again. "You don't have to ever talk about him, Rory. He's in your past."

"No, I want to say this. I need to. I was duped. He played me for a fool while he groomed girls at our school. He had been doing so for several years. He waited until they would turn eighteen, and then he had sex with them," she said dully, her eyes filling with tears. "I was in love with a man who was a sexual predator. I know now that he was never in love with me."

She swallowed. "I thought I loved him. I let him sweep me into a relationship, and yet I always felt there was something missing between us. The scandal was horrible. He resigned his position at school, and I moved out of the apartment we shared. I returned for the spring semester after our winter break, but I was ostracized, tainted by my association with him. People talked. A lot. Many thought I was in on what he had done. No one spoke to me. It was the loneliest time of my life."

Her voice broke on that final word. Walker's arms encircled her. She cried, dampening his entire shirtfront as she clung to him. Even as she sobbed, Rory thought of how she never cried. How she'd never had anyone to cry with about her problems. Her mom never wanted to hear about any kind of trouble. Anya had told Rory to suck it up and not be a baby. That tears made you weak, and your competitors would sense that weakness in you and strike hard to win.

Because of that, Rory never cried. Not even when she was shot. She'd pushed the pain pulsing in her shoulder and the agony of her fractured ankle to the side. Even through the months of grueling rehab, she had never cried, not even in frustration. She'd merely persevered.

That's what she did. That's what she was made of.

The only time she ever remembered crying was when she'd come to Granny Bea after she'd resigned her teaching position in Houston. Her grandmother, always stoic, had tolerated the tears and then told Rory she'd cried enough. That she had her health and a college degree and her whole life in front of her. That it was up to her to keep putting one foot in front of the other and not let the scandal with Bradley consume her life.

Walker was different. He wasn't telling her what to do. Forcing her to keep her feelings hidden. He allowed her to cry. To reveal what she truly felt.

To be herself.

Brushing away her tears, she looked up at him, seeing only sympathy. No pity.

"Thank you," she whispered.

"For what?"

"For just being here. For letting me cry when no one else thought I should. For listening to my tale of woe." Determination filled her. "You don't try to control me. You don't tell me what to do. You just let me ...be *me*."

He brushed his lips against her brow. "That's all I want, Rory. For you to be able to be you. I'm glad you're comfortable enough with me so that you don't have to hide your tears or your feelings."

Her fingers gripped his shirtfront, still damp with her tears. "I'm more than comfortable, Walker. And I am ready to get to know more about you."

With that, she jerked him to her, his lips crashing down on hers.

11

Rory hungered for this man. In a way she had never felt about any other. She didn't know why Walker seemed different. Special. But she was willing to find out.

No matter what the cost.

He gentled the kiss, easing back a little from its intensity. It was more now a kiss of exploration. She went with the flow and found she liked everything about the kiss. About this man.

Surprising her, he lifted her into his lap. The leisurely exploration continued forever. His large hands cradled her face. His shirt, which had been bunched in her fingers, would be terribly wrinkled. Rory released her grasp on it, resting her palms against the hard muscle of his chest.

Walker took his time, his actions deliberate and methodical, learning every crevice of her mouth. It didn't mean it took the passion from his kisses. Far from it. Instead, it was as if he lit a fire deep within her and was stoking it. Building it. She felt his kisses down to her toes. Long. Slow. Deliberate.

This man was different.

And suddenly, Rory found herself frightened beyond words by everything happening between them.

Sex during her figure skating days had simply been a way to blow off steam. Hot. Intense. Infrequent. No emotions involved, just a physical act that brought quick satisfaction.

With Bradley, it had been different. He had wooed her. Charmed her. Manipulated her into falling in love with him. Rory hadn't understood that at the time but knew now that he had sought her out for a reason, capitalizing on her lack of experience with a long-term relationship. If he were involved—attached—to another teacher, no one would ever suspect him of dallying with his own students.

She realized she had been emotionally stunted. Immature when it came to deep feelings involving men and love. Rory had never loved before Bradley, and the attention he paid her, along with his frequent compliments, made her confidence soar. She fell utterly, madly, deeply in love with him, all the while never understanding he didn't love her and never could. She doubted he was capable of love. Only manipulation and subtle domination, which he had exercised over her and his students.

Their sex life had been tame. Bland. Actually, boring to what she had experienced up until then. The frequency of sex was far less than what she wanted or expected, but she told herself they had busy lives, and his long hours made him more tired than most men. Bradley had not been one for kissing, wanting to move straight to sex without any kind of foreplay. She now believed he hadn't even been attracted to her, which was why he didn't linger over the act. Still, she had loved him desperately, with an intensity she'd never experienced. Since she'd never had a long-term relationship, she supposed this was what it was like.

But Bradley's betrayal now colored what was happening between Walker and her. She didn't know what was real and what wasn't. Suddenly, she believed she was making a huge mistake now.

Rory broke the kiss and tried to scramble from his lap, but Walker wasn't having any of that. His hands clasped her waist firmly, not letting her go anywhere.

"What's wrong, Rory?" he asked, his tone gentle. "If you want to stop kissing, we can. But I think there's more to it. Talk to me."

"Talk to you?" she looked at him, shaking her head. "I don't know how to do that, Walker."

He enveloped her in his arms, pushing her head to his chest, cradling her tenderly.

For the first time in her life, Rory knew she was safe. So safe that she could speak the truth.

"I've told you that I had a relationship which ended badly. How I was engaged to a monster. I'm scared now, Walker. I don't want to jump into something new too quickly. I need more time."

He stroked her back, and she felt him press a kiss to her hair. "You broke up more than half a year ago, Rory," he said quietly. "I know it takes time to get over things, but I don't want to lose you by pushing you too hard or too fast. I'm in your same boat, believe it or not. I haven't trusted anyone with my heart since Christine left years ago, but I feel something between us. I'm not going to give up on it. I'm not going to let you go because of some arbitrary timeline in your head. You can hurt over this asshole six months—or six years. You can let him own space in your head, or you can kick him to the curb where he belongs. I don't know him. But I know his type. Too many guys are like him. They have a true gem and throw it all away for some stupid thrill they think they'll get elsewhere.

"I want to get to know you, Rory. You. The real you. I think we have a chance of creating something special between us. I won't rush you physically or emotionally, but I am asking you to give me that chance."

She raised her head to meet his gaze. "I'm so afraid of being used again, Walker," she whispered. "I never had those years of being a teenager and liking boys. Dating. Learning about myself and how to navigate a relationship. Anya had me focused on one thing. Skating. No, winning. Nothing else mattered. I'm behind my peers as far as emotional maturity goes. I thought I had found lasting love with Bradley."

She swallowed painfully. "I'm so afraid. Of letting go. Of being hurt again."

His eyes fired with intensity. "I will never hurt you, Rory. I promise you that. Give us a chance to get to know one another. Either of us can step away at any time if we want. If it doesn't work, I can accept that and hope we can be friends. But if it does work? I will tell you now that I will be all in. For life."

How could Walker be so sure? Yes, they definitely were attracted to one another. The fire still smoldering between them was evidence of that. But why had he chosen her? Why did he think the two of them could build a lasting relationship?

The scariest thing she had ever done was not some dangerous skating combination. It would be this—giving the man before her a chance to win her heart. She decided she could go one of two ways. Step aside and be alone.

Or make the effort to see if they could create something special together.

She made the first move and leaned close, brushing her lips softly against his. She pulled back before either of them could get caught up in the kiss again.

"I think we should do a re-set and take things more slowly," Rory told him.

Easing off his lap, she sat next to him. Close but not too close. Offering her hand, he accepted it and shook it.

"Hello. I'm Rory Addison and new to Sugar Springs. I'll be teaching history at the high school this coming year."

His slow smile spread across his handsome face. "Nice to meet you, Rory. I'm Walker Cox and just moved home to Sugar Springs after leaving my law firm in Dallas. I'll be taking over my dad's practice, located on the town square. If you ever have need of a lawyer, I hope you'll drop by and let me help."

Rory could still feel the electricity between them and eased her hand from his. "It's nice to make a new friend, Walker. Since we're both new in town, maybe you can show me around sometime."

"I'd be happy to do so. Want to go for a drive now?"

She grinned. "Only if you promise to put the top down on your convertible."

He laughed, an easy laugh which rumbled in his chest. When Walker smiled, his entire face lit up. Once again, she couldn't help but compare him to Bradley, who had a brilliant, charming smile—which never quite seemed to make it to his eyes.

They both stood, and he escorted her to his car, opening the passenger door for her before he climbed into the driver's seat. While Rory had driven around Sugar Springs some on her own, Walker played tour guide, sharing tons of stories about the history of the town and his own time living there until he went away to college eighteen years ago. He drove to the square and parked, telling her about the different merchants' stores and their backgrounds. He took her by the police and fire houses, as well as the schools and a few churches.

Everywhere they went, he had an interesting or amusing tale to tell about the places he pointed out.

They drove by a bridge, which he said seniors in the Sugar Springs' graduating class always covered with their names and the year they were finishing school. He drove to Sugar Lake and they cruised around the entire perimeter as he showed her where couples from the high school would park and make out.

"Mine and Gid's specialty was to take girls out to the lake and roast marshmallows or hot dogs first before moving on to kissing."

"You mentioned you're still close to Gideon."

"Yes, we both went to SMU together, Gidon on a football scholarship. He was a great pro prospect until he tore up his knee early in his senior year. He put in the work, rehabbing all the months through graduation the next spring. Wasn't drafted but signed with a pro team. His blazing speed was gone, though. He decided he wanted to give back to others, and so he became a cop. A former fellow player on SMU's football team had a dad in law enforcement. Gid talked to him. That conversation convinced him to enter the police academy. He's worked his way up from patrolman to detective first grade."

"You'll miss living close to him."

"I will. I have hopes of him following me back here, though."

"Why? Is there an opening on the police force?"

"Not at the moment, but Mom and Dad mentioned that Police Chief Roscoe Hamilton is squawking about retirement. Dad's been close friends with him and Dr. Carpenter, a local PCP, for years and years. As boys, Gid and I were friends with Dr. Carpenter's nephew, who spent his summers here in Sugar Springs. In fact, Ford actually was a trainer for the SMU football team. He was a year behind us in school."

"I hope things work out and your friend does come home," Rory said.

They drove back into town, and Walker escorted her to the front porch. He slipped a hand around hers.

"I enjoyed spending this time with you, Rory. Would you like to try going on a date sometime?"

He looked so handsome and a tiny bit vulnerable. She spoke from her heart. "I was hoping maybe we could have dinner together now. Maybe even watch a little TV. That might be a nice way to spend the evening."

A boyish grin filled his face. "I'd like that. How about I pick up a pizza from Romano's? Did you like what we had the other day? Or maybe we could try some new toppings."

"Don't shoot me, but I'm not an anchovy fan. I like the taste of them, but I don't like what they do to my stomach."

He laughed easily. "Anything else you don't want as a topping?"

"No, I'm pretty much open to everything else." She paused. "That goes for pizza—and us, as well," she added softly.

He squeezed her fingers and released them. "I'll be back in half an hour with a pizza I hope you'll enjoy."

Rory watched him walk to his convertible, already talking on his phone. She assumed he was calling in their pizza order as he got into his car. He waved and she did the same. He drove off, and she finally entered the house.

Immediately, she went to her bathroom, brushing her hair after it being windblown by the ride in his convertible. She spritzed on new perfume, as well. She went to the kitchen and got out plates and napkins, realizing she hadn't had time to buy any groceries today. She texted Walker and asked him to include drinks in their order since she had nothing to offer him but tap water.

Rory then paced, full of nervous energy, until she saw him pull up in front of her house. She met him at the door and saw he carried the box of pizza and balanced four bottled waters atop it.

"That didn't take long," she commented.

"I hope you like what I picked up. It's another favorite of mine. Sausage, along with mushrooms, bell peppers, and onions."

"Onions? Hmm. I guess we're done kissing for the evening," she teased.

His gaze intensified as he said, "I don't think I would ever pass up an opportunity to kiss you, Rory Addison."

The look, along with his words, caused a delicious chill to tumble through her.

He gave her the bottled waters and told her to go sit on the couch, returning moments later with plates, forks, and napkins and pizza slices on the plates.

"I usually don't use a fork on pizza, but I know some people do," he said.

Rory laughed. "I'm a half and half kind of girl. I usually eat the first part of my slice with a fork and then when it's not floppy anymore, I pick it up by the crust and finish it off."

"Hmm. Learn something new every day. I think I'll try the Addison method of consuming pizza."

They ate their slices, Walker returning once to fetch the box and bringing it to the living room, setting it on the coffee table so they had easy access to more.

He asked her about how skating and teaching might be similar and what the differences were. Rory had never thought about it and talked to him about both her professions, linking some similarities for the first time.

In turn, she asked him about the kind of law he practiced and what it was like to be in a courtroom trying a case before a judge and jury.

"Probably a lot like what you've mentioned," he told her. "It's a performance. Subtleties matter. The pauses. The tone of my voice. My word choice. Very similar to what you do presenting information to your students in a classroom. Or even performing in a large arena as you skated. I do feel like a performer at times. An informed one. Trained in the law, backed up by facts I or my investigator have discovered. You try to win over audiences with your artistry and skill on the ice or the information you present to your students. While courtroom law is the same, I'm performing a delicate dance, trying to reel in the jury members to my interpretation of the facts, hoping they'll agree with me that the law has been broken and the accused needs to be punished."

By now, the pizza was long gone. They had talked for hours. Walker took her hand again and said, "Thank you for spending today with me, Rory. I liked getting to know more about who you were before you came to Sugar Springs. I know this is almost like the third act in your life. The first was skating all those years. The second was college and your first teaching job."

He smiled. "Hopefully, Sugar Springs will be your final act. I know it will be for me."

"Thank you for respecting my wishes, Walker. For understanding how fragile I am emotionally. For not taking advantage of me and agreeing to move slowly."

"Let's get this cleaned up," he said brusquely, helping her carry things to the kitchen.

He rinsed their plates and put them into the dishwasher, along with the forks.

"Walk me to the door?" he asked, a gleam in his eyes.

"Of course."

He threaded his fingers through hers, and they moved from the kitchen to her front door.

Walker took her other hand in his, facing her. "Goodnight, Rory," he said, bending and pressing the softest of kisses on her mouth.

For her, it was all too brief, leaving her wanting more. She had a suspicion he knew that but wouldn't call him out.

"May I call you tomorrow?" he asked.

"I'd like that."

He released her hands and opened the door, stepping onto the porch. She watched him moving down the sidewalk, his step confident.

She wasn't ready to cave yet.

But she definitely would be having sex with Walker Cox soon.

12

R ory collected the last of the papers as the final bell of the day rang. Her students filed out, and she paper-clipped what she had gathered and set the stack on her desk. No papers would be graded tonight. Not with the homecoming parade happening in a few hours.

It was now mid-October, and Rory had settled into life at Sugar Springs High School. She and Pam Holland had become close friends, being across the hall from one another and sharing the same conference period. She'd also become friendly with Sarah Meinholdt, the drama teacher who'd starred in Tanner Haddock's directorial debut, which was supposed to be released shortly before Christmas in a limited run. Other friends included the ironically named Frieda Painter, the art teacher close to Rory's age, and Linda McGregor, head of the English department, in her mid-thirties and divorced with no kids. The five women ate lunch together every day and even did the occasional happy hour on a Friday.

She was enjoying her classes immensely. While she had taught U.S. history previously, she welcomed the addition of World History, made all the easier thanks to

Paige's notebooks full of terrific ideas and stellar lesson plans.

Rory glanced down at her T-shirt, proudly bearing the logo of the Sugar Springs Knights. It was her usual Friday attire, but this week had been special because it was homecoming. She and Pam were co-sponsors of the National Honor Society, which would have a float in tonight's parade, which started at the high school at six-thirty, traveled a mile and a half and circled the town square, and then returned to the high school stadium, which sat adjacent to the high school itself.

Freddie Otts, whom Paige had told her would probably wind up being a movie mogul before he was thirty years old, was the NHS president. Rory and Pam were able to sit back and merely monitor activities because Freddie and his cadre of officers had everything well in hand. She would go down in a few minutes to where the NHS members would be putting the last touches on the club's float in the student parking lot.

Rory had never been happier in her life, not even when she was winning gold medals and ranked the number one figure skater in the world. Her life revolved around her students.

And Walker.

They hadn't slept together yet. Rory had said she wanted to be friends first and take things slowly. Walker had taken her at her word. They had spent quite a bit of time together, even with both of them settling into their new jobs. Walker's parents had left on their world tour, and he had familiarized himself with his dad's cases, picking up new clients of his own. They didn't see each other every day, but the rare days they didn't, they talked and texted. A lot. They had gone into Tyler several times on the weekends for dates, taking in movies and dinners, and once attending a concert at her former university.

They had also gone to all the Sugar Springs football games on Friday nights. Rory had known nothing about football, despite being a native-born Texan. The small, elite private school she had taught at only fielded soccer, wrestling, and lacrosse teams. The emphasis had been on the fine arts, with strong programs in music, art, and drama. Walker had been appalled that she didn't know a first down from a field goal, and he had made it his mission in life to explain the game of football to her.

Now, Rory was perhaps the loudest-cheering fan in the stands for the Sugar Springs Knights.

They also watched Dallas Cowboys games together on Sundays, and in little over a week's time, she would be hosting her first Monday Night Football get together when the Cowboys would play the Philadelphia Eagles.

She pulled a light jacket from her closet with the staff logo on it and heard someone say, "Hi, Beautiful."

Turning, she saw Walker standing in the doorframe, making her heart skip a few beats. He moved to greet her, kissing her lightly, and then holding up a sack.

"I brought you a sandwich. I was afraid if I didn't, you wouldn't take time to eat anything before the parade."

"Thank you. That was very thoughtful of you. I think I'll eat it now. Freddie told everyone to report to the parking lot by four-thirty for the last-minute adjustments to the float."

She slid into a student desk, and Walker turned one around, pushing it against hers so that they faced one another. She opened the sack and pulled out a sandwich, chips, and a plastic bag of grapes.

"This was so nice of you," she told him, biting into her sandwich and discovering it was ham and Swiss cheese, her favorite.

That was the thing about Walker. She said something—and he remembered it—filing away her favorite sandwich or song or chocolate bar. He was always performing small gestures which made her life easier and told her how much he thought of her.

In that moment, Rory determined they would consummate their relationship this weekend.

He retrieved her water bottle from her desk, and she took a sip from it, continuing to eat as he told her about a new case he had taken on this morning.

"The kid got swept up in something he didn't know how to say no to. It was a group of men in their early to mid-twenties who were committing a series of B&E's throughout Tyler. His older cousin, whom he idolizes, is part of the group and was the one who sucked him into trouble."

"Some cousin," she muttered, biting into a chip with relish.

"I agreed to represent him. He's sixteen, but they want to try him as an adult." Walker shook his head. "I did some dumb stuff when I was sixteen, but nothing like this."

"You'll help him. He's made a horrible mistake, but you'll be able to have a jury see that."

"You have a lot of faith in me, Rory."

"I do," she confirmed, their gazes meeting.

Pam stepped into the room. "Oh, hey, Walker," she greeted and then looked to Rory. "Thought I'd tell you I'm heading down to the float area. Sam is going to pick up the kids for me and feed them, and they'll be waiting on the square."

"I'll see you in a few minutes," Rory said.

She made quick work of the rest of her meal, slipping into her jacket and placing the grapes in her pocket.

"I'll nibble on these while I'm watching the kids. Will you be coming to the parade?"

He stepped closer to her, slipping his arms around her. "I wouldn't miss it."

Walker lowered his head and gave her a lingering kiss. Every touch—every kiss—from this man told Rory he was the one for her. She would have to be the one, though, who made the next move. He was too much of a gentleman to do so himself. He was operating on her timetable, and she was ready to accelerate and push ahead.

He walked her downstairs and then said he was going to return to his office for another hour or so, promising her he would be on the square in front of his office when the parade started.

"I'll look for you," she told him, being the one to pull him down for a quick kiss goodbye.

A sharp whistle sounded, and she glanced up to see Joe Bob Milton grinning at them.

"I believe we have a rule about PDA in the halls, Miss Addison," he teased.

"I'll remember that, Mr. Milton," she said, laughing.

Joe Bob shook hands with Walker. "See you at the parade," the principal said, moving down the hall.

Walker sneaked in one last, quick kiss, and they parted. Rory went to the parking lot. When she arrived, she saw Freddie and his crew had things well in hand. She joined Pam, and they talked about what had gone on at this morning's faculty meeting.

The NHS float looked good, better than what she might have expected from the small budget allowed. Soon, it was time for everyone to take their places.

Freddie gained access to a megaphone and started giving instructions to all the participants. People scrambled onto floats and behind the wheels of the trucks which would drive them as Freddie had each entry line up in the order he had previously arranged. Paige was right. Freddie one day might run a movie studio—or some international organization. Maybe both.

She and Pam climbed atop the NHS float with the other members, a student handing each of them a large bag of candy. They would toss this to the children who lined the streets and square as they passed.

Freddie gave the command for the first float to pull out and hurried over to the NHS float, giving his sponsors a thumbs up.

"Nice job in organizing everything, Freddie."

"'I'm in my element, Miss Addison, whether I'm bossing people around a parking lot or my team on the basketball court." He grinned shamelessly. "Dad said it's in my genes. That I get it from Mom's side of the family."

Freddie slid behind the wheel of the truck which would move the attached flatbed and started its engine, taking his spot in the line that was slowly easing out of the parking lot.

By now, the sun had set, and Rory was glad she had worn her jacket. The beginning of October had been warm, but a cool spell had blown in a few days ago. Walker had called it perfect football weather. The line of trucks and their floats continued, and she saw the first of the families lining the side of the road, tossing them pieces of candy. Children squealed, catching it, racing after the pieces which fell to the ground unclaimed.

It was an incredible feeling, being part of a community. True, she had belonged to the skating community for many years, but living and working in a small town was somehow different. She felt accepted as a teacher. She had made some good friends in a short time. She had a steady boyfriend whom she hoped would become much more than that.

Rory had found her home.

They finally made it to the town square and entered it. She could see all the happy faces in the crowd and heard the shouts of children as they clamored for candy. She and Pam, along with the students on the float, tossed pieces from where they sat on the edge of the flatbed, their legs swinging. Her eyes scanned the crowd, and she found Walker, who waved to her. She tossed a peppermint his way, and he caught it, winking at her as she blew him a kiss.

"I see Griff and Callie," Pam said excitedly, pointing to where her children and husband stood waving and shouting at her.

Rory threw several pieces of chocolates and suckers their way, and both kids squealed in delight as they scooped up their treats.

All the floats had now arrived on the square, and the parade came to a halt. Freddie jumped out of the truck, megaphone in hand, telling the crowd, "Remember to vote for your favorite float," and he reeled off the school's website. "Voting closes at nine o'clock tonight. Results will be announced at tomorrow afternoon's pep rally and again at the homecoming game tomorrow night. Crush the Cats!" he shouted, and the crowd echoed his words.

The parade started up again, and within twenty minutes, all floats were back at school. This time, however, they were parked along the street in front of the stadium so that fans coming to the game would be able to see them.

Rory and Pam thanked their NHS students for all their hard work, and she thought they had a good chance of winning best float. Freddie had designed a giant soda can with their opponent's logo of a bearcat on it. The students had built a knight in armor whose fist was coming down, moving back and forth, ready to crush the can. Crush the Cats had also been painted on the three banners that flanked their flatbed.

She and Pam climbed from the float and walked to the front of the school, saying their goodbyes before getting in their cars and heading home. When Rory turned on her street, her heart sped up, seeing Walker's car sitting in front of her house. He leaned against it, his arms crossed over his chest.

Pulling into the driveway, she hit the garage door button and eased into the garage. Walker followed her, coming up the drive.

She exited her SUV and took his hand, pulling him through the garage. She touched the button to close the garage door and opened the one to her house, stepping inside. He closed the door behind them and his arms encircled her.

The kiss was long and deep, stirring things inside Rory which made her restless.

Breaking it, she gazed up at him. "I'm ready, Walker."

"Ready for what?" he asked, his voice husky, desire burning in his chocolate eyes.

"I'm ready to make love with the man I've come to love."

13

W alker had finally heard the words which had been dancing in his head and embedded in his heart.

"I love you, too, Rory," he said, his throat thick with emotion. "I was never one to believe in something foolish such as love at first sight, but my feelings for you have grown since that day we first met. I've wanted to share them with you but was afraid you would back off if I voiced them."

He gazed deeply into her eyes. "Thank you for trusting me with your heart. Enough to say the words aloud. Especially first. I know that had to be hard. And I love you so much it hurts."

He bent and brushed his lips softly against hers. She moved into his arms, wrapping hers around his waist. The kiss was tender, full of unspoken promises that he would keep to her.

Now—and always.

She was the one who broke the kiss and took his hand, leading him to her bedroom. Walker hadn't stepped inside it since the day he helped her move in, but he had fantasized about being here with her many times. It was dark, and he didn't ask for her to turn on a light. He knew because of her past, this was a huge leap of faith for her to take. He didn't want to bring to a halt what was happening between them. He would see her not with his eyes, but through his touch. Memorize every curve.

The light from the living room was in the distance, and he could at least see her silhouette. He reached for the hem of her T-shirt and pulled it over her head. In turn, she unbuttoned the blue dress shirt he wore, slipping it from his shoulders and down his arms, dropping it on the floor next to them.

Walker reached behind her, unfastening the clasp to her bra, sliding it away from her. They were both now bared to the waist, and he hungered for her warm, smooth skin against his. He moved his arms around her, pulling her to him. Her small, high breasts pressed against his chest. As his hands moved up and down her back, his mouth sought hers greedily. They had gone no further than kissing before tonight, sometimes kissing for hours. He was ready now to kiss every place on her body. His mouth moved to her neck and kissed it, his tongue circling where her pulse throbbed.

"I love you, Rory," he repeated, wanting to be sure he drove that point home with her. "This isn't some one-night stand. Not a brief love affair. I want to know all of you tonight. And all the nights to come."

Her lips met his again, and the kiss brought shivers to him in its intensity. It was all the answer he needed from her, and Walker swept Rory into his arms, carrying her to the bed and placing her gently upon it. He slipped off the sneakers she wore and peeled away her socks, as well. He moved to the button of her jeans and unfastened it, sliding the zipper down, and then moved them down her hips and long legs, tossing them to the floor.

He slipped a finger beneath her bikini bottoms,

gliding it back and forth, hearing her breath hitch. Removing them slowly, he dropped them to the floor and sat on the bed, taking off his own loafers and socks before standing to strip off his slacks. He kept on his boxer-briefs, retrieving the condom he had carried in his wallet since the day after they had met, hoping to put it to good use.

Leaving it on her nightstand, Walker climbed onto the bed and began touching her. Learning her body. Listening for the little sighs and gasps which would let him know what pleased her.

He spent a long time on her breasts, flicking his tongue across the nipples and grazing them with his teeth. Kneading them as he kissed her over and over. His hands roamed her sleek body, finding the back of her knees to be a sensitive spot on her, causing him to chuckle.

Though he couldn't see her eyes, his hands saw her body. His fingers moved to her core, already slick. He pushed a finger inside her and stroked her deeply, causing her back to arch and a needy sound to erupt in her throat. He moved another finger inside her, caressing her until she panted and then gasped, bringing her to orgasm.

Walker then began at her mouth and worked his way down her body again, once more bringing her to orgasm with his tongue and teeth. Rory shuddered violently beneath him, and he knew he couldn't wait much longer before he exploded.

Quickly, he stripped off his boxer-briefs and tore open the wrapper to the condom, placing it over his swollen cock. He climbed onto the bed again, hovering over her, and asked, "Are you sure this is what you want?"

"You're everything I've ever wanted, Walker," she said

softly. "I just didn't know who you were and how badly I needed you. Until now. Make me yours."

He kissed her deeply and stroked her core, seeing she was ready for him. He pushed inside her in a single thrust, hearing her gasp. Slowly, he began to move, his tongue in her mouth mimicking what his body did below. Rory rose to meet him with each thrust. Joining together with her brought an exhilaration he had never experienced. It was an act of truly becoming one with her.

One with the woman he loved.

Reaching between them, he massaged her clit as he moved in and out and heard her moans of pleasure. Walker felt her orgasm ripple through her and found his own release, a wild ride which left them both exhausted by its end.

He collapsed atop her and then quickly rolled to his side, not wanting to crush her, but also not letting her go.

He would never let Rory Addison go.

Kissing her softly, he asked, "How was that?"

She laughed, sounding amused. "Do you need me to grade our performance, Mr. Cox? The teacher in me thinks you earned an A for your efforts."

"Just an A?" he teased, stroking her hair. "Not an A+?"

"I believe there's always room for improvement. I wouldn't want to inflate your ego and make you think you'd hit your peak your first time out of the gate with me."

Her fingers caressed his cheek lovingly. "Seriously, Walker? I've never made love with a man before. Everything up until now has been strictly sex. And now that I have this to compare it to, I know it was pretty mediocre sex, at that. Can I tell you something? Will you promise you won't laugh?"

Her tone was serious, and he captured her fingers and kissed them. "Promise."

"I've never had an orgasm before," she admitted.

Her words shocked but didn't surprise him, based upon what she'd just confided to him.

"You are a very considerate lover. You took care of me like no one ever has. I don't want to get into particulars. I don't think our past sexual histories should be something we overshare with one another. My hookups on the skating tour were merely that. Brief encounters. With my ex, he wasn't someone who was into foreplay. I realized later he might not have even been attracted to me. That I was too old for him, and he just used me as his cover."

He kissed her fingers again and touched her face, finding tears on her cheeks.

"No one ever took his time the way you did with me just now. I hope you can teach me what you like. What makes you feel as good as you made me feel."

He kissed her softly. "We have all the time we need, Rory. Time to get to know one another. That's what we've been doing up until now. I like knowing that butter pecan is your favorite ice cream and that you are one of the few people who enjoyed the finale of *Lost*.

"Our bodies will be the same way. We'll get to know them—each other—just as we have since you've come to Sugar Springs. We won't know everything about one another at first. We may even discover things about ourselves as we teach each other. But I'm ready to take this journey with you, Rory. Thank you for trusting me enough to want to do the same."

Walker fell silent, and his eyelids grew heavy. He drifted into sleep, Rory warm against him.

~

RORY AWOKE, enveloped in warmth, realizing Walker was wrapped around her like a glove. Her cheek rested against his chest, and she heard the beat of his heart, steady against her ear. Their limbs were entangled so she didn't know where she ended and he began.

Making love with Walker had been a series of revelations.

She had tamped down her feelings of fear, ones which wanted to make her run from him. Instead, she had embraced the fear without letting it swallow her whole. It had been important to her to be the one to move their relationship to the next level. To tell him that she loved him. To make love with him.

Making love ...

People used that phrase interchangeably with having sex—but they were two incredibly different acts. She'd had sex many times. The fast, frenetic times she'd coupled with other skaters, some who had barely spoken English. She'd had her share of times in her monogamous relationship with Bradley but understood he had never truly committed to her emotionally. She doubted he was capable of doing so. His emotional maturation was stunted. Her ex was only about control over women he could manipulate. Rory had gone along with everything Bradley had said or done. Their relationship reminded her of an old Julia Roberts' movie, *The Runaway Bride*.

In it, Julia's character had always adapted to the man in her life, hiding her true self. When Richard Gere's character asked how she liked her eggs, she had to seriously consider the question because it had changed with every man she'd been with. If he favored scrambled eggs, so did she. If he preferred poached, she did, too.

Gere's character had awakened something in her, and she learned to stand on her own two feet.

That's what Rory was learning to do now, with Walker's help. He didn't dominant her. Didn't push her into decisions or tell her how she should feel about things, as Bradley had. Instead, Walker wanted to know who *she* was. She realized they didn't have to like all the same things. That they could be individuals who sometimes had different opinions or liked different activities, and yet they could still come together and enjoy a relationship. They had already built a strong friendship. Now, she hoped tonight had laid the foundation for the physical intimacy which she hoped they would continue to explore.

Suddenly, her hunger for him consumed her. Rory didn't care if he might be sleeping. She wanted him again. Now. And she wanted to return the favor and help him to experience all the sensations he had made her feel.

Lifting her head, she began pressing soft kisses against his muscular chest. He began to stir, and she moved to his nipple, circling it with her tongue and flicking it back and forth. When he groaned and his arms tightened about her, she smiled, satisfied that she was on the right track.

She imitated what he had done with her before, kissing and touching all parts of him. Walker moaned in pleasure, letting her know by words and touch what he enjoyed.

Rory had never touched a man's cock but did so now, her hand encircling it, squeezing, stroking. She knew the pleasure he had brought to her and moved lower, her tongue stroking the tip of his cock. Walker gasped.

She grinned.

Circling the tip with her tongue, she slowly took his

cock into her mouth, moving her lips up and down it. His fingers pushed into her hair as she continued her actions. Until he pushed her aside.

Boldly, she started to climb atop him and take him inside her. She had never been the partner on top and looked forward to trying it with him. Walker shook his head, though.

"I don't have ...anymore ...condoms," he managed to get out. "Hop off, Rory."

She did as he asked, and he left the bed, heading into the bathroom. When he returned, he climbed into bed and took her into his arms. He kissed her, long and slow.

Breaking the kiss, he said, "I'd carried that single condom around for weeks, hoping I'd finally be able to use it with you." He chuckled. "Little did I know you'd be up for round two the same night."

"Then maybe you should keep a box of them in my nightstand's drawer," she said saucily.

Walker growled, pinning her to the bed, kissing her until she was breathless.

"I'll bring that box next time I'm here," he promised, releasing her and leaving the bed.

He reached for his clothes and began dressing.

"You're leaving?"

Slipping into his shirt, he bent and kissed her as he buttoned it. "I've got to. You've got a full day of school tomorrow. And your neighbors don't need to see my car parked in front of your house when they go out to get their paper or walk their dog. Especially nosy Mrs. Dunaway."

He stood, slipping into the boxer-briefs and then his pants. "Sugar Springs is a small town. Naturally, people will gossip about what they see. I'm not saying I won't spend an entire night with you in the future. I'll just need to park my car inside your garage. Same with you.

You've got students who live on your block. We need to be discreet."

Rory climbed from the bed and wrapped her arms around him. "I understand. It was different when I was engaged. We lived in an apartment which was about twenty minutes away from where we taught." She sniffed. "We didn't even know our neighbors."

Walker kissed her. "People already know we're dating. Even your students are used to seeing us together at games. But I know you have a reputation to maintain. I want to make sure we aren't gossiped about more than we probably already are."

She released him and went to where her robe hung on the back of her bedroom door. Slipping into it, she belted it and came toward him.

"Are we still on for the game tonight?" she asked.

"We're on for tonight—and any other night you choose, babe."

They kissed again, both reluctant for him to leave. Finally, he took her hand and walked her to the front door.

"It's four now. Try to go back to bed and get a couple more hours of sleep," he urged.

She burst out laughing. "I don't see how that's going to happen. I've just had the most amazing night of my life."

Walker grinned. "Then go back to bed and fantasize about what we're going to be doing after the game. And all weekend long."

Rory smiled. "That's a homework assignment I'm eager to start."

14

Walker left Rory's house on a natural high. He couldn't remember the last time he had gotten so little sleep and yet felt so amazing. He had no doubt about it.

She was The One.

He had done his best to let the ball remain in her court for play and let Rory be the one to make the first move. At first, he thought it would just about kill him because he wanted her so desperately. Instead, she had been right in insisting they build the foundation of their relationship with a solid layer of friendship. They had spent the last few months really getting to know one another, doing things he'd never thought to do with a woman before. One of the best activities they had pursued together was working on a puzzle of the Swiss Alps which was over a thousand pieces. They had wonderful conversations as they did so, sometimes even pondering pieces in silence, simply happy to be in one another's company.

He had told her of his mom's philosophy of doing dishes together and how the best dialogue between two people often occurred over washing and drying dishes.

She had taken to the practice and anytime they were together, they cleaned the dishes by hand instead of placing them in the dishwasher.

The investment into their friendship had only deepened their connection. Now, adding sex into the mix had changed things between them yet again.

No, not sex. They had made love, something Walker realized he had never done before, not even with Christine. Yes, he'd had a powerful physical attraction to his ex-wife, and their infrequent sex had been pretty amazing. But it had just been a physical act. He knew very little about Christine when they married and probably knew even less about her by the time they divorced. Already, his relationship with Rory was much deeper than any he had previously experienced, including his brief marriage.

Everything led him to believe—especially after last night—that Rory and he were meant to be together for the long haul. Walker sensed she felt the same way and hoped it wouldn't take long before they could be married. He had told her he was in his mid-thirties and ready to start a family. He still felt that pull toward fatherhood and wanted a marriage and kids soon.

Still, he would step gingerly for the present, not wanting Rory to feel as if he pressured her into anything more than she could handle. She was still bruised, fragile from her previous relationship with the asshole. At least Walker knew what was between the two of them was something meant to last. He hoped he could exercise patience because he wanted it all.

Now ...

He changed into running clothes once he got home, knowing sleep would evade him, and set out, running the darkened streets of Sugar Springs, the only illumination coming from the occasional streetlight. The run cleared his mind and refreshed him. When he returned home, he showered and then made coffee for himself and ate a bowl of cereal. As he ate, his phone buzzed, and he picked up his cell, seeing he had a text from Gid.

Can you talk?

IMMEDIATELY, Walker dialed his old friend's number, and Gid answered on the first ring.

"Hey, thanks for calling me back so quickly. I guess you're up."

"Have you solved the case?" he asked quickly. "Did you take a suspect into custody?"

Gid snorted. "I wish. Every time I think we're coming close, we hit a roadblock, but I have a favor to ask."

"Name it."

"The head of the task force knows we've been working seven days a week, around the clock, and he said we need a break to clear our heads. Hopefully, we'll come back with a new outlook and take in everything with fresh eyes. That means I have today off. I know you said it's homecoming tonight. Could I come in today and stay tonight with you?"

Walker couldn't disappoint his best friend. He knew how rough this current serial killer case had gotten. Although he had made plans to spend tonight with Rory, he hoped she would understand.

"Come on," he encouraged. "How soon can you be here?"

"If you're serious, I can be there by about eleven. I

haven't done laundry in forever, so I need to put a load on to wash and dry and then throw a few clean clothes in a duffel bag. I know it's a workday for you, but I can—"

"Today's a pretty light day, Gid. I would love to spend the day with you. This will give me time to go into the office and get a few things done, and then I can play hooky with you when you get here."

"Then I'll get the laundry done and be there around ten-thirty. Eleven at the latest. I'm looking forward to meeting Rory, by the way."

"I'm eager to put the two of you together. Stop by the square and my office when you get to town."

"Will do." Gid paused. "Thank you, Walker. I need the break more than you know. I'll only stay tonight and be gone by noon tomorrow. See you soon."

Walker felt a little better hearing Gid's plans. He would need to let Rory know, though, that they wouldn't be spending tonight together. He decided to FaceTime her because he needed to see her. She answered right away. Just hearing her voice and seeing her smile caused a rush of warmth to fill him.

"Hey, you. I hope this isn't too early to call." He could see she sat on the floor.

"No, I'm glad you did," she said. "I had just finished up a PiYo session."

"I need to let you know about a change of plans for tonight. I know I promised we would do something after the game, but Gid is coming into town for the day and leaving tomorrow."

"Has he cracked his murder case?" she asked eagerly.

He wanted to hug her for the enthusiasm in her voice. He couldn't think of a woman on the planet who would have been happy to hear plans had changed, especially after what had happened between the two of them last night.

"No. The task force has been told to take the day off. He's been burning the candle at both ends and said they all need a break. He knew it was homecoming, and he also wants to meet you after all I've told him about you. Would you mind if Gid came to the game with us tonight?"

"Not at all," she said. "I've been dying to meet him. You said he's only in for the day?"

"Yes, he said he would be leaving by noon tomorrow."

"Then we'll just have to make up for the lost time once he's gone, won't we?" she asked, and he saw the mischief in her eyes.

"I love you. For being so understanding."

"He's your closest friend, Walker. He needs you. He needs this break." She grinned. "And I need to check out Gideon Ross. I'm sure he's told you he wants to do the same with me."

"As a matter of fact, he is looking forward to getting to know you because he knows how special you are to me. Can I touch base with you later about plans?"

"You got it. Right now, though, I need to let you go so I can get ready for school."

"I'll talk to you later."

Rory smiled at him. "I love you."

He grinned. "I love you more."

Walker ended the call and finished his coffee. He dressed and went to the guest room, making sure clean sheets were on the bed and set out fresh towels in the bathroom before leaving for work.

He reached the office and told Margaret that they would be closing up once his friend arrived in town, no later than noon.

"I'll be in my office working on a few things," he told her.

Retreating there, he closed the door. By the time he finished what needed to be done, he printed out copies of it and shut down his computer. Collecting the documents from the printer, Walker went to Margaret's desk and handed the copies to her.

"These need to be filed in Tyler. If you wouldn't mind driving them over and doing so now, you can have the rest of the day off."

"Thanks, Walker," she said. "I needed to go to Tyler anyway. My son needs a new coat this year, and I can pick it up and a few other items."

As she gathered her purse and things, the door to the office opened. Gideon stepped inside.

"Hello, Counselor," he said, moving to Walker and throwing his arms around Walker.

"Glad you made it safely. Hope traffic out of Dallas wasn't too bad."

"A little construction slowed me down, but I made pretty good time."

He indicated Margaret. "This is Margaret Mason, my assistant and receptionist. Gideon Ross, my best friend."

The two shook hands. "Nice to meet you, Gideon," she said. "Thanks for coming to town. Your visit is allowing me to have most of today off."

"Happy to be of service, Margaret."

"I'll see you two at the game," she said and left.

Once the door closed, Walker said, "Margaret's divorced. Mid-thirties, with a ten-year-old son. Attractive and efficient."

Gid laughed. "Not interested. Thanks anyway. So, does the place feel like yours now? Or does the ghost of your dad still linger?"

"I actually feel as if it's mine," he said. "Rory and I

found a couple of things at First Monday in Canton earlier this month. I've got a new desk. A couple of paintings on the walls. Come on. Let me show you around."

He led his friend on the brief tour of the office, and Gid asked for a cup of coffee when he saw the coffeemaker in the small breakroom. Walker made a cup for each of them, and they went to the conference room, where he met with clients sometimes.

After seating himself, Gid asked, "Tell me everything about Rory that you haven't said in a text or the brief times we've talked." He grinned. "I mean *everything*."

Walker laughed heartily. "I can tell you that we've spent a helluva lot of time together, and I like her more each time I leave her. That it's hard *to* leave her."

Gid studied him a moment. "You're in love, aren't you?"

"That's a huge yes, Gid. And let me say this—it's love for the first time. I realize now what I felt for Christine was pretty damn shallow. We had a strong physical attraction, and we were both attorneys. Those were really the only two things we had in common. With Rory, it's so different. Yes, the physical chemistry is definitely there. I could—and have—kissed her for hours. But it's more than that. We have a lot of things in common. Our core values. We decided to be open with each other from the beginning. No topic is off-limits. We don't always agree on everything, but I know her better than any woman I've ever known."

Walker paused. "She's the one for me, Gid. I knew it from the beginning, deep in my bones."

"I haven't seen you looking this relaxed and content in years. Maybe never," Gid told him. "I'm eager to meet her and put my stamp of approval on your relationship. Shall I ask when the wedding is?" he teased.

He laughed. "I would marry Rory tomorrow, but we're taking our time. We did take a big step last night, however. We told one another that we loved each other."

Gid whistled low. "That is a huge step." He smiled. "I'm happy for you, Walker. I know you've wanted what your parents have for a long time. I can't think of anyone who deserves happiness more than you."

"Unless it's you," Walker said.

"I have something to confess. I have an ulterior motive coming to Sugar Springs today. Yes, I wanted to spend some time with you and meet Rory, but I'm also here at the invitation of Chief Hamilton."

He sat up. "I've heard whispers that Roscoe is thinking about retiring. You know he, Dad, and Dr. Carpenter have been tight for years and years. With Dad stepping away from his practice, I think it's causing a ripple effect. What do you think the chief wants to talk to you about?"

"I believe," Gideon said, "that he's going to offer me his job."

"Will you take it? Come back to Sugar Springs? I can't think of anything that would make me happier than having my best friend here with me."

"I'm not doing anything until I catch this serial killer, and I plan to tell Roscoe that today."

Realistically, Walker knew not every killer was brought to justice and asked, "What if that doesn't happen, Gid?"

"It's got to," his friend said, grim determination burning in his eyes. "In the meantime, I'll hear what Hamilton has to say. I'm supposed to meet him for lunch at Ida Lou's. I want you to come with me to lunch, Walker. If it's the three of us, no one will think anything about it. I can say that I'm here in town for homecoming, and no gossip will be stirred up by my presence. I'm supposed to text him when I'm heading to the diner and make it look as if we just ran into each other and want to talk a little shop. I'd be more comfortable if you tagged along."

"If that's what you want, Gid, I'm your wingman."

They sat and talked another half-hour, and then Gid texted Chief Hamilton that they were leaving Walker's office and headed to the diner. The police chief responded to the text, and Gid nodded at Walker.

"We're on."

He locked up his office since they wouldn't be returning, and they walked the short distance to Ida Lou's, entering and greeting the owner. She gave Gid a hug.

Chief Hamilton entered behind them, saying, "Well, look who's back in Sugar Springs. Our fancy Dallas detective."

The three men shook hands, and Walker did his bit, asking, "Are you alone, Chief? Would you like to join us for lunch?"

"Don't mind if I do, Walker. You can tell me where your mama and daddy are right now."

As Ida Lou led them to a booth, Walker asked, "You aren't following their adventures on Facebook or Instagram? Mom's been posting on both sites practically every day."

"I don't do social media," Hamilton said flatly. "Waste of time, if you ask me."

The three all ordered the brisket and beans special of the day, and Walker caught up the chief on where his parents currently were traveling.

"Mrs. Hamilton is on me to take her on a fancy trip, too. A long one." He paused. "Of course, that would mean using up all the vacation time I have—and then some. It might be ... better ... if I just put in my papers and retired. I'd need to have someone I trusted to step into my shoes, though."

Hamilton glanced around the diner, and his gaze returned to Gid. "So, what do you say, Gideon Ross? Can I convince you to come back to Sugar Springs and be its new police chief?"

15

Rory looked out over her classroom, wondering how the girls wore mums so large. Not having gone to high school in Texas, she had been unaware of the practice of boys giving mums to their homecoming dates, much less the enormous size of them. Some girls were covered entirely from their necks to their waists with the huge flowers and long ribbons adorned with glitter, which bore such phrases as *Crush the Cats* and *Sugar Springs*, along with the girl's name and year of graduation.

The P.A. came on, and Joe Bob Milton dismissed seniors to head down to the gym for the homecoming pep rally. Only one student exited her room, a boy who had moved to Texas from out of state this past summer and had yet to take U.S. history.

"Are you coming to the game tonight with Mr. Cox?" one of her girls asked Rory.

"Yes, and we're bringing his friend, Gideon Ross, with us."

"Gideon Ross?" a boy asked, perking up. "He's the best player Sugar Springs ever produced. My uncle played football with him and said no one could cover Gideon because of his speed and moves."

She hoped Gideon liked her because he was important to Walker. She had been surprised to hear that Gideon had come to town today because Walker had tried to get his friend to Sugar Springs several times before now. The murder case Gideon was working dragged on and kept him busy, however. The number of murders attributed to the Dallas serial killer now numbered eleven red-headed females and had even made the national nightly news. Rory couldn't imagine the kind of pressure Gideon and his task force must be under to bring the killer to justice.

The P.A. sounded again, with Joe Bob asking for all juniors to report to the gym at this time. Her classroom was less than half full because many of the students had been summoned earlier since they were either football players, cheerleaders, or members of the drill team or band.

"Let's move on down to the gym," she said brightly, waiting until the last student exited before locking her door and slipping the keys into the pocket of her jeans.

As she walked down the corridor, she saw Pam and Linda waiting for her at the top of the stairs. It was so good to have friends again at school. To talk with over lunch. To share little things. She hoped to remain friends with these two and the other women she ate lunch with every day.

"Ready for the homecoming pep rally?" Pam asked.

"Each week, I'm surprised how these pep rallies get louder and better," Rory said.

"I still can't believe your last school didn't have homecoming. Or a football team," Linda said. "Why, that's like having a birthday cake with no icing or candles on it. What's the point?"

They chuckled and joined the mass of students moving toward the gym. Once they arrived, she found herself caught up in the beat of the drums and the chant of the cheers. The fight song began to play, and the football team entered the gym, led by new head coach Cole Johnson. He had guided his team to an undefeated season so far, and everyone in town expected the Sugar Springs Knights to make it deep into the playoffs.

Class cheers were followed by a dance from the drill team and a skit by some of the senior boys, naturally led by Freddie Otts. The cheerleaders did a dance of their own, and then a jalapeño-eating contest was held. One of Rory's homeroom students claimed victory, and she whistled loudly, a newfound skill taught to her by Walker.

Glancing across the gym as they sang the school song to close out the pep rally, Rory truly felt a part of things. She wanted to stay in this town forever. Raise her kids here. See them march in the band or tackle opponents on the football field.

And more than anything, Rory wanted to do it with Walker by her side.

Their relationship had certainly changed last night. Not only had they taken a serious step by making love, but they had both voiced their love for one another. She had come to the realization that if she were ever to trust a man again, it could only be Walker Cox. The attorney was everything her ex wasn't. Walker was a man of integrity, with a sterling reputation, one who was eager to give back to his community. He wanted to sink roots deeply into Sugar Springs and have children. Bradley had told her that he wasn't interested in ever having a family. That they spent all day, every day, around kids, and he wanted to escape to a quiet, peaceful home at the end of a long day of teaching and coaching.

Though Rory wanted children, at that time she had wanted to please Bradley more and went along with whatever he wanted, pushing her own feelings aside. She had made so many mistakes in that relationship.

That's why she enjoyed being with Walker now. He listened to her and treated her as an equal. He didn't try to cram his opinions down her throat. They had lively discussions, oftentimes about politics since they sat on opposite sides of the spectrum, but she knew Walker respected her and her opinions. He would never try to make her into someone she didn't want to be. It was liberating, knowing she could be her true self with him.

The school song ended, and the band struck up the fight song again as the crowd cheered the football team exiting the gym. Rory returned to her classroom for her purse and jacket, leaving her briefcase behind for the first time this school year. She had no intention of grading any papers this weekend, not with homecoming happening and Gideon Ross in town.

And whatever she and Walker might do after Gideon departed.

She texted when she got to her car, letting Walker know that she was leaving school. He replied that they would pick her up at five-thirty so they could attend the alumni tailgate party, which would be held in the student parking lot next to the stadium.

Rory arrived home, collecting her mail and going through it before freshening up. She picked up her sketchbook and began drawing, soothing her nerves, killing time until Walker showed up.

The doorbell startled her, bringing her out of her reverie, and she hurried to answer it. She found Walker and Gideon on her porch, both dressed in jeans and ancient-looking sweatshirts with the Knights logo emblazoned on the front.

She had seen pictures of Gideon with Walker at the Coxes' house, but she was struck by how handsome the

Dallas detective was in person. He was slightly taller than Walker and had hair black as a raven's. It was his gray eyes, though, which drew her in.

"Come on in. It's nice to finally meet you in person," Rory said.

"I'm glad to meet you, Rory," Gideon said, taking her hand and shaking it. "This guy talks about you constantly. I needed to check you out and see if you're really the angel he says you are."

Her cheeks heated. "I hope he hasn't bored you."

A smile played about Gideon's lips. "Not at all. If anything, I'm glad he's found you."

Walker's cell rang and he frowned, looking at it. "I need to get this. Give me a moment." He walked toward the kitchen.

Gideon said, "You've changed him, Rory."

"I hope that's not a bad thing," she said, unsure of where their conversation headed.

"No, I definitely mean it as a compliment. I haven't seen Walker this lighthearted in years. He's always been my best friend. For as long as I can remember, though, it seems he's carried the weight of the world on his shoulders. We spent this afternoon at Sugar Lake, fishing, and had a lot of time to talk. I know leaving his high-profile firm and practicing small-town law has helped decease his anxiety level, but I know you are the real difference in his life. Why he's so damn happy. He loves you. You make him ... a better version of him. That alone makes me want to be your friend."

Gideon wrapped her in a bear hug and whispered, "Thank you," in her ear.

"I'm glad you were able take a day off and come to Sugar Springs," she said.

"I've done nothing but work seven days a week for several months now. I'm reaching my breaking point. If we don't find this killer soon, I don't know if I'll be able to live with myself. Every new murder takes a piece of my soul."

She placed a hand on his forearm. "This little respite will be good for you. Twenty-four hours away from the case may bring new insight once you look at the evidence your team has assembled."

"That's what the head of our task force said. Mandatory break for all. I hope it works."

Walker stepped back into the room. "Sorry."

"Is anything wrong?" Rory asked.

"Nothing that can't wait until Monday morning," he told her, giving her a warm, reassuring smile.

"Hey, did you do these?" Gideon asked. "They're really good."

She turned and saw he had picked up her sketchbook. "It's just something I fiddle around with. I used to skate competitively, and I designed my own costumes."

"I've tried to encourage Rory to pursue some kind of arrangement with her designs," Walker told his friend.

"Well, these are amazing. I've never watched figure skating, but I think Walker's right. You have talent and should try to partner with some manufacturer. Or at least with individual clients and someone who can make costumes from your pictures." Gideon grinned. "You were a big name in the skating world. I Googled you after Walker told me he was seeing you. I think skaters would be thrilled if they were wearing a design by Rory Addison."

"I'll think about it," she said, taking the sketchbook from him and placing it on the coffee table. "Let me get my jacket. It's going to be cool tonight."

In unison, the two men exclaimed, "Perfect football weather!"

Walker drove them to the high school, and they

parked and walked to the tailgate, the smells of sizzling burgers wafting through the air. Since this was Rory's first homecoming, she wasn't sure what to expect, but she found a good number of graduates from the high school had returned for this tailgate and the game which followed.

Walker introduced her to people he had played football and baseball with, as well as others she hadn't met who lived in town. Some returning alumni were even friends from his Scouting years.

"Rory Addison?" someone asked.

She turned and saw a gorgeous, dark-haired stranger her same height, standing in front of her. The woman had curves in all the right places and striking eyes which were the color of amber.

"Yes?"

"I'm Vivi Romano, Paige's best friend." Vivi smiled. "She told me to look for you tonight when I told her I was driving in for the tailgate and game. How are you liking her house?"

"Quite a bit. It's the perfect size and in a great location. You're in Dallas, aren't you? I think your mom told me both you and your brother work in restaurants there."

"Yes, I'm a sous chef at a steakhouse. Dante, my brother, is about to leave where he cooks and open his own Italian restaurant in Dallas. He's aiming for December."

"Is he also here?"

Vivi laughed. "No, Dante wouldn't take off from a Friday night service to come back to a little hole in the wall like Sugar Springs."

"But you did," Rory said, wondering about the difference between the siblings.

Vivi grew reflective. "Sugar Springs has been good to

my family and me. While I enjoyed leaving and training as a chef and I like my life in Dallas, there's something to be said for living in a small town. Kind of like Cheers— where everybody knows your name. I think of Sugar Springs as one big family."

"You need to grab a burger or hot dog," she said. "Are you here with anyone? If not, why don't you sit with us at the game?"

"That would be terrific," Vivi said. "Let me get something to eat, and I'll be right back."

Once the tailgate ended, Rory and Vivi accompanied Walker and Gideon into the stands. As they watched the game, she got to know Vivi much better and could see why Paige liked Vivi so much.

When the game ended, Vivi asked, "Would you like to come back to Romano's for some pizza? Mom and Dad will be expecting a big crowd, but we could go upstairs to the office for a little peace and quiet while we eat."

"I'm all in," Gideon declared. "It's been too long since I ate a Romano's pizza. Nothing in Dallas comes close to what your dad makes."

Vivi accompanied them to Walker's car, saying her mom had dropped her off, so she didn't have a car to claim. On the way to eat, Vivi called and put in an order for them.

"It'll be ready shortly after we get there," she told them.

They parked on the square and headed into the pizza parlor, which was already half full and buzzing with energy after tonight's victory.

Viv took them through the kitchen, which was crazy with activity, and they got drinks before going up a staircase. The office had a sofa that would fit three of them, and Vivi pulled the chair from behind the desk and rolled it over. Mrs. Romano arrived with the largest pizza Rory had ever seen, placing it on the coffee table.

"Here you go," Mrs. Romano said. "If you need anything else, just let me know."

They devoured the pizza over the next hour. Rather, Walker and Gideon ate the majority of it, while Rory and Vivi each claimed one large slice.

"I know you ate two burgers at the tailgate, Walker," she said. "How do you have room to put that much away?"

"You can't turn down a Romano's pizza, babe," he said. "Besides, I can't let Gid eat more than me. It's a guy thing."

Vivi talked a little bit about the restaurant she worked in, and Walker promised that he and Rory would drive into Dallas some weekend and eat there.

"Let me know when you're coming, and I'll make sure you sit at the chef's table," Vivi told them. "You, too, Gideon."

"This is my one night out," the detective declared. "I'm like Cinderella. Once this night is over, I'm headed back to Dallas in the morning and my task force." He held up his beer. "But I want to make a toast."

They all raised whatever they drank as Gideon said, "To this night's victory on the field—and for friends, both old and new. Cheers."

"Cheers," they echoed.

Mr. and Mrs. Romano appeared, having closed down the restaurant, wanting to wish them all goodnight.

"We should get going," Walker said, and they accompanied the Romanos downstairs, saying goodbye to Vivi and her parents.

He drove Rory home and walked her to the front door, slipping his arms around her.

"I hope tonight was okay, and you didn't mind us spending it with Gid and Vivi."

"No, it was perfect. It gives me an idea of what our life in Sugar Springs could be like together."

Walker dipped his head, kissing her.

He broke the kiss. "We have a lot to talk about tomorrow. And the dance to chaperone. I'll call you once Gid has left for Dallas."

"I really like him, Walker."

"He likes you, too." He leaned in and brushed his lips softly against hers. "See you tomorrow, babe. I love you."

"I love you, too," she said, watching him return to his convertible.

She waved as they drove off, then she entered her house, a feeling of immense satisfaction rolling through her. She had a great job she thoroughly enjoyed. She was becoming a part of the Sugar Springs community. And she had the love of the best man she had ever known.

Rory finally had learned to trust once again.

16

W
alker turned in bed, propping his hand against his head, his elbow pressed against the pillow as he drank in Rory. Her lips were swollen from kissing, and her auburn hair was loose and wild about her shoulders, catching the light streaming in from the window, making it appear to be on fire. He touched her cheek as she rolled to face him, his thumb stroking the smooth skin.

He had made his way to her the minute Gid had left town. They'd gone for a long run together this morning and then come back and talked over bacon and eggs, tossing out the pros and cons of Gid leaving the Dallas police force in order to take charge of the smaller police department of Sugar Springs.

Gid had asked that Walker keep their discussion with Chief Hamilton to himself, not ready for it to be made public knowledge in any way. He had given Walker permission to tell Rory about it, however. His friend had given his seal of approval and said he was ready to be tapped as the best man whenever the pair decided to marry.

For now, though, Gid would remain in Dallas. He had told Roscoe Hamilton at their lunch yesterday that he had to see this particular case through to its conclusion. Walker knew Gid wasn't a quitter and would persevere until he found this serial killer and saw him locked away. In the meantime, the police chief had agreed to stay on in Sugar Springs and not mention retirement until Gideon was available to replace him.

Walker hoped for his friend's sake that would be soon.

After Gid was gone, Walker had raced to Rory, and they had spent the rest of the morning and early afternoon in bed, exploring one another. He recalled the physical attraction he'd felt toward Christine, but what he had with Rory was completely different. They had laid a firm foundation of friendship before ever consummating their relationship, and he had high hopes they would be partners for life. He wouldn't broach the subject of marriage just yet, but Walker hoped by Christmastime they might be engaged and marry when his parents returned from their world tour in May.

She placed her palm against his cheek, lovingly stroking it with her thumb. Just a simple touch from this woman made Walker melt. He looked forward to building a life with Rory and starting a family together.

"I suppose we should get up and eat something," she teased. "After all, you can only live on love for so long before stomachs start to growl."

Hers did at that moment, and they both laughed as his gurgled in response.

Climbing from the bed, he held out a hand, pulling her from it and into his arms.

As he wrapped them about her, Walker said, "I never knew how good—how right—something could be. It's taken me a long time to find you, Rory Addison, but I'm never letting you go."

As he kissed her, his belly rumbled loudly again, and he broke the kiss, both of them laughing again.

"Let's get in the shower," he suggested. "Then we can feed the beasts."

They showered together, which wasn't an easy feat in the small space from the decades-old bathroom. He made a mental note to add a large shower to his list of must-haves, which he would present to Tamara Heath, the local realtor. They'd already had one conversation when they ran into one another on the square a few weeks ago, and he'd told Tamara in vague terms what he was looking to purchase but that he was in no rush.

Now, though, Walker wanted to find a place to live with the woman he wished to make his wife.

They stepped from the shower, and he toweled her off, watching her dress as he dried himself. Rory unpinned the hair she had placed in a knot atop her head and shook it out. It fell past her shoulders, and he stepped toward her, wrapping his arms around her from behind and studying their image together in the mirror. He wanted to ask her to move in with him, but he was aware how gun-shy she still was. He could be patient when necessary, and so he merely nuzzled her neck and then released her.

They finished dressing, and she made grilled cheese sandwiches for them, heating tomato soup to go along with it. They talked about the homecoming dance, which started at seven this evening, and how they were committed to chaperoning it.

"The dance ends at ten," she told him, "and my NHS members will stay and clean up afterward. With Freddie in charge, it shouldn't be more than half an hour before we can leave."

"Then maybe you could come and spend the night at my place," he suggested. "You could pack an overnighter and leave it in the car. We could go straight from the dance back to my place."

She gave him a dazzling smile. "I would like that. Very much."

Her cell rang, and Rory went to retrieve it from where it sat on the counter.

"Hmm, it's Sarah. I wonder what she wants." Answering it, Rory put it on speaker and said, "Hello?" as she sat at the table again.

"Hi, Rory. It's Sarah. I really need you to come over ASAP. Can you do that?"

"Sure, I can leave now. I'm with Walker. Do you mind if he tags along?"

"Bring him. If you don't want to accept, then maybe he will," her friend said cryptically. "See you soon."

Rory frowned. "I wonder what that's about?"

"Let's go find out," Walker said, taking her hand and leading her to his car.

They drove the six blocks to Sarah's house and got out, knocking on her door.

Sarah answered right away, inviting them in, and leading them into the kitchen where Mrs. Berry sat, her Irish setter sitting by her feet.

Rory had told Walker she had met Mrs. Berry once before when she'd dropped by to see Sarah. The widow who lived next door was known for her green thumb and had been working in the flowerbed of her front yard. Both Walker and Rory had passed Mrs. Berry several times separately during their morning exercise, and the widow had her dog on a leash, doing the same.

"Have a seat," Sarah said.

They sat at the kitchen table, their curiosity growing.

"I know Rory has met Mrs. Berry, but I don't know if you have, Walker," Sarah said.

He offered his hand. "Not officially. We've just passed

on the street. I do know you and Mr. Berry have been clients of Dad's for a long time."

"Yes, Campbell handled our wills for us. I lost my husband about eighteen months ago."

"I'm sorry to hear that," he said.

"I'm sure you wondered why Sarah called you over, Rory," Mrs. Berry said. "Let me explain. My daughter lives in Houston with her husband and two little girls. They're two and five and the light of my life. I drive down to see them once a month and stay for about a week. Sarah has been kind enough to dog sit Comet for me when I do so."

"She's the sweetest dog ever," Sarah said enthusiastically, leaning down to pet the dog. "Comet definitely gets me out of bed and is eager for a walk each morning."

"My daughter is pregnant again," the widow continued. "This time, it's a boy. My son-in-law just found out he's being transferred to Chicago, and they've asked for me to come along and live with them. In fact, they'll be heading up there the day after tomorrow and asked me to come down and keep the girls while they're gone. They'll be house hunting in the suburbs and want to find a place with a mother-in-law suite, so I'll have a bit of privacy."

Mrs. Berry paused. "The thing is, I can't take Comet with me. My son-in-law is allergic to dogs and cats, which is why I always leave Comet with Sarah when I travel to Houston. I had gotten her about six months ago because I was getting a bit lonely with my husband gone. I can't take her with me to Chicago, however."

"And I don't want to take on the responsibility of a dog," Sarah added. "I've been talking with Tanner Haddock as he edits *Shadows of the Past*, and he believes the acting offers will roll in for me once it releases. This will be my chance at my dream—to be a film actress. I'll be resigning at the end of the school year and hopefully will have a few acting gigs lined up by then. An actor's life is too nomadic, and I don't want to have to leave Comet in doggy daycare for weeks or months at a time, especially if I have to go on location to film."

Sarah smiled. "I remembered, though, that you mentioned wanting to adopt a dog, and that Walker was also interested in getting a pup."

Mrs. Berry said, "I know Comet isn't a puppy. She just turned a year old. She has had training, though, and is housebroken. I'll admit that I didn't realize how active Irish setters are when I got her. They enjoy a lot of physical activity and are also good with children. If you haven't found a puppy that you're interested in adopting, I hope you'll do me a favor and consider taking Comet."

Walker glanced at the dog lying on the floor. She looked up at them with her warm, brown eyes, melting his heart.

Rory looked to him, and he nodded in approval. She looked back to Mrs. Berry and said, "I would be happy to make Comet a part of my family."

Tears welled in the widow's eyes. "Thank you, Rory. I wanted her to go to a good home. Comet is a real sweetheart. I can leave for Chicago, knowing my baby will be in good hands. Would you like to come over and collect her things?"

"You want me to take her *now*?" Rory asked, surprise in her voice.

"I think a clean break would be best," Mrs. Berry said, wiping away a falling tear. "I'll contact Tamara Heath and have her put my house on the market immediately. I leave for Houston soon and will probably spend most of my time down there, helping my daughter pack up the house for the big move. I believe it would be best if Comet went to her new home during this transition."

"Then I'll be happy to take her home with me now," Rory said.

Everyone stood, and Walker accompanied Rory and Mrs. Berry next door, Comet following at the widow's heels.

"She loves to walk fast and would probably enjoy running," Mrs. Berry said. "Do you do any running, Rory?"

"No, ma'am, I'm strictly a walker, but here's your runner," she said, her thumb pointing to him.

"I'd be happy to help exercise Comet, Mrs. Berry," Walker said. "How did she get her name?"

The older woman chuckled. "Because she's so darn fast. Like a comet zipping across the sky. She's a streak of light when given the chance to really cut loose."

Mrs. Berry spent a few minutes gathering the Irish setter's toys and food. She went over when and how much to feed the dog, and Walker took the items to his car, placing them in the trunk. When he returned, Mrs. Berry asked them to come into the backyard with her, where she went through a series of commands with Comet.

"I want you to be familiar with what she knows how to do," Mrs. Berry said. "We went to an obedience class when I got her six months ago, and she was the star pupil."

Both he and Rory practiced giving the setter instructions, which Comet readily followed.

The widow bent and wrapped her arms about her dog, kissing the pup on her forehead. Walker held out his hand and helped her stand again.

"Thank you for doing this favor for me, Rory. I know we hardly know one another, but Sarah has talked of you frequently and thinks the world of you. My Comet is going to be taken care of, and that is such a relief to me."

"Can we trade cell numbers in case I have any further questions?" Rory asked. "I'm also happy to text you pictures of Comet if that won't upset you."

"No, it wouldn't at all. I would love to see her every now and then that way."

The women exchanged phone numbers, and Rory snapped the leash onto Comet's collar, leading her to Walker's convertible. Walker followed, taking what Mrs. Berry said was the dog's favorite blanket, and he spread it across the back seat. Comet leaped into the car and curled up on it.

Mrs. Berry stood on the sidewalk and said, "She just had all her shots last week. I take her to Dr. Bisch here in town. You might want to give his office a call and let his receptionist know that Comet has moved to a new home."

"I'll call first thing Monday morning," Rory promised.

Walker started the car and waved goodbye. The widow smiled sadly and turned away, hurrying toward her house.

Rory faced him. "I didn't know we would be dog parents so soon," she said, glancing to back seat where Comet sat regally. "I hope she won't miss Mrs. Berry too much."

"We'll simply lavish her with love," he promised, adding, "just like I plan to do with you."

A blush stained her cheeks. "I think Comet and I will like the attention," she said saucily. Then hesitating, she added, "It's good to know Irish setters are good with children."

Walker knew exactly what she was saying without

the words being spoken aloud. "Yes, it is good to hear that the breed is kid-friendly."

He slipped his hand around hers, lacing their fingers together.

This had been a weekend for the books. They had verbally and physically expressed their love for one another, and now they had a dog.

Walker grinned to himself, thinking things were definitely on schedule.

Rory and Walker both stretched, he for his run, and she for her walk. Comet stood nearby, eagerly awaiting to be exercised.

The Irish setter had been a blessing in many ways in the weeks since they had taken her off Mrs. Berry's hands. Comet was friendly and intelligent and a wonderful companion. She did enjoy a high level of exercise and started her day with Walker each morning, who took her on runs lasting between five and ten miles.

Ever since they had adopted Comet, Walker pretty much had moved in with Rory. It amazed her how quickly their love had deepened and how comfortable they were with one another. They wanted to spend as much time together as possible, and Walker said he preferred Paige's cozy house to his parents' larger one. He did stop by the Coxes' house daily to make sure everything was in working order, but after work, he spent all his time with Rory and Comet.

They would be driving to Dallas today in order to have dinner at the steakhouse where Vivi served as sous chef. They would also do a little shopping for Christmas while there. It was the week of Thanksgiving, and Rory's school district had the entire week off. Walker had said he didn't have much going on at his law office and had given Margaret the whole week off, as well. She had taken her son to visit family in Louisiana. Walker would check messages to see if anyone had called his office, but he didn't think anything of importance would arise during this holiday week.

They had plans to spend Thanksgiving Day with Pam and Sam, and Rory was looking forward to the two dishes she would be preparing for their holiday feast. She'd learned that most people in Texas celebrated Thanksgiving at lunch so that dishes could be cleared and everyone was in front of the TV to watch the Dallas Cowboys play that afternoon.

"I'll run by Mom and Dad's while Comet and I are out and see if all is well there. I'll meet you back here, and we can shower and get on the road."

"Don't forget that we need to drop Comet at Pam's on our way out of town," she reminded him.

Sarah was not available to dog sit this week. Instead, she had flown to California and was going to spend a few days with Tanner and Paige. *Shadows of the Past* would open on Christmas Day in four large markets— New York, Chicago, Los Angeles, and Dallas. After the new year, it would be in wide release.

Sarah also mentioned that Tanner wanted to talk with her about her career and was pushing for her to re-sign at the semester instead of the end of the academic year. She would make that decision while in California. Although Rory would miss her new friend if she did leave Sugar Springs, she had a feeling they would con-tinue to stay in touch, no matter where Sarah's career took her.

Walker signaled to Comet, and the setter hurried to him. Walker snapped the leash onto Comet's collar and gave a wave goodbye.

Rory set out a few minutes later on her walk, thinking over the activities her students would be completing during the three weeks after Thanksgiving and before winter break. She had settled into her classes and, despite lesson planning and grading papers, had a little bit of free time on her hands and used it to work on her skating costume designs. Walker had continued to encourage her to do more than draw, but she wasn't ready to commit to anything specific at this point. Frankly, she didn't think after so many years that many in the skating world would even remember her, much less clamor for her designs.

Still, she had gone so far as to contact Sylvia Golding, the woman who had sewed Rory's costumes years ago when she created her own practice wear and competition costumes. Sylvia had enthusiastically agreed to work with her again in case she picked up any clients.

Ever since then, Rory had been doing her homework. After she had been forced from competitive skating, she had never watched another competition, either in person or on TV. Because she was so unfamiliar with today's skaters, Rory had spent many hours reviewing footage on YouTube of some of the most popular skaters in the world, hoping to reach out to a few in the US to begin with and see if there might be any interest on their part regarding her creations. She might have been gone from that world seven years now and though she was no longer relevant, she believed her designs could be. It wouldn't hurt to test the waters.

She returned to the house and hopped into the shower, only to be joined by Walker. Shower sex had become one of her favorite things, and Walker did not disappoint this morning. Their sex life was very active, but more importantly, it was meaningful. They continued to learn more about what pleased each other, and Rory hoped things were leading toward a more permanent arrangement. Possibly, a marriage proposal. Although they had only known each other since summer, she knew Walker Cox was her soulmate and was eager to spend the rest of her life with him.

They both dressed and packed bags for their overnight stay in Dallas. Vivi Romano had recommended a boutique hotel for them to stay in. It was only a few blocks from her steakhouse. Rory looked forward to seeing her new friend tonight. Ever since they had met at homecoming, she and Vivi had cemented their friendship by texting frequently. Rory knew that the Romanos were interested in Vivi taking over their pizzeria sometime in the near future and hoped that would happen. She wondered if Gideon also returned to town, whether he and Vivi might get together. The four of them had had such a nice time together eating pizza after the homecoming game, and she knew from Walker that Gideon had an opportunity to come back to Sugar Springs and take over its police department if he wanted to do so.

So far, that had yet to occur because the serial killer he sought was still on the loose.

Walker placed their bags in the trunk of his car while she gathered Comet's toys and food and draped his favorite blanket on the back seat. They drove to Pam's house, and her friend greeted them as they pulled into the driveway.

"The kids are thrilled to be keeping Comet," Pam shared. "This will be a good test run for us. We've never had a family pet before. Sam said if this works out, he would be willing for us to look into getting a dog."

"Comet already loves Griff and Callie," Rory said. "I know the three of them will have a good time together while we're gone."

They accompanied Pam inside, where the twins were curled up on the couch watching TV. The minute they saw Comet, however, they squealed in delight and scrambled from the sofa, giving the dog hugs and pets.

Walker supervised kids and dog while Rory went into the kitchen with Pam, setting down Ziplock bags with the Irish setter's food and treats.

"Thanks again for keeping her while we're in Dallas. We should be back by dinner tomorrow night."

"We'll be here," Pam assured her. "We don't have any plans. Other than a little grocery shopping for Thanksgiving dinner on Thursday, I'm enjoying this week off from school. My lesson plans are done for the rest of the semester. I'm caught up on grading papers. I'm devoting this week to the twins. And Sam, of course."

They hugged goodbye, and Rory went with Walker to his convertible, the top up due to the cold weather. On the way to Dallas, they talked about everything from the NFL games coming up to politics and a new movie they wanted to watch on Netflix over her break.

Walker took her to lunch at a diner he had frequented during his days living here, and Gideon met them there. The detective talked a little about the case he was working on and how his gut told him they were getting close to identifying the killer.

"He's made a few mistakes lately. Nothing that we've leaked to the press, but I have high hopes he'll be taken into custody soon." He paused. "Just watch your redhead while you're in Dallas, Walker. Our killer only targets redheads."

A chill ran through Rory. While she had known about the victims Gideon was working to bring justice to, it had never struck her that she was a redhead, as all the murdered women were. She supposed the killer felt wronged by a redhead in his past and killed over and over, trying to get back at that particular woman. Rory was glad she had Walker with her during this visit to Dallas.

They bid Gideon goodbye and went to check into their hotel. It had a European flavor and reminded her of various places she had stayed while she traveled the world, competing in skating events.

Walker suggested they take a nap since they had both been up so early, and they curled up on the large bed. Rory fell asleep quickly and awakened two hours later to Walker's kiss. They made love leisurely, her orgasm shattering her. She framed his face and kissed him softly.

"I don't know what I did before I met you."

"Same," he echoed. "I love you, babe."

They dressed up for this special dinner, Rory in a peacock blue silk dress, and Walker in a charcoal gray suit, with white dress shirt and red tie. They decided to walk the few blocks to the steakhouse so they wouldn't have to bother parking Walker's car. They were to eat at the chef's table during the early service, which suited them since they both liked eating early and going to bed by nine or ten each evening.

The hostess greeted them, and Walker gave his name. Immediately, the woman's eyes lit up.

"Ah, you're Vivi's friends. May I take your coat?" she asked, and Rory handed it over. "Right this way, please."

The woman seated them, and Vivi came out in her chef's whites, her eyes bright. "I'm so glad you could make it to Dallas and join us this evening," she said.

"You can make all our selections for us," Rory told her friend. "I know you'll take good care of us."

Vivi smiled. "I'll do just that. You're in for a treat." She glanced at the server who had arrived and said, "Bring them a bottle of our best cabernet. You don't need to take their order. I know exactly what I want to feed them."

The server nodded. "Very well, Miss Romano."

They ate like kings. Their large ribeye steaks were marbled throughout and flavorful and tender. The steaks were accompanied by cold, crisp Caesar salads, with scalloped potatoes and roasted vegetables.

When it came time for dessert, Rory wasn't sure she could eat another bite.

Vivi stopped by the table again. "Have you enjoyed your meal so far?"

"It's been absolutely the best meal I've ever eaten," Walker declared.

"I agree," Rory said. "But as much as I want it, I don't think I have room for dessert."

"I can box it up for you if you'd like," Vivi suggested.

"That sounds perfect," Rory told her.

"I'll be right back," Vivi told them and disappeared.

Walker linked their hands together and smiled warmly at her. "I hope we look back on this meal years from now and remember it. For more than just the food."

He gazed at her intently, and Rory's heart began beating in double-time.

"I don't want to harp on my age," he said. "But I don't want to waste any more time, Rory. You're the one that I want. The one I can't live without. You have made me happier than I ever dreamed possible. Would you do me the honor of marrying me?"

Tears flooded her eyes. "Yes," she whispered, and then more enthusiastically, she said, "Yes," joy bubbling from her.

Walker kissed her, a kiss she would not forget any-time soon. When she opened her eyes, Vivi stood at the table beaming at them, a sack in her hand with their desserts inside. Her friend beamed at her. "Anything you want to tell me?"

"We just got engaged," Rory said, still not quite believing it herself.

Vivi squealed, leaning down to hug her. "I'm so happy for you both. I knew this was coming. And there's no charge tonight. This meal is on me, including the tip. I'm so glad to celebrate your happiness."

They thanked her profusely, then met the chef of the steakhouse. He asked how their meal had been and congratulated them upon hearing the news of their engagement.

"Dante is opening his own restaurant next month," Vivi shared. "You'll have to come back and eat at it."

"Let us know when you want us, and we'll be here," Walker said.

They slid from the booth and went to the front of the restaurant to claim Rory's coat. Then she heard her name being called and turned. She immediately recognized the young woman standing in front of them. She had been an up and coming junior in the figure skating world as Rory was leaving, and now she was ranked the number two women's figure skater in the US.

"I saw you and just had to come and introduce myself. I'm Candace Smith. I worshipped you when I was growing up, Rory."

"Thank you, Candace," she said. "You've had quite the career yourself. May I introduce my fiancé, Walker Cox?" Rory delighted in saying that and watched as the two shook hands.

"May I ask what you're doing now, Rory?" Candace asked.

"I'm teaching high school history in a small town in East Texas," she replied.

"Do you remember that cobalt blue outfit you wore at the second Olympics? The one you designed?"

She smiled, the image in her head bringing back fond memories. "That was one of my favorite creations. It was comfortable and stylish, two musts. I also liked how it contrasted with my hair."

"I know you've been out of figure skating for quite a while, but I have always remembered that costume. Also, the cornflower one. And that bold yellow, too. I was impressed how you designed your own costumes and even choreographed your own programs. You did it all, Rory."

Candace hesitated a moment and then added, "I may be overstepping here, but I was wondering if you might consider creating a few outfits for me. Nationals and Worlds are coming up. I would be thrilled to wear anything you might design for me."

A thrill shot through Rory. Candace was tall, with a willowy frame, and would look good in numerous types of designs.

Walker squeezed her fingers in encouragement, and Rory said, "I would be happy to do so. When would you like to meet and discuss what you'll need?"

"If you are available tomorrow anytime, I'd be happy to work around your schedule. I leave Dallas to head back to Colorado and train on Friday morning, and I won't return until after Worlds next March."

The two women exchanged cell numbers and decided to meet at nine tomorrow morning at an apartment Candace kept nearby.

"Thank you so much," Candace said, spontaneously hugging Rory. "You were my idol for years. Every goal I have, I made to live up to what you did in figure skating. I'm so happy to be working with you."

"I feel the same," she replied.

Walker helped Rory slip into her coat, and they strolled back to the hotel.

On the way to their room, she said, "I wish I would've known I would run into Candace and commit to dressing her for the upcoming championships. I would have brought my sketchbook with me."

"We can pick up a blank one for you tomorrow before your meeting," he said. "And after you meet with her, I want to go look at rings. I knew I would propose tonight, but I have no idea what you might wish for in an engagement ring. I thought we could look and decide together."

"As long as you make it my Christmas present," she told him. "I don't need anything else but you." She grinned. "And my ring."

They changed into pajamas and decided they had room after all to eat their desserts. Vivi had packed crème brûlée for them both. It was sweet and light and hit the spot.

Shortly after, they got ready for bed and went to sleep. At one point, Rory woke and reached for Walker, but he wasn't there. She supposed he had gotten up to use the bathroom and closed her eyes, falling asleep again.

The next time she woke, he was next to her. She danced her fingers lightly across his forearm, just enough to wake him. He pulled her close and soon they were making love. She didn't think life could get any better. Until she got out of bed and saw something sitting on the nightstand.

A sketchbook and tin.

Picking up the sketchbook, she asked, "How did you find a store open? And when did you even get this?"

She began flipping through the pages, only to realize

it was *her* sketchbook, filled with drawings she had been doing all fall.

"Walker?" she asked, confused.

He moved to her, wrapping his arms around her, softly kissing her mouth. "I thought you might need it to show Candace. So, I went and got it for you."

Her jaw dropped. "You drove all the way back to Sugar Springs? For me?"

He brushed his lips against hers. "There isn't anything I wouldn't do for you, Rory. I hope you know that."

Tears misted her eyes. "No one has ever taken care of me the way you do, Walker. I love you so much."

She pulled him down to her, kissing him with everything she had, wanting to show him how much she loved him.

A man who would drive ninety minutes each way simply to retrieve a sketchbook and colored pencils in the middle of the night was a man who was definitely a keeper.

Rory would spend every day of the rest of her life letting Walker know he was the only one for her.

18

Thanksgiving Day dawned, and Rory and Walker walked Comet together early that morning. They would be heading to Pam's house for their one o'clock holiday luncheon. They had arranged to FaceTime with their loved ones who were overseas this morning.

Good to her word, Granny Bea had done exactly what she had told Rory she would do—grab some Red Hats and take an international trip. Granny Bea and her friends were currently on a fourteen-day vacation through England, Scotland, and Wales. Fortunately, today the women would be finishing their latest sight-seeing adventure early and returning to their hotel in Wales. Rory had decided to wait three days to tell her grandmother about her engagement until this call, when there would be plenty of time to talk about it face-to-face. They had traded a few emails, but she was bursting to give Granny Bea her good news.

They would follow up this conversation with a call to Walker's parents, who were in Eastern Europe now. Walker FaceTimed with his parents once a week, catching them up on the happenings in Sugar Springs, while hearing about their travels. Rory hoped the

Coxes would be excited about their son's engagement to her.

They showered and dressed, eating a light breakfast, and then Rory got out everything she would need to make the two dishes she had promised to bring to Pam's. They were two classics, according to her grandmother. One was a cornbread dressing, which other parts of the country called stuffing. Here in Texas, though, it was dressing that accompanied a turkey, and the more cornbread in it, the better. Granny Bea was going to walk Rory through what to put in the dressing because no actual recipe existed. It was more a throw a little of this and that in. She did mix up two pans of cornbread now, however, and put them in the oven to bake, per Granny Bea's instructions. Once they came out, Rory dumped the tins upside down and let the cornbread cool on paper towels spread across the counter.

The other dish, which Granny Bea reserved for holidays such as Thanksgiving, Christmas, and Easter, was green bean casserole. Although her grandmother was all about using fresh ingredients, ironically, this casserole called for the use of canned green beans, along with canned mushrooms and soup. Rory didn't care what was in it. She only knew it tasted heavenly and that her grandmother had made it for every holiday meal when Rory had lived with her grandmother during her college years. Using the recipe she had, she went ahead and mixed the ingredients for it, setting it aside, eagerly anticipating the upcoming FaceTime call.

Walker came into the kitchen, carrying her tablet, which he set on the table, and asked, "Ready to do this?"

She smiled at him tenderly. "I'm ready," she said, a wave of love rolling through her, knowing this good man would be hers for life.

Rory set the oven at the correct temperature so it

could heat up as Walker called Granny Bea. By the time her grandmother answered, they were both sitting in front of the screen.

"Happy Thanksgiving, Granny Bea," they said in unison after her grandmother answered.

"Oh, my, it is good to see both of you. Do you have everything ready for us, Rory? We need to get the dressing mixed up and baking in the oven. Then we can talk."

She glanced to Walker, and he nodded.

"I'll come back after the cooking is done," he said cheerfully, exiting the kitchen and leaving her alone.

Rory picked up the tablet and moved it to the counter, holding it so Granny Bea could see everything sitting there.

"It looks as if you have what we need, honey. Okay, first thing? Grease my special baking dish and crumble that cornbread into the largest bowl you have."

Her grandmother then walked her through the process, and Rory made mental notes she would later write down so she would have the recipe for cornbread dressing in the years to come. Granny Bea was in excellent health, but she didn't want to be one of those people whose relative passed away and the knowledge of the family's favorite dish went with the deceased.

She held the tablet up after following her grandmother's instructions to the letter, and Granny Bea said, "It looks just like it should, sweetie. Stick it in the oven."

Rory did so and took a seat again at the kitchen table, calling for Walker to join her.

He did, smiling at Granny Bea, and said, "I can't wait to taste your cornbread dressing, Granny Bea."

"Well, it may be my recipe, but your girl put it all together. I only wish I could be there to eat some with you.

Instead, I'll be going to dinner soon and having cawl cennin, onion cake, and Welsh rarebit."

"About that," Walker began. He paused, deferring to Rory to share their news.

"I'm not Walker's girlfriend anymore, Granny Bea. I'm his fiancée."

Her grandmother's smile was blinding. "I'm so happy for you two," she exclaimed, pulling a handkerchief from her sleeve and dabbing her eyes. "I prayed this day was coming. I think you are perfect for one another. Tell me all about it."

They walked Granny Bea through the magnificent dinner they'd eaten at Vivi's restaurant and how Walker had proposed at the end of it.

"We went ring shopping the next day," she said, holding up her hand to the tablet's screen so her grandmother could see the one-carat Marquise solitaire engagement ring. Walker had wanted her to get something larger, but Rory fell in love with this ring and told him that anything larger would be too ostentatious for her. At the same time, they had picked out matching wedding bands and purchased them, as well.

"I suppose you'll wait for your parents to come home before you tie the knot," Granny Bea mused.

"We're calling them today after we finish talking with you," Walker said. "While I want them at our wedding, I don't know if I can wait to marry this woman until they return home in May."

Granny Bea smiled at him. "When it's right, it's right," she said sagely. "I can understand that—and I think your parents will, too." She paused and quipped, "Just don't do it before I get home next Tuesday," and they all laughed.

They spent a few minutes hearing about the places

the Red Hats had visited the past few days on their tour, and then a knock sounded at Granny Bea's door.

"That's my signal to tell you goodbye and head to dinner." She blew kisses to them. "I love you both and can't wait to be home again. Bye-bye."

The screen went blank, and Walker let out a long breath. "Well, Granny Bea took the news well. Let's see how my parents do. Do you need to do anything, cooking-wise, before we call them?"

"No, I just have to keep my eye on the clock and slide the green bean casserole into the oven when the timer I set goes off."

"Okay."

He didn't sound okay.

"Are you worried about telling your parents that we're engaged?"

He took her hands in his, bringing them to his lips, tenderly kissing them. "No, babe. Not at all. I'm ready to shout our news from the rooftops."

The only people who had known up until today about their engagement were Vivi, who had witnessed it, and Gideon, whom they had seen before they left Dallas on Tuesday. They hadn't wanted anyone in Sugar Springs to know because they wanted to be the ones to tell their loved ones about the upcoming wedding. She worried, though, that Walker somehow had doubts.

"Stop furrowing your brow," he teased. "What I'm worried about is not telling them that we're engaged. It's telling them how soon I'm going to marry you."

"What?" she asked. "We haven't even talked about a date yet. It's been enough simply to bask in the glow of being engaged."

He gazed deeply into her eyes, and Rory saw the tremendous love for her in them. "I don't want to put off starting our life together, babe. While I would love for

Mom and Dad to be at our wedding, I want it to happen now. Before the end of the year. I was hoping I could convince you to marry me over your Christmas break."

Her throat grew thick with emotion. "I would marry you today if we could," she told him. "Of course, I don't think we can apply for a marriage license on Thanksgiving Day, much less find someone to perform the ceremony. I'm happy to marry you wherever and whenever you wish, Walker, but I don't want to hurt your parents."

"Let's just share our news, and then we'll go from there," he said. "We have five minutes until we're supposed to call them. I'll tell you now that I talked with Tamara Heath yesterday. She already had some ideas of what I was looking for in a house, and she called to tell me that one which has a lot of what's on my wish list is about to come on the market."

Rory grinned at him. "So, what *do* you want in a house?"

He grinned right back. "Besides you in it? A few things."

He told her how a large backyard was a priority, so kids and dogs would have plenty of room to run around. He discussed how many bedrooms he wanted and how he wanted wood floors throughout and a gas stove in the kitchen and a fireplace in the family room. Walker also wanted any updates already done if the house were an older one because he didn't want to take time away from Rory to do them.

"I don't care if it's a single-level ranch or a rambling two-story," he finished. "I just want something with a lot of room, inside and out."

"That sounds wonderful," she said, picturing them sitting in front of that fire, having put their kids to bed, Comet—and possibly another rescue dog—lying next to the fire.

"Besides all that? We need to make sure we have designated space for your office."

She laughed. "I can grade papers anywhere. At the breakfast table. On the sofa. It doesn't really matter."

"It *does* matter—because I don't know how long you might be teaching."

Rory frowned. "Wait a minute. You're not some old-fashioned guy who doesn't want his wife working, are you? Even when we have kids, Walker—and I know you want them as much as I do—I still want to work. I might take some time off while they're young, but I like teaching. I like being useful. I want to make a difference."

"Babe, I think your design career is about to explode. Candace Smith already adores you, and you said she fell in love with several of the designs you showed her."

Since Walker had gone and retrieved Rory's sketchbook, she'd been able to show the figure skater many already conceived designs. Rory had also sketched a few new ones as she talked to Candace about the program she would perform at Nationals and Worlds. She had taken Candace's measurements and after ring shopping, Rory had dragged Walker to a specialty fabric store, where she had purchased yards and yards of different materials to be used in making up the outfits.

Rory had then had them go to the closest post office, and they had shipped the fabrics to Sylvia Golding, who would create patterns and sew the costumes. Rory had followed it up by a lengthy, detailed email to Sylvia, which included not only Candace's measurements but pictures of Rory's sketches. Rory had texted Sylvia to read the email first and then call her. The entire way back to Sugar Springs, the two women had talked about the costumes to be sewn, nailing down the smallest details. Sylvia lived in Boulder and would take the outfits to Candace where she trained in Colorado early after the new year began and allow the figure skater to try on everything, making any necessary adjustments.

"You really think I might be busy enough to stop teaching?"

"You are clever and creative, babe. A rock star. Candace already is your biggest cheerleader. Word will get out—and other skaters will want you to design for them. I believe you'll need the home office space to do so."

"It would be nice to be able to work from home," she mused. "Especially since we hope to have kids soon."

He kissed her fingers again and released her hands. "We'll get there. Let's talk to Mom and Dad now. One step at a time."

They established the FaceTime connection, and Betty and Campbell Cox appeared in the shot.

"Hello," Betty called, waving at them.

"Hello, yourself," Walker said. "Happy Thanksgiving."

Campbell frowned. "It just doesn't seem right to be gone and not eating turkey and dressing and watching the Cowboys kick butt on Thanksgiving Day," he grumbled.

"Rory just mixed up the cornbread dressing. It's in the oven now," he told them. "We'll be sharing our Thanksgiving dinner with Pam Holland, the teacher who took your place, Mom."

Betty smiled sadly. "I'm with your father. It's been amazing seeing the places we have, but I miss being home for the holidays. I miss you, Walker, and you, too, Rory." She paused and then said, "We've decided to come home early."

"What?" Walker exclaimed. "What about your trip around the world?"

"We've talked it over, and we think we've just been gone from home too long," Campbell said.

Betty nodded. "We've already seen Central and South America. The UK and Northern Europe. We're in Eastern Europe now, and it's got some of the most spectacular landscapes either your father or I have seen, but we're homesick, son. Your father has already talked to the cruise director. We can get off at a port soon and fly home. They always have a waiting list and can rebook our stateroom for the remainder of the cruise from their standby list. They'll give us a credit, and we can simply fly to the port we want to start from and go from there at a later date."

"How soon will you be home?" Rory asked.

"If everything goes as planned, we should fly into Dallas the first Saturday in December," Betty said.

She looked at Walker, who beamed at her, and they both turned back to the screen.

"Well, that's really good news—because you'll make it home in time for a wedding," he said.

"A wedding?" Betty exclaimed. "Who in Sugar Springs is getting married? You haven't even told us about anyone getting engaged recently." Then she stopped, and Rory could see the wheels turning in her future mother-in-law's head. "It's the two of you, isn't it?" Betty squealed in delight.

Rory held up her hand to the screen, showing off her diamond engagement ring. "Yes, we just got engaged a few days ago, and Walker has informed me he wants a wedding by the end of this year."

"Oh, Campbell! We may need to come home even sooner to help Rory plan the wedding."

"No!" both men said, and Walker added, "We want to keep this simple, Mom. There won't be a whole lot of planning. Besides, you'll be home in plenty of time before the wedding happens, so you can take care of little details we might have missed."

"What's the date, son?" Campbell asked.

Walker laughed. "I guess we need to get out a calendar and see when Rory's break starts. I think I would prefer having the ceremony performed before Christmas, so I can wake up on Christmas morning next to my wife."

Betty smiled radiantly. "This is the best news possible. I want you to remember, Walker, that we told you we were coming home before you told us about your wedding."

"Duly noted, Mom."

They spent several minutes telling the Coxes everything about their engagement and then they hung up, Betty promising to FaceTime them again in a few days to check on their plans.

Walker ended the call and faced her, letting out a long sigh.

"I'm glad they were homesick," he said. "I didn't want to have them cut their trip short once they heard the news about the wedding. You know they would've done that."

"We could have waited until they got back next May. But I'm glad you want to get married now."

"I'm ready to start making babies with you, Rory Addison. I'm ready for us to start our lives together as man and wife."

He pulled her into his lap and kissed her slowly, a perfect kiss that she felt all the way to her soul.

A timer dinged, causing Rory to break the kiss.

"Time to put in the green bean casserole," she said, pushing from his lap and collecting the covered glass dish, slipping it into the oven next to the bubbling cornbread dressing.

Rory set a timer again and looked at her fiancé. Smiling, she said, "See that timer counting down? You've got me until it goes off and things need to come out of the oven."

He pulled her into his arms, laughing. "If there's one thing I know how to do, it's take advantage of every opportunity I get."

19

Walker came home from his run with Comet, having gone by his parents' house to see if all was well. Knowing now when they would return to Sugar Springs, he would make certain that the house was cleaned from top to bottom and that new sheets would be on the beds and the refrigerator stocked with fresh food. Rory had already suggested making a lasagna and taking it over to them, so they had something to eat off for a few days after they arrived home. Knowing Mom and Dad, they would expect Rory and him to stay and share the meal with them, as his Mom pumped them about wedding details.

He entered the house, letting Comet off her leash. The dog trotted into the kitchen and straight for her water bowl and the food Rory had just finished putting out. Walker kissed her and opened the drawer, retrieving a pod and placing it in the coffeemaker. The microwave dinged, and she removed a cup of hot water, dunking a teabag into it and placing it on the kitchen table. He loved how they already had a smooth routine of domestic bliss in the mornings, one which would only grow stronger once they were officially man and wife.

"Are you very hungry?" she asked. "I think I'm still

stuffed from all the food I ate yesterday. I should have passed on the turkey sandwiches during the Cowboys game. And definitely turned down that second piece of pumpkin pie at halftime."

"Same with me. Want to just do a bowl of cereal?" he asked.

"No. I think I'll go with Greek yogurt and some blueberries," she replied.

They each made their own breakfast and sat at the table to eat together.

"I've already checked online this morning, and the Smith County Courthouse and Annex are open for business," Walker told her. "I thought today would be the perfect time to apply for our marriage license. That way, you don't have to take off a day from school for us to do so."

Rory giggled. "We are on the same wavelength. I already looked up the requirements and downloaded the marriage application. We're supposed to bring that completed app with us, as well as our ID. Our Texas driver's license will work." She paused. "The only thing they might need is a certified copy of your divorce decree."

"Being the prepared attorney that I am, I have a copy of that in my personal files. Those are in my bedroom at Mom and Dad's. We can stop by and pick it up on our way. Anything else?"

"No. Just a credit or debit card to pay for it. The license is good for ninety days, so it will be good to have it on hand now."

"Then let's finish breakfast and get ready and drive into Tyler," he suggested. "I'm waiting until it's eight o'clock before I text Tamara. If we're lucky, we can see the house she mentioned to me when we get back from Tyler."

Rory's phone rang. "Hmm. Pam. Wonder what she wants. Hello?"

Walker took his cereal bowl and coffee mug to the sink, rinsing them and placing both in the dishwasher. He heard Rory agreeing to something, and then she hung up.

"Sam wants to borrow Comet again," she said. "Pam said he's this close to committing to a dog, but he wanted to know if Comet could spend today and tomorrow with them. We can pick her up on Sunday."

"Griff and Callie will be all over that," he said. "They were both disappointed when we didn't bring Comet to lunch yesterday."

He gathered up a few toys and Comet's food, and after they were ready for the day, they stopped at Pam's to drop off the Irish setter.

Sam answered the door. "Hey, thanks for loaning Comet to us," he said. "I'm ninety percent sure we'll get the kids a dog for Christmas. Not a puppy, though. One about Comet's age. I like that she's already trained and definitely like that she's housebroken."

"It would be easier that way," Walker agreed, handing over the sack of food and toys and the folded blanket. "Text us on Sunday when you're ready for us to pick her up."

"Comet!" Callie came running and threw her arms around the dog's neck. "I love you," the little girl proclaimed.

"See you soon," Walker said, returning to the car, where Rory waited.

They stopped by to pick up his divorce decree. He had two certified copies of it. When he'd obtained them, he hadn't been thinking of a second marriage down the line. In fact, that had been the last thing on his mind. His dad had always taught him to be prepared, though, and so Walker had gotten the official copies of his divorce decree and filed them away. Little did he know how much he would want to dive headfirst into marriage again.

Of course, he hadn't known Rory Addison at the time. She had changed his outlook on a lot of things.

They drove into Tyler, with very little traffic on the road. He knew many offices gave their employees the day off after Thanksgiving and was glad the courthouse was actually open. On their way, Rory filled out the marriage application, which was a single page and very straightforward.

Arriving at the county courthouse annex, Walker cut the engine and said, "Let me text Tamara before we go in. It's just a few minutes after eight now. I doubt there's going to be a huge line to obtain marriage licenses."

He let the realtor know he and Rory were interested in seeing the property she had mentioned to him as soon as possible.

Immediately, the realtor texted him back, asking if today at ten-thirty might be convenient.

"Tamara asked if we want to see the house this morning. That okay with you?"

Rory nodded. "I'm eager to see it. That sounds fine."

Walker fired off a quick text, telling Tamara they would meet her at her office at ten-thirty and received a thumbs up emoji.

"We're set."

He got out of the car and went to open Rory's door, helping her out. They entered the courthouse and went to the county clerk's office. As he suspected, no line had formed this early on a day after a major holiday. In fact, the place was dead. Walker's heart began to beat more swiftly than usual, anticipating the huge step they were now taking.

"May I help you?" a dark-haired woman asked.

"We're here to apply for our marriage license," he said proudly, glancing at Rory and seeing her smile matched his own.

"You came at a good time, as you can see," the clerk said. "Today, people are either shopping in person or online, or they're sleeping in on a rare day off. Have you already filled out our online application?"

"Yes, I have it right here," Rory said, handing the paper over.

The clerk inspected it and nodded. "This is good. No mistakes or anything left blank. I wish more people could get it right the first time as you have. Okay, folks, I need to see some ID. Texas driver's license if you have that."

"We both do," Walker said, pulling his license from his wallet and handing it to her.

Rory did the same, and the woman looked them over, once again nodding to herself. "Here you go, Walker," she said, returning his license to him. "And here's yours, Aurora."

Hearing the name took him aback. "*Aurora*?"

Rory blushed. "It's my given legal name, but my parents called me Rory from the start."

The clerk frowned in disapproval. "If you don't even know your fiancée's given name, sir, you might want to take time to get to know one another a little better before you get married," she admonished.

Walker didn't care what this clerk thought. He knew Rory down to her soul. That's what mattered.

Removing his credit card, he handed it over. "Here you go, ma'am."

She sniffed, seeing he was going to ignore her advice. "That will be eighty-two dollars," she said primly, running his card through her machine and then handing him a credit slip to sign.

He did so, and she gave him a copy of the receipt.

"Your license is good in any county in Texas or any in the United States. You have ninety days to make good on it. If you haven't used the license by then, you will have to apply for a new one and pay the fee again."

He grinned. "No chance of that happening. We'll be getting married over Aurora's Christmas break. She's a teacher, and I'm going to make certain she has her papers graded so that we can enjoy our marriage and what comes after during her school break."

"Let me run the copy of your license, sir. I'll be right back."

The moment the clerk stepped through a door and was out of sight, Walker pulled Rory into his arms. He gave her a kiss and broke it, saying, "I'm glad at least I found out now that your given name is Aurora. I might've had to stop our wedding ceremony and asked to know what else I didn't know about you before we said our I do's," he teased.

"I really can't remember the last time I even thought about that being my name. It only comes up every few years. Whenever I renew my driver's license or passport. That kind of thing."

He kissed her lightly again and said, "Well, it's a beautiful name. I'm glad it's yours—and I'm glad you're mine."

The clerk returned and handed over their marriage license to him. "There's a list of the different officiants you can ask to perform your wedding on our website if you're getting married locally."

"I saw that when I downloaded the application. Thank you for your help today," Rory said, taking Walker's hand and pulling him from the office before he could cause any more trouble.

They returned to Sugar Springs and drove straight to Tamara Heath's office.

Walker glanced at his watch. "It's only a couple of minutes after ten, but I don't think Tamara will mind if we're early."

Going inside, he called out, "Hello? We're here, Tamara."

The realtor appeared in the doorway. "Ah, you're early. I like that in a client." She glanced to Rory. "We haven't been introduced yet. I'm Tamara Heath. I already know you're Rory Addison. My son has you for World History and simply adores you. I wasn't able to make Open House, but he told me that was fine. That he wouldn't be causing any trouble in your class because he enjoys it so much."

"Ah, you must be Tim Heath's mom. Tim is a terrific student. Always engaged and full of creative ideas."

Tamara laughed. "He's always full of some idea. I wish he were as well behaved in his other classes as he is in yours. I've had long talks with his math and English teachers recently. Maybe you could pass along some tips to them on how to keep Tim's attention."

The realtor glanced down. Her eyes widened and she grabbed Rory's hand, pulling it up. "My, that's a lovely engagement ring." She looked at Walker. "You did really well, Walker," she said, releasing Rory's hand. "I see that this house is not just going to be yours, but Rory's, as well."

"We also have a dog. Comet. She's an active Irish setter and needs that big back yard I've mentioned to you."

"Well, you're going to love the Slater place. I don't have properties this nice or large open up very often here in Sugar Springs. Come into my office, and let's talk a little bit about it before I take you to see the place."

They accompanied Tamara into her office, and she flipped through a few file folders, opening one and handing each of them a sheet containing the highlights of the listing.

"Look over that a moment while I bring up the property on my computer."

Walker studied the picture of the front of the house and then skimmed over the particulars, seeing that it was close to thirty-five hundred square feet, with five bedrooms and recent updates throughout the inside.

"Come over and click through the pictures of the various rooms," Tamara said. "Then we'll talk."

She rose from the chair, and Rory took the vacant seat, Walker leaning over her shoulder as they viewed the various rooms of the listing. When they finished, Rory relinquished her seat to the realtor, and they sat across from Tamara again.

"This listing hasn't gone live yet," Tamara informed them. "It's what we call a pocket listing. I have, though, been given permission by the owner to go ahead and show it to you before it goes on the market Monday morning. It's owned by a couple who usually bounce between their properties in Jackson Hole and San Francisco. Mr. Slater has recently retired. They'll be spending more time at their vacation home in Wyoming, while still keeping their home in San Francisco."

"Who are the Slaters?" Walker asked. "I don't recognize the name."

"They are very introverted and never really assimilated into Sugar Springs because they spent so little time here. The property belonged to Mr. Slater's grandfather. He left it to his grandson upon his death more than twenty years ago. Mr. Slater and his wife both worked in San Francisco and have split their time between the previous two homes I mentioned, so they've only come to Sugar Springs on rare occasions. They have no family in the area.

"The house sits on a cul-de-sac," Tamara continued, "with only three other homes on it. The neighbors pretty much have kept an eye out on the place since the Slaters are never in Texas."

"Why now?" Rory asked. "If they've owned the property for so long, why sell it at this point?"

"I asked that same question when they contacted me and said they wished to list it," Tamara replied. "They held onto it for sentimental reasons, but they have no reason to visit here. With both of them retiring now, they are also selling a few other properties they've invested in over the years and consolidating their portfolio. They knew, though, that the house was horribly outdated. I'm talking shag carpet and wood paneling in the family room. Laminate countertops in the kitchen and bathrooms. They told me what they wanted done and how much they were willing to spend to make the updates and get it in proper condition to sell. I met with a local contractor and hired him and his crew to make all the changes. I think you'll be pleased with what you see today."

Tamara smiled brightly. "Are you ready to go take a look at what could be your future home?"

"More than ready," Walker said. "I'm know I'm not supposed to tip my hand, but I can tell you now that I'm very eager after seeing the pictures and looking at the specs."

The realtor offered to drive and took them to a neighborhood not far from where Walker's parents lived. They turned on a street that had a sign saying it was a dead end, and Tamara told them the cul-de-sac was just to the right before the dead end occurred.

When they turned onto the cul-de-sac, his heart sped up as he spied the house. It was a two-story Colonial with tremendous curb appeal.

Tamara pulled into the long driveway and stopped the car. "What do you think so far?"

"The outside is gorgeous," Rory said. "I love the color of the brick and the imposing columns. The landscaping is perfect, too. If the inside looks as good as the outside, I think you just might have a sale, Tamara."

The realtor laughed. "Come on inside."

They entered the house, which was a little chilly.

"Let me crank up the heat," Tamara said. "They usually keep it down, but not so cold that pipes would burst if the temperature dropped severely."

The realtor walked them through the house as it warmed up, pointing out various features and the updates which had been completed. Walker found himself liking almost everything he saw. The primary suite was on the first floor and twice the size of his parents' bedroom. It featured a walk-in closet for each of them and an ensuite bathroom with a shower large enough that he and Rory would no longer have to twist and turn as they did when they were together in her shower. He glanced over and saw her grinning, knowing she was thinking the same thing.

"As you can see, I had all the rooms painted in neutral shades. If you need more of a splash of color, it would just be a coat of paint here and there."

"I actually prefer neutrals," he said.

"So do I," Rory echoed.

They toured the entire bottom floor and then went upstairs. A lofted area was at the top of the stairs and would make for a good playroom for their future chil-

dren. The remaining four bedrooms were all located upstairs, along with two bathrooms.

They returned downstairs to the kitchen, and Rory
commented on how her favorite part of the house was
the large island in the center of the room.

"This is quartz," Tamara said. "I made sure the island
was large enough that not only a cook would have a
nice-sized prep area, but you can pull several stools up
and use it as a breakfast bar in the mornings. Shall we go
see the outside?"

Once outside, Walker saw they had quite a bit of
land. The area was fenced, but he couldn't see the end of
the property from where they stood.

"It's the width of a normal backyard," the realtor
said. "But it runs two acres in length. The entire backyard is fenced. I know you mentioned dogs, so you don't
need to worry about them getting out. I know it's just
grass here. I didn't want to do too much to the outdoor
space. I know you had mentioned wanting an outdoor
kitchen and possibly a pool. Sorry to disappoint you on
that front, but it's something you could easily put in this
spring if you choose to buy the property."

"I didn't want to do updates inside a house and dis-
rupt things while we tried to live in our new place," he
said. "But I can definitely see how we could make our
mark outside in the backyard. I'd like to build a deck
here," he indicated. "Put a fire pit over there. Have the
kitchen run along here. And then the pool could go
lengthwise."

"I have the name of a few people whom you might
wish to use for the job," Tamara volunteered. "The contractor who did all the inside work to the house and
painting the outside, as well, could do the outdoor
kitchen and deck for you. You'd have to have someone in
from Tyler, I'm guessing, for the pool, though."

"Do you mind if we walk through it again slowly?" Rory asked. "I was a little overwhelmed the first time. I'd like to take some time in each room and familiarize myself with the layout."

Tamara looked at her watch. "I do have a showing in half an hour nearby. I'm meeting my client there. It won't take fifteen minutes to go through the house because it's small. Why I don't I leave you here and come back afterward to get you when that's done? Hopefully, you'll have made up your minds by then, and I can write up the paperwork."

They bid the realtor goodbye, and Walker entered the house again with Rory.

"What do you really think?" he asked.

She beamed. "Oh, I want this house so badly I can taste it, Walker. I just didn't want Tamara to know how eager I was. Now that we're alone, though, I really would like to go through each room and talk about how we might wish to furnish it."

"Sounds like a terrific idea," he said.

They started in the entryway again, with Rory talking about the kind of table she would place there.

"I'd like a small clock in the center. It's one Granny Bea has already passed along to me. It could go here. And photographs. Lots of framed photographs. Of us— and the kids."

He slipped his arms around her waist and kissed her. "I can see us here with those kids, Rory. I think this is going to be an amazing place to raise our family."

They spent the next hour going through each room, talking about the kind of furniture they would need to purchase in order to fill the entire house. Walker told her he had sold his condo with all the furnishings left behind, while she didn't have anything to contribute since Paige's house had come totally furnished.

"It will be special. Us furnishing our house together," he said. "We don't have to do it all at once. But hopefully over the next year, we can fill each room and make it our own."

One room on the first floor was designated as an office, with beautiful French doors closing it off for privacy. He told her this was where he wanted her to work, be it grading papers or designing skate wear.

"There's really no place for you to have a home office if I take this room," she said. "Unless we make one of the bedrooms upstairs into your office."

"I don't want an office at home," he told her. "I spent so many hours at my Dallas law firm. Most of my waking hours were there. I went home to eat, sleep, shower, and that was about it. I didn't even own a TV set because I wasn't home enough to watch anything. The few times I could catch part of a football game, I would simply meet Gid at a sports bar."

He took her hands in his. "I have my office here in town. I want to keep decent hours and not have to bring home work. On the rare occasion I have trial prep, I could drive a couple of miles into the office and work from there. I'd rather the bedrooms here stay bedrooms for our future kids or guests."

"As much as I have enjoyed teaching these past few years, I really like the creativity of design work," she admitted. "If my partnership with Candace works out and I can gain other clients, I would be happy to take this room as my office and work from home. I don't want to quit my day job just yet, however. I know we'll need my salary."

Walker laughed, releasing her hands and framing her face with his, stroking her cheeks with his thumbs.

"Now I know you're not marrying me simply for my money," he joked. "If you ever do grow tired of whatever you're doing and just want to stay home to raise kids, Rory, we'd be fine financially. I made an obscene amount of money before I left Dallas, especially after I made partner. Working as many hours a week as I did, I didn't have time or inclination to spend my salary on anything except my sports car, and even then, it's several years old. We're set as far as money goes. If you want to quit teaching at the end of this school year and focus on designing figure skating wear? I'm happy to support you in that endeavor. Emotionally and financially."

"Hello?" Tamara called out.

Walker took Rory's hand, lacing his fingers through hers. "Let's go tell Tamara we're ready to put in an offer."

20

R ory and Walker headed to Dallas again on the Sunday before she was supposed to return to school from her Thanksgiving break. Their offer on the Slater property had been accepted, and they'd had an inspector out the same day. Tamara had shared that Mr. Slater was relieved to have received an offer so quickly, even before the listing was made public, especially since she had warned them this was not an ideal time to put a property on the market, much less one so large and expensive.

They would be closing sometime in the next week to ten days, but for now, Walker had said they needed to use the little time she still had off and begin furniture hunting. They had gone to Tyler yesterday and found a wonderful set for their great room. It included an extra-large sofa, loveseat, and two different chairs with ottomans, along with a few end tables. She had spied a globe there, three feet in height, and portraying the world as mankind knew it around the eighteenth century. The historian in her immediately wanted it, and Walker agreed, seeing as how he loved history himself.

Today, though, they were driving to Dallas to go to a showroom the designer who had put together Walker's condo had used. He had given her a call, and she had left his name at the desk so they would be allowed entrance. She told him if he found any pieces he wanted, to have them tagged with her name, and she would see they were held and delivered to him once ownership of the house was passed on to Rory and him.

They stopped for brunch in downtown at what was considered a hot spot, and Rory could see why. Her Eggs Benedict contained crab instead of ham and was absolutely the best breakfast dish she had ever eaten. They had asked Vivi and Gid to join them, but only Vivi was able to do so. It was good to see her friend again, and they told Vivi all about the Slater place.

"Things are moving along for you," Vivi commented. "Have you chosen a wedding date yet?"

"We picked up the marriage license in Tyler on Friday, and Walker would like to get married the Saturday after I get out of school on Friday. The way winter break runs this year is that there's pretty much a full week before Christmas and a full week after it."

Vivi frowned. "I was hoping to make the wedding, but Fridays and Saturdays leading up to the holidays are some of our busiest times."

Disappointment filled Rory, but she knew how important Vivi's job was to her.

Then Walker asked, "What if we got married on a Sunday? Maybe that afternoon. Say, one or two o'clock. Would you be able to make it then?"

Vivi brightened. "That would be ideal for me, Walker, but I don't want to throw a kink into your plans."

He laughed. "The plans are to get married. Period. That's about as far as we've gotten. I had mentioned to Mom and Dad that we wanted something small." He looked to Rory. "I never really thought to ask you. While it's my second time around, it's your first marriage. Am I rushing you? Do you want a large wedding?"

"I thought you knew me better than that," she said. "For me, the smaller the wedding, the better. A more intimate wedding is more special in my eyes. In fact, if we just had your parents and Granny Bea, along with a few close friends to act as witnesses, that would be more than fine with me."

He grew thoughtful. "I have an old fraternity brother who's now a judge in Tyler. I'll bet he would be willing to come in on a Sunday afternoon and marry us in his chambers."

"That would be ideal," she said.

They finished their brunch and parted from Vivi. She was spending the rest of the day in the new space which Dante would open in a few weeks.

"I've been helping advise Dante on the menu, since it's Italian. The furniture has come in, and we'll be placing the tables and booths today."

"Good luck with that," Rory told her friend, hugging Vivi goodbye.

She and Walker went to what was known as the Design District in Dallas, and Walker gave his name to the security guard at the door. They were granted permission to enter and wandered the place like kids in a candy store. Rory saw so many wonderful pieces which would work in their new home. Fortunately, she and Walker had similar tastes as far as furnishings were concerned.

"I know we had aimed to furnish the great room, our bedroom, and the kitchen, but I think we might be able to complete a few more rooms than that with what we're seeing here," he told her.

"I agree."

They walked through the warehouse, snapping pictures with their cell phones so they had an easy reference as they moved throughout. In the end, they wound up choosing a dining room set which seated twelve and a sideboard to accompany it. They also selected their bedroom furniture. That room was so large that they picked out a king-sized bed, dresser, chest of drawers, and armoire, as well as a nightstand to go on each side of the bed. Since the room had a good-sized nook, they also decided upon two club chairs and a table to go between them.

She had always been mad for plaid, and they came across a fun plaid pattern that covered a large sofa and small loveseat.

"How about these for the playroom?" she asked Walker. "We could also put up a TV there. It would still have plenty of room for things such as a play kitchen and shelves where we could place baskets for toys and books. Eventually, it could become a hangout spot as the kids get older, and they could watch TV in the loft with their friends."

"Great idea. Let's get it."

They also found a desk for her office, which would go well with the built in bookcases already present in the room. Rory found the perfect chair and a table and lamp which would sit beside it in her office.

"The only other item I want in my office is a drafting table, but I'll need to go to a specialty store for it."

They had an assistant tag all the items they wanted, and Walker texted the list to his designer so that she could handle things on her end. He told her he'd let her know once they received their closing date and delivery of all these items could be scheduled.

"We still don't have a kitchen table or any outdoor furniture," he said.

"I say we wait on any kind of outdoor furniture and accessories until the deck is built. It would be nice, though, to find a table for the kitchen since it is eat-in. And maybe barstools for the island."

"If you're still up for a little more shopping, I know of a couple of furniture stores which are nearby. Want to check them out?"

She agreed, and after another hour of searching, they found the perfect kitchen table that sat six and would look wonderful in the space. The table was round and its chairs quite comfortable. They also found barstools which would be a good match with the kitchen furniture.

"I did like one bedroom suite we saw," Walker said. "It would make for a nice guest room. That way, if anyone came to stay with us, they would have a place to sleep. We can wait and furnish the other bedrooms and nursery when the time comes."

He gave her a wolfish grin. "Speaking of that, maybe we need to get working on it again."

Since their engagement several days ago, they had given up using condoms, knowing they would be married soon and not wanting to waste any time in getting pregnant.

"Yes, I know which set you're talking about. The modern farmhouse look. We both talked about how much we liked it."

"That's the one," he said.

"Let's go ahead and get it. There may be a time when Granny Bea comes to visit, and I don't want her to drive back in the dark to Tyler. It would be good to have a room for her to stay in overnight. Gideon could also use it when he comes to visit."

They found a salesman, and he wrote up their large order. Walker explained they would be closing on a house soon and that they wanted to wait on delivery until then. The salesman assured them it wouldn't be a problem. He gave Walker his card and said to call when they were in the house and ready for their new furniture to be delivered.

Returning to the car, Rory said, "We've put in a full day. I can't believe so much of the house will be furnished."

He reached for her hand and squeezed it. "We're a good team. In every sense of the word."

They drove back to Sugar Springs, stopping to pick up Comet on their way home. Sam thanked them for the loan of the dog and said they would be looking for one of their own in the near future.

"I would take Comet if I thought you would give her to us," Sam joked.

"No way," Rory said quickly. "Comet is already family to us."

They arrived home, and she changed into comfortable sweats. Walker asked if she might want pizza for dinner, and she agreed. He called in an order for delivery and once their Romano's pizza arrived, they settled on her couch, turning on the TV.

A text came in, and Rory picked up her phone, frowning at the message. The sender was unknown, and the message told her to turn on a news magazine show which was about to begin.

She showed it to Walker and asked, "I wonder who might've sent this."

"Let's check out the program they're recommending," he said, picking up the remote and changing the channel.

The program began moments later, previewing each of the stories tonight. The last one was a feature on Candace Smith and her skating career.

"Do you think Candace has a new phone, and she's the one who texted me to watch this interview?" Rory mused.

"You can check with her after the show ends. Eat your pizza while it's hot."

They sat through a story about a water shortage in Africa and wells being dug there with funds from an international humanitarian group. A second segment was about the latest tech wizard and the new phone he had invented, which would hit the American market a week before Christmas.

Finally, the story featuring Candace came up.

"I recognize that reporter," she told her fiancé. "Her name is Monica Wethersby. She was the last person to interview me before ... my last night I skated."

Walker put an arm around her shoulders, and she snuggled into him.

The interview was a good one. Monica did a thorough job of interviewing Candace, covering her career prior to this interview, and discussing her hopes for the upcoming Nationals and Worlds competitions.

"I've traded ownership of the U.S. title the last couple of years," Candace told Monica. "Susan won last year, but I took the U.S. crown two years in a row before that. It's time I wore that crown again."

Candace paused, smiling mysteriously. "I guarantee I will be the U.S. Women's Figure Skating Champion this coming year," she declared. "I have the perfect music to go along with a spot-on short program and free skate. And a secret weapon."

Monica showed interest, leaning in slightly. "Oh? Do you have a new choreographer? A new coach?"

"No, I'm happy with my current team, but I've added someone to it. Someone very special. She is designing not only my practice wear but the new costumes I will be wearing at both Nationals and Worlds."

Rory's mouth grew dry as Candace continued.

"I'm sure you know her, Monica. Everyone in the skating world knows Rory Addison."

Surprise showed on the journalist's face. "*The* Rory Addison? Holder of two Olympic gold medals and seven world titles? How on earth did you connect with Rory? She hasn't had anything to do with the skating world since she was forced into retirement."

Rory sat up, wondering what Candace would say next.

"She's teaching now. In a little town in East Texas called Sugar Springs. I admire how Rory went back to school and earned her degree. She is very good at what she does now."

Rory couldn't help but chuckle. Candace had no kind of idea what kind of teacher Rory was.

"I approached her recently, however, remembering how she had designed several of her own competition costumes, along with creating her own skating choreography after she broke with her coach. As a young skater, I truly looked up to Rory Addison. She showed that a woman could do anything on the ice, and I was determined to follow in her footsteps. I particularly remember a cobalt blue skating outfit she wore during her free skate at her second Olympics."

Suddenly the screen filled with an image of Rory gliding gracefully along the ice, wearing the very outfit Candace described.

"So, Candace, you have teamed with Rory Addison, and she's creating your skating wardrobe now."

The camera switched back to Candace, who smiled like the Cheshire Cat. "Yes, Monica. And that is my secret weapon. When a woman feels terrific—especially a female athlete—she will go out and kick ass when she performs. I'm going to feel beautiful and perfect on that ice when I'm wearing my Rory Addison creation."

Monica wrapped up the interview, and Walker picked up the remote, turning off the TV.

He smiled broadly at her. "Candace dropping your name like that? That is advertising worth its weight in gold. I would be shocked if you don't pick up several clients after this interview has aired."

Her phone rang, and Rory reached to the coffee table to retrieve it.

"Unknown again," she said.

"Answer it," Walker urged. "It's probably Candace wanting to give you her new number."

Rory answered, not wanting to sound hesitant. "Hello?" she asked firmly.

"Hi, Rory. It's Monica Wethersby. I hope you don't mind that Candace shared your cell number with me. I told her we had done an interview together years ago. Your last interview." Monica paused. "I'd like to change that if you're agreeable. I want to interview you again, Rory. Hear about your teaching career and your new foray into designing for athletes.

"So, what do you say? Are you ready to sit down and open up about this new chapter in your life?"

Rory went with her gut. "I'd be happy to have you interview me, Monica."

21

Rory's emotions were swinging violently this Saturday. Elation filled her because they had closed on the Slater place yesterday. Even now, Walker was driving back from the airport with his parents. She was eager to see them and show the Coxes and Granny Bea, who bustled around the kitchen now, the home in which she and Walker would live and raise their family.

The fear was due to the interview which would occur later this afternoon. Rory had spontaneously agreed to speak with Monica Wethersby. She had liked the journalist when they had previously met and thought Monica could give a fair, balanced picture of Rory's life now. Walker had enthusiastically supported her decision, telling her that this would be good PR and give her a higher profile than she'd had in years. She knew if she were to launch a new career as a designer in the figure skating world, this national exposure would prove critical.

Yet she was almost paralyzed with fear, thinking about how everything regarding her relationship with Bradley Bolton would come out.

Walker had volunteered to sit in on the interview, not

as her fiancé, but as her attorney. If she gave him the high sign, he would ask for the cameras to stop rolling. In fact, Walker said Rory should state up front which topics were to be off-limits. Either Monica would agree or not. The interview could hinge upon that.

She was torn, though. Part of her was afraid the new life which she had built in Sugar Springs would unravel with such exposure of her link to Bradley. At the same time, her story might be able to help someone out there.

Rory decided to trust her instincts and make the call when the interview began.

For now, though, she was helping Granny Bea put together a welcome home lunch for Campbell and Betty Cox. They had flown into New York yesterday afternoon, planning to spend the night because they knew they would be exhausted and need to adjust to the time change. After a good night's sleep, the couple had boarded their plane at eight o'clock this morning and flown into Dallas, landing shortly after ten. Walker helped them collect their luggage and had texted her when they left the airport. The five of them were going to have lunch together at the Coxes' house since they had a table which would seat all of them, unlike her place. Then Walker and Rory would take everyone to the Slater place. No, she needed to stop calling it that in her head. It was the Cox homestead now.

Granny Bea asked Rory to set the table, and she did so, happy her grandmother had been able to come and meet Rory's future in-laws today instead of being introduced for the first time at the wedding.

"They should be here in the next few minutes," she told her grandmother. "I know you're going to like them."

Granny Bea took Rory's hands in hers. "The important thing is that you like them—and they like you. It's a good thing you got to know them a bit before they left on their extended trip."

"I think they'll make for great in-laws," she said, bending to stroke Comet.

"We're here!" Walker called out, and warmth spread through her. Just hearing her fiancé's voice could put her on top of the world.

Rory and Granny Bea went to greet the Coxes, Comet bounding into the room and heading straight for Walker. Betty was already moving toward them, and she threw her arms around Rory, hugging her tightly.

"Oh, Rory. It's so good to see you. I'm thrilled that you're going to be a part of our family." Betty released her and smiled, enveloping Granny Bea in an embrace. "And you're Granny Bea. Walker has said such lovely things about you to us."

"Your son is a wonderful man," Granny Bea said. "I think our two will do quite well together." Then a mischievous grin spread across her face. "I'm hoping we'll have babies soon. Lots and lots of babies."

Rory laughed as Betty nodded enthusiastically. She smiled at Walker and Campbell, who had brought in the suitcases.

Campbell was kneeling, petting Comet, and said, "I think I may steal this one from you. I can tell she's a good girl."

"Where do you want your luggage, Mom?" Walker asked.

"Just take all the suitcases into the bedroom, dear," Betty responded. "I'll need to sort through everything and begin a laundry marathon. But that's for later. Right now, I want us to talk and go see your new house. I think I know where it is."

Campbell rose and came to Rory, embracing her.

"How are you, Rory? I hear you have an important inter-view today. And hello, Granny Bea. I'm Campbell."

Nerves ran through her again at the thought of talking with Monica Wethersby. "I'm a little shaky if I'm being truthful," she told him.

"Well, you charmed Betty and me and certainly have captured Walker's attention. I think you'll do just fine with this reporter. Walker told us you even know her from a previous interview."

Soon, the lasagna was out of the oven, along with a crusty French bread. Granny Bea had also tossed a salad and made up her special dressing for it, which the Coxes raved about.

"You simply must share this recipe, Granny Bea," Betty insisted.

"I will pass it to Rory upon my death and not be-fore," her grandmother said. "It's my secret sauce for salads."

They heard about some of the adventures Betty and Campbell had experienced over the past several months.

"I'm so glad you documented your trip via social me-dia," Rory told them. "Looking at your pictures and reading your posts, I couldn't help but feel as if I had gone along on the trip with you."

"I agree," Walker said. "I think half of Sugar Springs has followed your journey. Except Roscoe Hamilton."

Campbell snorted. "Roscoe is a Luddite. He only uses a computer when he's forced to. He did email me a few times, though. Said he's thinking about retiring in the next year or so. Do you know anything about that?"

"He mentioned it briefly when I had lunch with Gid and him at the diner about six weeks ago. Gid came in for homecoming. So did Vivi Romano. Her brother is opening a restaurant in Dallas next weekend."

"Dante was always such a polite, handsome young

man," Betty remarked. "He had excellent grades in my class. I'm sure his restaurant will do well."

"We need to get this cleaned up and go over to the house. Rory's interview is at three this afternoon," Walker said.

"Where will it be?" Betty asked.

"Where I'm living. At Paige's house," Rory said.

"Honey, why don't you go on home and get ready for it?" Granny Bea suggested. "Walker can show us your house and tell us a little about how you'll furnish it."

She glanced at the clock, seeing it was already half-past one.

"I agree," her fiancé said. "Look at the time. Let's clean up, and we can be on our way."

"Go ahead, Walker, and take everyone to the house. I'll handle everything here and then go home. It'll give me time to think through a few thoughts I have." She also mentioned that she would leave Comet here, not wanting the dog to be a distraction to the film crew, much less interrupt the interview.

Walker promised to head to her place after the tour ended, and she was grateful he still planned to sit in while the interview took place.

"Don't rush," she told him. "Monica said it would take at least half an hour to get all the lighting set up. As long as you're there by three-thirty, we should be good."

Once she had the house to herself, Rory put away the leftovers in the fridge and loaded the dishwasher, starting it. She made sure everything in the kitchen had been put back in good order and then drove home. Butterflies ravaged her stomach, making her regret ever having agreed to this interview.

She thought about changing clothes and then decided to remain in what she wore, a wool tunic of pale yellow and slim, black pants. She brushed her teeth and applied new lipstick. Too nervous to sit and do anything, Rory paced the small house until she heard car doors slamming and looked out the window. She spied Monica Wethersby and a man getting out of a van. He reached for a camera, and her mouth grew dry. She hurried to the kitchen and downed half a bottle of water.

Two more vans pulled up, and more people spilled from them, removing equipment. She began doing deep breaths, trying to force herself to relax.

The doorbell rang, and Rory went to answer it, finding only Monica on the porch.

"Hello, Rory," said the journalist. "It's good to see you again. Thank you for agreeing to sit for this interview with me." Monica waved a hand, indicating the people starting to gather behind her. "This is the crew. They'll need to set up. Deal with lighting. Your hair and makeup. Test sound levels. I don't want you to worry about anything. I'm going to take good care of you."

The invasion happened, a good ten people spilling into her small space. One woman who said her name was Reva took charge of Rory, leading her to the bathroom to touch up her makeup and hair.

"I know this may look a little heavy as you glance into the mirror, Rory, but I guarantee you that it will keep you from looking washed out under all those bright lights."

"No, I understand that from my skating days," she revealed. "I learned how to do my own makeup for the ice. It always seemed a bit much, but it photographed well for TV and looked good at a distance to the audience who gathered in the arena."

By the time Reva finished working on Rory, wires ran everywhere, the lights almost blinding her. She saw the furniture had been pushed aside and two chairs had been placed beneath the lights, one for her and one for Monica.

The door opened, and Walker came in. Immediately, she went to him, and he wrapped his arms around her.

"I guess I should be glad they let me through," he said. "There's a security guy on the porch to keep anyone from interrupting the interview. Everyone loved the house, by the way. Mom and Granny Bea have already designated us to host holidays once we get settled."

Just his presence had calmed her. "I'm glad you're here."

"I wanted to be here for you. Whether I'm in the room as the interview is conducted or right outside."

"Stay. I'll tell Monica I want you here."

Rory led Walker to the journalist and introduced them, explaining how she would appreciate if Walker could be present while they spoke.

"I was going to give you a topic to steer away from," she told the reporter. "Knowing how thorough you are, I know you've investigated me and know what I've been up to since I left the skating world."

"I know the subject you're referring to. I do want to speak with you about it, Rory. I will say this—and I have never agreed to do this with any other person whom I've interviewed. I'd like to ask you whatever I wish, and once I've put a rough cut together, I'll let you view it. If there is anything that makes you uncomfortable—any part of the segment you don't wish to air—my editor and I will cut it."

"I can agree to that," Rory said. "That's very generous of you. I do think I have a story to tell and that others might learn something from it."

"Good," Monica said brightly, glancing about her. "I think we're about ready to begin. Walker, you can stand over there. Rory, we'll face one another, you in this chair."

The two women sat, and Monica pointed out where the different cameras would be as an assistant attached a mic to Rory's shirt and they tested the sound level for each woman.

"Each of these three cameramen will be filming the entire interview," the reporter explained. "Then my editor and I will splice things together, showing different angles throughout the interview. If at any time you need us to stop, Rory, just let me know. You can take a break. Clear your head. Run to the restroom. Get something to drink. We can make certain everything looks seamless in the editing room."

Monica indicated a glass of water already to Rory's right. "Sip on that anytime you need to," she suggested. "Are you ready for us to begin?"

She nodded.

"I'll start slowly at first, building on what you did in the past, and then work up to what you're doing now. We can talk about any future plans you might have." Monica smiled. "Just pretend it's the two of us having a conversation. Ignore everyone and everything around us. Concentrate on me, and you'll be fine."

"About how long will this segment run?" Rory asked. "And when do you think it might air?"

"Anywhere from fourteen to twenty minutes. It depends upon what other stories are being presented that particular week. The order the executive producer wants them placed. I have a feeling that we'll get the last spot, which will lean closer to the twenty-minute mark. We will talk at least an hour today if not more, though, then I'll whittle the footage so that it will fit into the timeframe I'm given. As to when it airs? That's up to the network. Right now, they've penciled it in for about six weeks from now. Don't worry about those details, Rory. Just take a deep breath and relax," Monica advised. "Let's have some girl talk now."

Rory inhaled deeply and expelled the breath slowly, placing her hands in her lap. "I'm ready."

"I'll be doing a voiceover intro which will tell a little bit about who you were and are now, so it may seem like an abrupt start as we begin. It will flow well when you see the piece. I promise."

Monica cleared her throat and then said, "Rory, you left the skating world more than seven years ago, at the top of your game. Tell me what it was like to be a world and Olympic champion."

"It was never about the titles for me," she said honestly. "Yes, they were the proverbial icing on the cake for all the hours I had put in. But it was always the work itself which was most important to me. I loved every minute of skating. Choosing the music which would express what I wanted my audiences and the judges to feel. Working on putting together the short program and free skate. Seamlessly weaving in the required elements, and mixing them with the artistry of what I wanted to convey on the ice. I loved the physicality of skating. I enjoyed the artistry of it. I loved the marriage of these two elements."

"You let Anya Moranova go after many years of serving as your coach. You chose not to replace Anya."

"No, I didn't want or need a coach or choreographer. By that time, I had a good sense of who I was and the kind of skater I chose to be out on the ice. I had a vision of what I wanted my programs to consist of. My practices informed me what moves I could execute. I trained a bit differently from other skaters, not spending as much time on the ice. Instead, I walked and lifted weights, as well as doing Pilates and practicing yoga. All that helped my endurance and especially helped build my core and leg muscles."

Monica continued asking a few questions about Rory's skating days and then said, "And then that night came which shattered the skating world. You've never spoken of that night, Rory. Can you take us into your head? I know this is difficult for you."

"It *is* hard to speak about," she admitted. "I've never really done so before. I've never said the shooter's name aloud because I didn't want him to take any more from me than he already had."

She described the eerie experience of being shot on national TV, as well as the painful ankle break which had occurred when she landed wrong after the bullet struck her shoulder. Rory discussed the grueling recovery and how she continued to exercise even now, wanting to keep her body in good shape. Monica asked why Rory hadn't returned to skating.

"I could have competed," she explained. "Just not at the level I had been. And if I couldn't give each performance my all, then I knew it was time to move on. Most of my education was done by home schooling, and I discovered a deep love for history. I decided to start anew, in a totally different career, and earned my teaching degree here in Texas, where I was originally from before I moved to Colorado for training. I lived with my grandmother during my college years. Being an older student, I didn't really fit in on campus. I was happy, though, because Granny Bea is the wisest person I know, as well as full of fun."

Monica led Rory through a few anecdotes about Granny Bea and had the journalist laughing by the end of them.

"On a more serious note, Rory, I wanted to ask you about your teaching career. Specifically, your relationship with Bradley Bolton, your former fiancé who left the school you both taught at under a dark cloud."

Rory had known these questions were coming, and she took a calming breath.

"I'll be honest, Monica. Age-wise, I was an adult, but my emotional growth was stunted. Being homeschooled, I never had the opportunity to date and participate in social activities like others did. For years, almost every waking hour was spent on the ice or thinking about being on the ice—or at competitions. I kept to myself during my college years. My first teaching job was really the beginning of my interacting with large groups of people."

Rory paused. "I was naïve and taken in by Mr. Bolton's charm and good looks. Unfortunately, the relationship was never one between equals. I wanted to please him and tamped down my true feelings, subordinating myself to him. I was a watered-down version of myself. I liked what he liked, from music to movies to food. I did what he wanted to do. Frankly, I disappeared in my desire to please him, and so I compromised being my true self."

She took a deep breath and slowly let it out. "My lack of dating experience was a factor. I probably missed signs that other women might have picked up on, but I will say this. I think there are men out there who don't reveal their true selves to the women who love them. Mr. Bolton had a dark side that I never saw. One which I never even knew existed."

"And that dark side involved grooming young women," Monica prompted. "For sex."

The bluntness of the question threw Rory, but she kept her composure.

"It did. I never observed a hint of this part of Mr. Bolton. I only saw the charming man who spent hours outside the classroom, coaching the girls' wrestling team. He was careful. He never had a sexual relationship with any of his athletes who were under eighteen. He waited until they legally became adults in the State of Texas before nudging them into physical intimacy."

"Let me get this straight. You're telling me you *never* saw an inkling of this?" Monica asked, clearly incredulous.

"No, I didn't," Rory said firmly. "Mr. Bolton was very careful. He only let me see what he wanted me to see. It was the same with the faculty at our school. And the other students and parents. He was acknowledged as a wonderful teacher and coach. No one suspected him of living this double life. I only learned about his multiple affairs after the fact."

She paused, feeling raw and exposed, but knowing she needed to continue.

"Was I devastated? Yes. I ached for those vulnerable young women. They may have believed the relationship they had with Mr. Bolton was consensual, but I firmly believe he took advantage of them."

"Do you see Mr. Bolton now?" the journalist asked pointedly.

"Never," she said emphatically. "I immediately broke our engagement and moved out of our shared apartment once I learned of the accusations. I've moved four times, and he doesn't know where I currently reside. Although I had no involvement in his activities with his students, I also chose to resign at the end of the academic year, realizing I was a distraction to my students, through no fault of my own."

Staring at Monica—and knowing the camera was probably moving in for a closeup, Rory said, "I don't think of Mr. Bolton. Ever. He's not worth my time. I've started a new life. I'm happy. Fulfilled. I've matured and learned a lot about myself."

"I know this new life includes a fiancé," Monica said.

"Yes," Rory said, smiling, the tension leaving her. "I am extremely fortunate to have found a good man. One who knows all about my past. He's kind, thoughtful, and allows me to be exactly who I am, warts and all. Mr. Bolton had told me he never wanted children, something I had longed for, but I put aside my wishes because I thought I loved him. My new relationship is different in every way from the old one. I feel cherished by my fiancé. I understand now that love is both giving and taking. Love has brought joy into my life. My fiancé supports me in every endeavor."

"I hear he is the one who pushed for you to do something with your designs."

Rory spent a few minutes talking about how she had created the skating costumes she'd worn in competitions and how that process had always satisfied her tremendously.

"Although I enjoy my time in the classroom with my students, sketching designs for workout and competition skating outfits is quickly becoming my new passion," she shared. "I am working now with Candace Smith, an immensely talented figure skater. I hope we can partner for several years to come."

"Do you think working with Candace will bring in new clients?" Monica asked.

"I hope so."

"It seems that you are dipping your toe back into the world of figure skating, Rory. Would you ever consider doing more than designing outfits? Maybe creating choreography? Or even coaching?"

She smiled enigmatically. "You never know, Monica. Right now, I have a full-time job teaching and a part-time one working with Candace. We'll see what the future brings."

Monica thanked her for the interview, and the crew applauded enthusiastically. An assistant removed Rory's mic. Monica pulled her own mic and handed it over to the assistant.

"That was wonderful, Rory," the journalist praised. "We got some very good material."

"It seems as if we talked a long time," she said.

"My habit is to assemble a couple of different versions. A shorter one and a longer one. I usually show both to my producer. Once a decision has been made as to the length of the segment, I head back to the editing bay with my editor." Monica paused. "I think the timeline will speed up, though, this time."

"Why?"

"I want my producer and the executive producer of the news magazine to see the raw footage before I cut it. I have a feeling they'll want to air it sooner than they had planned. I'll keep you in the loop," Monica promised. "I'll see to the edits and then play for you what we have, and we'll go from there. I do think the portion regarding Bradley Bolton is important, though. I hope you'll allow it to remain in the final cut."

Rory took a deep breath, nodding in agreement. "You did an excellent job of not sensationalizing it, Monica. I appreciate that. It was the most difficult time in my life. Every friend I had abandoned me. I was extremely lonely and despondent. Fortunately, I came to Sugar Springs. This community has embraced me."

"I'm happy for you, Rory. We'll be in touch." Monica turned to the crew. "Okay, guys. Let's strike everything and get out of Rory's hair. I want to roll in fifteen minutes and make that flight back to New York tonight."

Walker appeared at her elbow, taking it and guiding her into the kitchen. He gave her a slow, delicious kiss.

"You did so well, Rory," he praised.

"I was nervous going in, but Monica was right. I forgot about the lights and the crew. I just concentrated on her and her questions and telling my story."

"You told your truth. I'm very proud of you."

He kissed her again, and the familiar stirrings of desire filled her.

"Did Granny Bea stay at your parents? Are we expected back there?"

"Your grandmother left for Tyler when I came over here. Mom and Dad are exhausted and still running on European time." He stroked her hair. "As soon as this crew clears out, it's just you and me."

She smiled. "Less than fifteen minutes."

"Then let's use that time wisely," Walker said, his lips grazing hers.

22

The bell rang, and Rory dismissed her class, closing the door after the last student exited the room. It was her conference period, and she had one more class after that before she would be done for the day.

It was finals week at Sugar Springs High School, and she couldn't believe the semester had flown by so quickly. The way things were shaping up, however, she would only have one more semester in her teaching career.

Her interview with Monica Wethersby had been put together quickly. Instead of airing sometime in the next month or two, the journalist told Rory how excited the network was about the interview, and they had moved it up, airing it this past Sunday night.

True to her word, the reporter had allowed Rory to watch the version they hoped would appear on TV. She didn't ask for any changes and thought the piece could run as it had been edited. Rory liked what Monica had done in the intro, a brief encapsulation of Rory's skating career to refamiliarize viewers with her. The journalist had even woven in shots of Sugar Springs and the high school, showing Rory's current life. A lone cameraman had been sent back to get a few shots of her teaching a class and even leaving the house for a walk with Walker and Comet.

The segment flowed extremely well, and after she had watched it with Walker, he had enveloped her in his arms, telling her how proud he was of her.

One thing Rory had allowed was for Candace Smith to share Rory's cell number with a few select figure skaters. Since the segment had aired three nights ago, she had spoken to three skaters in the U.S., along with ones in France, Norway, and the UK. She explained to each skater that teaching was her full-time job but that she was willing to work with a handful of skaters, thinking those in the U.S. would be the easiest to work with at the start. The European skaters had been understanding, but all had asked if she changed her mind and left teaching to design full-time, to keep them on a waiting list since each was eager to partner with her.

With Nationals and Worlds coming up so quickly, however, she told the three U.S. skaters that she would work with them after those competitions ended, wanting to devote all her time to Candace's needs. Still, Rory offered to design some practice wear for them in the meantime, just to let them see if they would still want to work with her regarding their competition wardrobe.

Last night, she and Walker had talked about this for a long time, and they had come to a joint decision that she would finish out the academic year and then resign to pursue this new design career. She would tell Joe Bob Milton sometime in the spring so he would have plenty of time to replace her. The gruff principal was already grumbling about the fact that Sarah Meinholdt had resigned mid-year, and he was worried how he would replace her, saying drama teachers didn't grow on trees.

Rory was excited for her friend, though. Tanner Haddock believed Sarah had a promising career ahead of her in the film industry. Rory couldn't wait to see Sarah's performance in *Shadows of the Past*. It would premiere on Christmas Day in Dallas, but she and Walker would be hosting family in their new home and wouldn't be able to attend.

Since they had closed on the new house, a few furniture deliveries had been made. In fact, Walker would be heading to the house within the next hour to meet the truck which would bring the final bit of furniture they had purchased. It was easier for him to do so since he worked for himself and made his own hours. They had already discussed the layout of where to place each piece, and Rory was going to go over to the house after school. First, though, she would stop by Paige's house and grab a load of clothes to transfer.

Their goal was to be in the house by the end of this week. With the semester ending on Friday and their wedding on Sunday afternoon, they would be hosting their own wedding reception in the new place. It would be a very stripped-down reception, consisting of a mound of pizzas coming from Romano's, along with some appetizers, and a wedding and groom's cake provided by Rolling Scones, the local bakery. Instead of being married in the judge's chambers, the judge was making it easy by coming to them, and they would marry in their own great room. Gid would be Walker's best man, while Vivi and Sarah would stand up with Rory.

They would spend the few days before Christmas getting settled into their new residence and after hosting a Christmas Day luncheon for their relatives, they planned to fly to New Orleans for their honeymoon. It was less than a ninety-minute flight, and they were eager to visit a place neither of them had been to before. They would head out to where the Battle of New Orleans had taken place, scratching their itch for history, as well as visiting the World War II Museum. Walker had also lined up a few tours of the town, even one of the local cemeteries. Friends had been recommending different places for them to eat, and Rory thought she would probably come back ten pounds heavier if she ate everything which had been suggested to them.

Since today was a review day and all her papers were graded, she pulled out her phone to touch base with Candace. Sylvia had been quick to jump on the costumes for Nationals and had driven those to deliver to Candace today.

Candace answered quickly and since they were FaceTiming, Rory saw that she wore the skating outfit designated for the first day of competition at Nationals. Candace smiled, her excitement obvious.

"Hey, Rory. I'm going to let Sylvia hold the phone so you can get the full effect."

She passed the phone to the seamstress and stepped back.

Rory said, "Turn slowly for me."

The skater did so, and Rory saw how well the costume fit Candace. When Candace had made the full circle, Rory applauded.

"Sylvia said it doesn't need any adjustments," Candace said. "I love the color and the way it fits. It's like a snug glove but so comfortable. I feel like I could skate to the moon and back."

She laughed. "That's what we're aiming for, Candace. We want you not only to look beautiful but feel competent and confident in it—and skate your heart out."

"Let me change into the free skate's outfit. I'll be right back."

The skater vanished from view, and Sylvia turned the phone around, saying, "She really likes what you've done, Rory."

"I had the idea, Sylvia. You're the one who brought it to life. Frankly, it looks better than I had envisioned."

"Candace has a beautiful frame. I can't wait to see her on the ice, wearing these outfits."

The pair chatted a few minutes about the other costumes Sylvia would be sewing for Worlds, along with the practice wear.

"I actually finished two of the practice outfits," the seamstress said. "I know from working with you how you've said so much of skating is a mental game. I want Candace's confidence to go through the roof, and that includes during her practice sessions."

"I heard that," Candace said off-camera, and Sylvia turned the phone so that it faced the skater again. "My brother plays baseball, and he's told me ninety percent of it is mental. When he goes up to the plate, he has to believe with every swing that he's going to make contact with that ball. He's been in slumps before and said he had to get his head in the right space to get out of them. I do agree that if my practices go well, my confidence soars."

Candace swept her hands down her body and twirled. "And *this* will push me to the top spot on the podium when I perform my programs at Nationals."

Once more, Rory had the skater turn slowly, asking her to hold up her arms, imitating some of the choreography she would use in her free skate.

"This one fits just as well as the other one, Rory," Candace said. "I can't thank you and Sylvia enough. For the first time in my skating career, I feel as if all the stars are aligning. Yes, I've won a national title before, but this is giving me a huge boost, pushing me over the top."

They talked a few minutes about how Candace's practices were going and some of the combination jumps she would be doing. Rory made one suggestion regarding the choreography, and Candace nodded thoughtfully.

"My coach records some of my practice sessions for me to watch. Could I send one of those videos to you? Just to see if you spot something I might be able to tweak or adjust?"

"I don't want to step on your coach's toes," Rory said cautiously.

"It should be my decision in the long run, shouldn't it?" Candace insisted. "I know you broke with your coach because she wasn't listening to you. Mine is very flexible, however. I know we both would appreciate your input."

She knew this was a small ask on the skater's part. She also believed if she watched the video and recommended any changes that it might also tip her life in a new direction.

The thought excited her.

"I'd be happy to view your routine, Candace. Text the video to me."

"Thank you, Rory!" The skater blew kisses at the screen. "I need to go now, but I did give your number to one of my Canadian friends, Brian Harris. He is really promising. I know you said you just wanted to work with people in the U.S., but Canada's right next door. I'm sure he'd be happy to fly down and talk with you in person."

"I'll have to think about it. Remember, I'm still teaching."

The skater laughed. "Not for long. From what I see on social media, the skating world is buzzing about you and that interview which just aired. And you're welcome," Candace said pertly. "I'm going to take credit for reintroducing you into the figure skating world."

"I will talk to you soon," Rory said, laughing.

Sylvia turned the phone so it once again faced her. "I'll keep working on the outfits for Worlds. Let me know about your decision on adding clients."

"Will do, Sylvia. If we don't talk before, I hope you have a very Merry Christmas."

Rory ended the call and saw that she had one voicemail. As she suspected, it was the Canadian skater. She had never thought about designing for men, but ideas immediately flooded her now. She would talk it over with Walker and sleep on it, but she had a feeling she was going to say yes to this Canadian skater.

She went to the office and checked her mailbox and then stopped and talked with Frieda Painter for a few minutes, hearing what the art teacher's time off from school would encompass during her winter break.

Rory returned to her room, and the bell rang for the final class of the day.

She played a review game with her students and was proud when it went so well, knowing they would be prepared for the exam. The day ended with the final bell, and she reminded her students she would be available for tutoring the next morning in case they had any questions.

One student hung back and approached her after the others had left, a shy smile on his face. Javier Rodriguez had exited the ESL—English as a Second Language—program the previous year. He spoke English well, but sometimes he had trouble expressing his thoughts on paper. Rory had worked with him throughout the semester and had been amazed at the progress Javier had made.

He held up a brown paper bag with handles and

passed it to her. She recognized his artwork on the out-side of the bag, having seen many of his sketches over the past few months.

"What's this?" she asked, touched that he had thought to give her something.

"It's for you, Miss Addison. You have helped me very much. I appreciate your help." Javier smiled broadly. "I made this for you."

"Then it will mean even more to me, knowing that," she told him, "because I will think of you every time I see it."

Opening the bag, she pulled out an object wrapped in tissue paper. She unwound it and saw it had a wooden base and on it sat *MRS. COX*, written in script.

"You carved this?" she asked, awed by his artistic ability.

"Yes, Miss."

"I think you have a future as a woodworker and artist, Javier."

Rory hugged the teenager, and he smiled bashfully at her.

"I need to go study. I promise I will do good work on your exam."

"I have no doubt you will ace it, Javier. That means you will do extremely well on this exam."

A smile light his face. "Ace it. I like that."

The boy left, and Rory smiled at the nameplate in her hands. Soon, she would be Mrs. Cox and proudly display this on her desk. For now, though, she wrapped the gift in the tissue paper again and placed it in the bottom drawer of her desk. It would be the first thing she brought out when she returned to school for the new semester, ready to be known by her married name.

Gathering her coat and purse from the closet, she

left her classroom and locked the door. Then she saw Freddie Otts coming down the corridor.

"I'm glad I caught you, Miss Addison."

"Aren't you supposed to be at basketball practice, Freddie?"

"I talked Coach into giving us today off so we could study for finals."

"You can be persuasive," she said, and they both laughed.

"I was studying in the library and heard Miss Meinholdt say she needed you. I volunteered to come up and get you for her."

"Hmm. I wonder what she needs. Thanks for letting me know, Freddie."

"I'll walk down with you," he said cheerfully. "My books and backpack are still in the library."

On their way, they talked about the basketball season, which had started not too long ago. She and Walker had attended two of the games, and Rory had been impressed by Freddie's athleticism and leadership on the court.

"I hope that we can be district champs," he told her. "Coach says I'm a shoo-in for second team All-District. He's pushing me, though. We're hoping I might even make first team."

"If you continue to play the way you did during that Deep Creek game, I think you'll accomplish that goal."

They reached the library, and Freddie held the door for her. Rory thanked him and stepped inside, only to see the library full.

"Surprise!"

She felt her cheeks heat as her eyes skimmed the room. She saw so many of the friends she had made here, along with some of her students, as well.

Next to her, Freddie said, "It's a wedding shower for

you, Miss Addison. Miss Meinholdt and I put it together."

Tears swam in her eyes as she hugged the teenager. "Thank you, Freddie."

He escorted her to a beautiful sheet cake, which bore her and Walker's names and the date of their wedding.

Sarah joined them, and the two women hugged.

"You don't know how hard this was to keep from you," her friend said. "I think everyone was bursting at the seams to tell you."

"I am very surprised. No one spilled the secret."

Pam brought her a piece of cake, and Rory spent several minutes circulating, talking to those who had come to the shower.

"We need to begin opening presents," Freddie announced. "After all, some of us have to go home and study."

Everyone laughed as Rory took a seat and opened numerous gifts. She was touched by the generosity of both staff and students.

After she had opened the last present, she said, "I am so glad I came to Sugar Springs."

"That's thanks to me," Joe Bob called out, causing everyone to chuckle.

"Seriously, though, I have found a true home here. I'm so excited to be marrying a native of Sugar Springs, and I can't wait for the day I walk through these doors with my own children. Everyone, you've been so gracious and welcoming to me. I can't think of a better spot to live and teach."

Freddie rounded up the NHS officers, and they loaded Rory's car with the presents she and Walker had received.

Sarah accompanied them to the car, and Rory hugged her friend tightly.

"I'm going to miss you so much, Sarah."

"I'll always have roots here in Sugar Springs, Rory. I know we'll be friends for life. Let me know if you need anything else done before the wedding on Sunday."

"I think we've got all the bases covered, but I'll let you know."

Freddie handed Rory her keys, along with a sheet of paper. "Everything's packed in your car, Miss Addison. Here's a list of each present and who it's from so you can write your thank you notes."

She thanked him and the students and then got into the SUV, deciding to head to the new house and drop everything off since her car had no room for her to bring over a load of clothes.

As she drove up, she spied the large truck in front of the house. Two men exited it, carrying the dining room table down a ramp leading to the ground. Walker stood on the porch and waved to her.

She pulled into the driveway and got out, gathering a few gift bags, and heading toward her fiancé.

"They had a surprise shower for us at school," Rory told him, accepting his light kiss. "My car is full of wonderful gifts."

"I'll help you bring things in," he said. "Let's put all the bags on the island, and we can sort through and find a place for everything later."

They made several trips, taking the items to the kitchen as the movers continued bringing in chairs for the dining room table. Comet eagerly ran around, her tail wagging.

"I think I'll go home and grab the clothes I left on the bed this morning," she told him. "Should I take Comet home with me?"

"No, leave her here. I'll stay until the movers finish up and then bring her home with me." He kissed her.

"I'll grab something from the diner for dinner if that's okay with you."

"Sounds good. I'll bring the one load of clothes here and then meet you back home."

She returned to her now-empty car and drove the short distance home. That's what she liked about a small town, being able to get wherever she needed in only a few minutes, with very little traffic. The only traffic jams she had been in were those going to the Sugar Springs football games.

Rory touched the remote, raising the garage door, and then went into the house, humming.

Suddenly, a familiar voice said, "You only hum when you're happy. Bugged the shit out of me."

She froze.

A disheveled Bradley Bolton stood in the kitchen.

With a very large gun pointed at her.

23

Walker thanked the movers and tipped them. He returned to the dining room, Comet trailing after him, and stood in the doorway, admiring the dining room. The large table would accommodate twelve people. He looked forward to the time when every chair would be filled with family and friends in the coming years.

Everything was coming together quickly, much sooner than he had anticipated. All the furniture they had chosen had now arrived with this afternoon's delivery. While they would still need to find a few area rugs and place knickknacks and photographs to help personalize the space, the house was beginning to look like a home. They had all day Saturday to get everything looking as good as possible for the wedding and reception, which would be held here on Sunday. And if things weren't perfect, it wouldn't matter. Family and friends would be celebrating his marriage to Rory.

The one area they lacked in was kitchenware. Dishes. Pots and pans. Baking sheets. Glassware. Fortunately, Mrs. Romano was taking care of bringing plates and silverware for the reception. She also told Walker that she would handle the wine, champagne, and other beverages that would be served at the reception. It, along with the accompanying food, would be the Romanos' wedding gift to them. Mr. Romano had insisted they would need to feed their guests more than pizza, and he was planning to bring along several appetizers. After consulting with Rory, they had decided on stuffed mushrooms, bacon wrapped scallops, sausage cream cheese crescent rolls, prosciutto wrapped persimmons with goat cheese, and caprese skewers with balsamic dipping sauce.

He liked that Rory hadn't minded a more casual wedding and reception. Not many brides would agree to serve pizza at their reception. At least they were going traditional as far as cake went. Rolling Scones would be providing both a wedding and groom's cake, and Linda McGregor and Frieda Painter, two of Rory's colleagues, had offered to serve as cake cutters.

He turned out the lights and locked up the house, Comet on his heels the entire way. After they'd adopted the dog, Walker had read up on Irish setters, finding many times they suffered from separation anxiety when their owners left for work each day. Since he was his own boss—and Comet was exceptionally well-behaved —he had gotten in the habit of bringing her to the office with him. The dog thoroughly enjoyed being around people. Visits to a law office could be tense for a number of reasons, but Comet worked her magic every time. He believed his clients enjoyed petting the Irish setter and that it relaxed many of them, making the time with their attorney more palatable.

"Let's go, girl," he told the dog, watching Comet bound down the porch stairs and to his waiting car.

Walker called ahead, placing an order for two of the daily special—pot roast, mashed potatoes, and mixed veggies. He drove the short distance to the town square and left Comet in the car.

Ida Lou greeted him. "Your order's almost ready, Walker. Are you looking forward to the big day?"

He smiled. "That—and every day after with Rory."

"You got a good one in her," the diner's owner said. "But she's also lucky to have you, too."

He paid for the dinners, and a server brought a large takeout bag with handles, handing it to him.

"I had them place a mix of cornbread and rolls to go along with it," Ida Lou said. "And I put in a big bone for Comet to gnaw on."

Walker thanked her and returned to the car, telling Comet she had a surprise when they got home. He actually thought the Irish setter understood what he was saying because she broke out in a huge grin.

As he backed out of his parking spot, his phone rang. He saw it was Gid and hoped his best friend wasn't calling to say that he couldn't make it to the wedding.

Putting his sedan into drive, he tapped a button so the call would be on speakerphone.

"Hey, Gid," he said cheerfully.

"Where are you?" Gid barked at him, the sound of a siren blaring in the background. "Is Rory with you?"

"No. We both just left the new house. I stopped at the diner for dinner, and she went home to put a load of clothes in her car to drive over."

"Fuck, fuck, fuck!" Gid said, clearly frustrated, although Walker had no idea why.

"I'm on my way to Sugar Springs now," Gid said tersely. "I need to call Roscoe Hamilton."

His gut lurched. "What's wrong, Gid? Tell me. Now."

"I think my serial killer is Rory's ex-fiancé."

That was the last thing Walker had expected to hear.

"What?" he asked, dumbfounded, trying to make sense of the words.

"Her ex is Bradley Bolton. Bolton was arrested over some beef at a homeless encampment under a freeway. A guy said Bolton had taken his shoes and sleeping bag. Bolton was arrested and released."

"What's that got to do—"

"Bolton's prints taken at the station matched prints we pulled at our serial killer's last crime scene, Walker. There was a delay after Bolton was booked and printed for the petty theft and making the connection to our killer. By the time the match came in, he'd been released."

A cold fear pillowed deep in his belly. "Do you know where Bolton is now?"

"We tracked him to a homeless shelter in downtown. He's not there. The director says sometimes he shows up. Some nights he doesn't. If they're not inside the shelter by nine each night, the doors are closed, and they're locked out until the next morning." Gid paused. "The thing is, every victim has had red hair. Like Rory. We hadn't had anything to go on until these prints were found at the last crime scene. We eliminated others' prints as people known to the victim. When Bolton was arrested and the computer match made, we put out an APB with his faculty picture, the last one he had taken at the school he and Rory taught at, as well as his picture from the recent arrest."

Walker put his foot into the gas, anxious to be home. "I'm headed to her now. Why do you think she's in danger, Gid? Why are you headed here? How would he even know to come here?"

"Because one of the homeless guys heard us talking to the shelter's director. He heard me mention Bolton by name. He ambled over and said he'd been razzing

Bolton earlier today about the interview Rory had given on TV. How Bolton had taken this guy's cell and brought up the YouTube video of the interview and watched it. Left the shelter, cursing, saying he was going to get even. The minute I heard that, I jumped into my car and headed east."

Gideon paused. "It gets worse, Walker. Just as I was leaving the shelter, a patrolman contacted me about a carjacking that took place a couple of hours ago. Near White Rock Lake. The victim gave a description of the man who took her car. She said he kept mumbling something about Sugar Springs. How he had to get there. The patrolmen showed the vic the pictures our team had put out of Bolton and contacted me. She identified the carjacker as Bolton.

"He's headed Rory's way. He may not have her address, but he's coming for her, Walker. I need to let you go. I'll call Roscoe now so he can have men sent to her house. Text me the address."

Gid hung up. Walker pulled to the side of the road, his hands shaking as he sent his friend Rory's address. Immediately, he called her. The call went to voicemail.

Maybe she had her hands full of clothes and would call him right back. Or she couldn't answer.

Because Bradley Bolton was already there.

He tossed his phone in the cupholder and whipped back onto the street, narrowly missing an SUV, who honked at him.

He didn't care. He had to get to Rory. He had to stop Bradley Bolton.

Because life wasn't worth living if Rory wasn't with him.

~

RORY'S THOUGHTS RACED, questions flashing through her mind.

Why was Bradley here?

Where did he get a gun?

Would he use it on her?

She tamped down the fear racing through her, knowing she had to keep a clear head if she were going to have a chance against him. One thing she did know. She was a stronger, more confident woman than she ever had been when she was with him. And she wasn't ready to check out of this world anytime soon. She wanted a life with Walker.

And not even a crazed ex-fiancé with a gun would keep her from that.

"I didn't know you despised my humming," she said, looking directly at him, but also seeing past him, her mind scrambling to locate anything she could use against him as a weapon.

He was between her and the main part of the kitchen. The only things near her were the café table and two chairs. He wasn't close enough to her for her to strike him, but she could grab one of the chairs, raise it, and charge him.

Rory did have her purse on her shoulder. If she slipped it off quickly, she might swing it at him and knock the gun from his hand. She would need to make a choice soon. Unless she could get him talking. Buy herself some time. Let her inch a bit closer.

"I despised a lot about you," he said, sneering at her.

"I wish I would have known that."

He laughed. "Why? So you could try and change that about yourself? Everything I said to you, you worried about. You made yourself over, trying to be what you thought I wanted you to be—when I didn't want you at all."

"I was too old for you," she said.

"Damn straight," he admitted boldly. "I like my pussy young and untouched. You were already too old when we met, but you were stupid as shit. You hung on my every word. It didn't take much to reel you in and make you think I loved you."

Rory took a small step toward Bradley. "You're right. I'd been confident—maybe overconfident—when I was a figure skater. Then that stalker shot me. All the painful rehab. The night terrors and doubts. Then knowing I could never go back on the ice again. That I'd lost my competitive edge. Younger skaters waited in the wings, ready to take over and pursue the titles I'd won."

She cleared her throat, moving another small distance toward him. "I lost belief in myself. I began to find my way professionally in teaching, but my personal confidence was shot. I was attracted to you. You were so complimentary to me. I fell for you. Hard."

He laughed. "It didn't take much to make you fall for me. It was obvious you'd never been in love before. You even told me what a lonely life you'd led. Training. Traveling. Competing. How you weren't close to anyone except your old granny." He shook his head. "You were the perfect cover for me. A little attention and a few *I love yous*, and you were mine. You would've defended me to the ends of the earth. You believed every lie I told you. You were a stupid, naïve leech, clinging to me."

"Where have you been, Bradley? You don't look so good."

It was true. The normally well-groomed Bradley Bolton appeared unkempt, several days growth of whiskers on his face. His hair was long and greasy-looking. His clothes looked as if he had lived in them for days, if not weeks. And he reeked. She shuddered to think when his last shower might have been.

His face reddened in anger. "It's all your fault," he growled.

Anger sizzled through her. Rory moved slightly toward him, barking out, "*My* fault? I wasn't the one whispering sweet nothings into the ears of inexperienced teenagers. I didn't make promises to them. I wasn't the one who was inappropriate with student athletes I coached."

"You left me!" he shouted, causing her to cringe. "I tried to get you to come back. I would've made it up to you."

"You just told me you didn't even like me, Bradley," she said calmly. "Not to mention you never loved me and thought I was too old for you. Yes, you came to my apartment after I moved out and said you wanted to get back together, but why would I do that? By then, I already knew I wasn't enough for you. I wasn't who you wanted."

Rage spilled from him in waves now. "I lost everything. I *needed* you. And you *abandoned* me. You moved. I couldn't find you. I couldn't find a job. Everyone knew what had happened. I went from being one of the premier wrestling coaches in the state to a washed-up nobody overnight."

Rory wanted to tell him it wasn't her fault he'd literally screwed students and had paid the price for doing so once he'd been caught. She needed to find a way to calm him, though. She was almost close enough to use her purse as a weapon against him.

"If I had known you were in trouble, I would have helped you, Bradley," she said, her tone laced with understanding, hoping to soothe him so she could catch him off-guard. "You know I still care about you."

He glared at her, waving the gun about. "Really, Rory? I watched your fucking interview. I know you've moved on pretty quickly. I see the ring you're wearing. It didn't take you long to find someone to replace me."

The interview. That must be how he located her.

"When I couldn't find you? When I couldn't find a job? I discovered a way to get back at you." Bradley gave her a chilling smile. "I killed you. Over and over again. To get back at how you betrayed me."

Confusion filled her. "I don't understand."

"I found redheads. Ones like you. And I killed them. As painfully as possible."

She gasped. "In Dallas? *You're* the serial killer they've been hunting?"

Nausea swept through her. This was so much worse than she ever might have imagined. Knowing it was Gideon's case, Rory had followed the news accounts, sickened and disheartened by what this murderer had done to women, hoping Gideon and his task force would find the twisted killer and bring him to justice. To think *she* was at the center of it all, that in Bradley's twisted mind he'd been punishing her, again and again, made her feel responsible for those women's deaths.

But if anyone could stop Bradley Bolton now, it had to be her. It had come down to this moment.

With a loud cry and a quick motion, she slipped her purse from her shoulder and swung it at the hand holding the revolver. The purse connected, knocking him off-balance. The gun went off, the noise deafening as the bullet hit the kitchen's ceiling. She released her grasp on the purse's strap. Knowing her legs were the strongest part of her, she thrust one out, slamming it into his groin.

Bradley was already going down. The blow merely sent him to the ground more quickly. And with a helluva lot more pain. He fell on his back, his head hitting the floor hard and bouncing, the breath knocked out of him.

Still, he aimed the gun he'd managed to hang onto at her.

Rory launched herself from the ground as she had thousands of times on the ice, her arms held tightly against her body. Rotating. Feeling the heat of the passing bullet as she spun. Grateful that it had missed her. She timed her landing and came down directly on Bradley's chest, her entire weight driving into him. The gun fell from his hand.

And suddenly Walker was there. Kicking the gun across the kitchen floor. Grabbing her wrist and pulling her off Bradley and into his arms. She heard sirens. Loud sirens. The front door forced open.

Then the kitchen was flooded with people in blue uniforms. Officers from the Sugar Springs Police Department. Two yanked Bradley to his feet and cuffed his hands behind his back, even as he cursed loudly at Rory. The pair led him from the kitchen. Walker pointed out the gun, and a third officer retrieved it.

Roscoe Hamilton appeared, worry etched into his face. "You all right, Rory?" he asked.

By now, she was shaking. Cold flooded her. She nodded, her teeth chattering.

"It's adrenaline, babe," Walker told her. "Let's go sit."

He took her to the next room and eased her to the sofa, picking up a throw and wrapping it around her.

The police chief followed them, saying, "We'll need to get a statement from you, Rory. It can wait an hour. I'll have the EMTs look you over. Okay?"

She bobbed her head up and down, words impossible to get out at this point.

Walker sat next to her, encircling her in his strong, steady arms.

"It's going to be all right," he assured her. "Gid's almost here. He warned me Bolton might be heading this way. Gid's the one who called the police."

Rory nodded, feeling incredibly sleepy all of a sudden. She snuggled against him and closed her eyes.

She was alive. In Walker's arms.

Everything else could wait.

EPILOGUE

DENVER—FOURTEEN MONTHS LATER

Rory and Walker used the passes provided by Candace Smith to gain access to the area where the group of international women figure skaters were getting ready for their free skating program performances to crown the next Olympic champion.

"Does this take you back?" Walker asked.

"Yes, but I don't miss those days at all," she declared. "Now that I have you and the twins, I have everything I need."

"Don't forget your business," he reminded.

Her designs were now being worn by a dozen skaters, including Brian Harris, the Canadian who'd taken Olympic silver last night. Brian had been the first male she'd designed for, and she had two more whom she'd added to her select client list, one a U.S. figure skater and the other one part of a U.S. ice dancing team. She'd had fun designing this team's costumes for competition, simply because ice dancing was a bit more flamboyant. The couple had skated together for over six years and had married two years ago, and they had taken bronze for the U.S. earlier today.

Unfortunately, Rory and Walker had only seen Brian's performance on TV and would watch the ice dancers' program after they returned to Sugar Springs, where that performance sat on the DVR. They couldn't be gone long because of the twins. Rory had pumped as much as she could before she left home this morning, and she continued to pump while in Denver for this brief trip to the Olympics. Thankfully, the games were being held in the U.S. for the first time since the 2002 ones, which had taken place in Salt Lake.

She couldn't help but grin, and Walker said, "Are you thinking about Remy and Jack again?"

Laughing, she nodded. "I can't help it. Those babies are the lights of my life."

He kissed her. "It was a stroke of genius on your part, having two our first time out."

Only after she had delivered two healthy babies had Rory learned that she herself had been a twin. Granny Bea confided that another girl had been stillborn. Her parents had never mentioned this to Rory, and it still stung a bit to learn she'd had a sister whom she never knew about.

She and Walker had already talked about when to get pregnant again. Her obstetrician advised to wait at least eighteen months before they started trying, saying it was necessary to give her body time to bounce back. She hoped since she had gotten pregnant quickly the first time, this next time would also happen sooner rather than later.

Candace spotted them and sailed over, looking confident, as a national champion should. The figure skater had won the U.S. title wearing one of Rory's designs last year, and the buzz of the win and the sleek, elegant costumes Candace wore for both her short program and free skate set the skating world on fire. Rory had been inundated with requests for her to design for over thirty skaters.

She had kept her clientele small, however, only adding to it once she resigned from her teaching post last May. Already four months pregnant by the end of the school year and finally feeling good after having reached her second trimester, Walker had taken her on a driving trip to various battlefields. They had visited Civil War battle sites in Vicksburg, Manassas, and Gettysburg, as well as Revolutionary War parks at Guildford Courthouse, Princeton, and Saratoga.

They wrapped up their trip with a week in Washington, D.C., spending time visiting various Smithsonian museums and memorials dedicated to men such as Lincoln, Roosevelt, King, and Jefferson. For two history buffs, it had been the perfect vacation, and she was eager to return someday with their children in tow.

The trip had renewed her creatively, and Rory had plunged into designing with gusto and joy. All her clients were competing in these Denver Olympics. One day, she hoped to bring their children to see the games in person—but she would never want them to be a competitor as she had been. She had loved skating, but she longed to give their kids a much more normal life than the one she had led.

A Sugar Springs upbringing.

Rory hugged Candace, and they talked briefly about how her short program had gone. Candace asked for Rory's advice on one jump combination, and she replied honestly.

"Go into this free skate tonight as if it were a practice session. Stay loose. Know what combos you want to do before you set foot on the ice—but live in the moment. If your performance is going well and you believe you can win by sticking to your planned set, do so. But if you need something to push you over the top, based upon your competitors' scores, don't hesitate. Just go for it."

The skater hugged her again. "I knew you would understand. I'm first now in the standings, but I've heard the girl from France and that new teenage sensation from Japan both have something up their sleeves. Since they'll skate before me, I'll know exactly what numbers I need going into my skate." Candace laughed. "And besides, I'm wearing one of your designs. How can I lose?"

"Knock 'em dead," Rory said.

Walker accompanied her to their seats, and they settled in for the performance. Brian joined them, along with his coach.

"I'm sorry we weren't able to also make your event," she apologized.

"I know the twins are keeping you busy," the Canadian said. "It was surreal. The fact I went out there and had the skate of my life. I repped my country—and your brand, Rory. I was so proud to be wearing your designs. It gave me the edge I needed."

"I hope Olympic gold is in your future someday, Brian," she told him.

"Hey, I'm thinking about a world title next month."

The skater had already been fitted for what he would wear at the championships next month, and she hoped he would continue to skate well for years to come. Men traditionally stayed in figure skating longer than women, and Rory could see herself working with Brian for many years to come.

As they watched the performances, Rory quietly told Walker different things to look for in various skaters' programs. He had started watching figure skating competitions with her, now that she was designing for several clients, and they rooted for them from the comfort of their couch.

Then it came time for Candace to compete. As the skater had predicted, the Japanese skater was currently in first place, closely followed by the French one. Another American—and client of Rory's—was in fourth. Both the Japanese and French women had skated clean programs. Each woman had taken risks with difficult combinations. It would be up to Candace to be absolutely perfect if she were to take the gold medal.

Walker's fingers engulfed hers, and Rory held on tightly, barely breathing each time Candace launched herself into the air. Every jump was super-clean, however, and not only was the figure skater's athleticism on display, but her artistry shone through, as well.

Her husband's lips grazed her ear as he said, "She looks amazing. Everything she does looks better because of what she's wearing. You've done that for her, Rory. She's fearless out there—because of you."

Candace moved into place for her final combination, gliding across the ice as the music swelled. She pushed off, gaining great height, and spun magically in the air, landing seamlessly.

The arena went wild, and Rory knew her client would be wearing a gold medal around her neck tonight.

The program ended, and the cheers from the audience went on for a long time. Then the crowd began chanting, "Candace! Candace!" It reminded Rory of the times they had done the same for her. But she felt no jealousy. She had no regrets. She was in a new phase of her life. Wife. Mom. Designer.

It was more than enough.

"Kiss and cry time," Walker said, making her laugh, since he hadn't known the term when they married. Her husband had taken time, though, to get to know her sport and her clients, which meant a great deal to her. Walker was more than a husband. He was her lover. Her cheerleader. Her best friend. And the best dad in the world to Jack and Remy.

When the results were announced, Candace and her coach leaped to their feet, embracing, crying, jumping up and down. The skater rushed onto the ice for a final victory lap, inundated with flowers thrown onto the ice to celebrate her victory.

"I guess we'll need to change the copy on your website's bio now," Walker said. "Update it to let others know you're not only an Olympic champion—but that you design for other medal winners." He beamed at her. "I'm so damned proud of you, Rory Cox. I never knew how happy I could be."

As he kissed her, Rory felt exactly the same. Life with Walker and their children, along with her new career, made her feel as if she were on top of the world.

ALSO BY ALEXA ASTON

ABOUT THE AUTHOR

A native Texan and former history teacher, award-winning and internationally bestselling author Alexa Aston lives with her husband in a Dallas suburb, where she eats her fair share of dark chocolate and plots out stories while she walks every morning. She enjoys travel, sports, and binge-watching—and never misses an episode of *Survivor*.

Alexa brings her characters to life in steamy historicals, contemporary romances, and romantic suspense novels that resonate with passion, intensity, and heart.

KEEP UP WITH ALEXA
Visit her website
Newsletter Sign-Up

MORE WAYS TO CONNECT WITH ALEXA